P9-CAN-140

## "You're crazy if you think I'll live with you!"

Juliet almost choked with rage. "I don't intend to put up with your insults every day for the next six months!"

"Then finish the book early and you'll be free to go," Mark suggested smoothly. "I'll do everything I can to make it easy for you. And frankly, it's a relief to know you despise me so much you won't change your tactics and try to get your money-grubbing little paws on me."

"You're safe, I assure you," Juliet said in a frozen little voice. "And whether you believe me or not, so is James. Not even the pleasure of spending the Bannerman millions would reconcile me to the prospect of having *you* as my brother-in-law!"

# WELCOME
## TO THE WONDERFUL WORLD
## OF *Harlequin Romances*

Interesting, informative and entertaining,
each Harlequin Romance portrays an appealing
and original love story. With a varied array
of settings, we may lure you on an African safari,
to a quaint Welsh village, or an exotic Riviera
location—anywhere and everywhere that adventurous
men and women fall in love.

As publishers of Harlequin Romances, we're
extremely proud of our books. Since 1949,
Harlequin Enterprises has built its publishing
reputation on the solid base of quality and
originality. Our stories are the most popular
paperback romances sold in North America; every
month, six new titles are released and sold at
nearly every book-selling store in Canada and the
United States.

For a list of all titles currently available,
send your name and address to:

HARLEQUIN READER SERVICE,
(In the U.S.) P.O. Box 52040, Phoenix, AZ 85072-2040
(In Canada) P.O. Box 2800, Postal Station A
5170 Yonge Street, Willowdale, Ont.  M2N 6J3

We sincerely hope you enjoy reading
this Harlequin Romance.

Yours truly,

THE PUBLISHERS
*Harlequin Romances*

# Island
# of Dolphins

## Lillian Cheatham

# Harlequin Books

TORONTO • NEW YORK • LONDON
AMSTERDAM • PARIS • SYDNEY • HAMBURG
STOCKHOLM • ATHENS • TOKYO • MILAN

Original hardcover edition published in 1984
by Mills & Boon Limited

ISBN 0-373-02683-8

Harlequin Romance first edition April 1985

Copyright © 1984 by Lillian Cheatham.
Philippine copyright 1984. Australian copyright 1984.
Cover illustration copyright © 1985 by Will Davies.

All rights reserved. Except for use in any review, the reproduction or utilization
of this work in whole or in part in any form by any electronic, mechanical
or other means, now known or hereafter invented, including xerography,
photocopying and recording, or in any information storage or retrieval system,
is forbidden without the permission of the publisher, Harlequin Enterprises
Limited, 225 Duncan Mill Road, Don Mills, Ontario, Canada M3B 3K9. All the
characters in this book have no existence outside the imagination of the
author and have no relation whatsoever to anyone bearing the same name
or names. They are not even distantly inspired by any individual known
or unknown to the author, and all the incidents are pure invention.

The Harlequin trademarks, consisting of the words HARLEQUIN ROMANCE
and the portrayal of a Harlequin, are trademarks of Harlequin Enterprises
Limited; the portrayal of a Harlequin is registered in the United States Patent
and Trademark Office and in the Canada Trade Marks Office.

Printed in U.S.A.

# CHAPTER ONE

'THERE may be a little difficulty in placing you,' Miss Posenby said slowly, frowning down at the papers on her desk. 'Having worked for no one but your stepfather makes it a little awkward in the realm of experience, but there's no question about your efficiency. You scored perfect in your shorthand and typing tests.'

Juliet smiled ruefully. 'I had to be quick,' she explained. 'When Dad dictated, he didn't like to be stopped or interrupted or he would lose his train of thought. Sometimes he would start working at midnight and he thought nothing of continuing until dawn.'

'Indeed?' Miss Posenby's dry voice gave no hint of her immediate conclusion that Juliet's stepfather sounded like a tyrant. It was obvious that the girl had been devoted to him and was devastated by his death. Her wan, drawn look attested to that. As head of her own employment agency, Miss Posenby had had years of experience in sizing up people at a glance, and her analysis of Juliet had been shrewdly accurate. The girl was a beauty, of course, that much anyone could tell. She had a slender yet curvaceous body, shoulder-length black hair, dark-fringed violet eyes, and her luminous skin was reminiscent of a magnolia. Her face was a perfect oval, with the high cheekbones and clean lines of a model. Also, she had an instinct for clothes—she wore that crisp oatmeal linen with a natural flair, but Miss Posenby recognised that the linen had been a sale item last week—without the scarf and belt that gave it its present chic. Age? Well, that was more difficult. On the basis of her record, she had finished college and worked several years for her stepfather, but there was a curiously unawakened look about her that gave her an innocence that was decidedly out of step with today's jaded world.

Miss Posenby was no one's fool. A well preserved sixty, with hair that looked like cotton candy and had been tinted blue to match her eyes, she looked like somebody's fairy godmother until one noticed that those eyes were too down-to-earth to ever dwell in fairyland. They were observing Juliet curiously now, as though she had just heard something that caught her attention.

'Your stepfather was a writer, then?'

'Not really,' Juliet admitted. 'His books were all scientific ones. He was a scientist first of all.'

'A scientist?'

'Yes. His field was dolphins.'

'Dolphins? You mean—*fish*?'

'Dolphins aren't fish,' Juliet corrected her smilingly. 'A lot of people think they are because they live in the sea, but actually, they're mammals. They must breathe air to live and they suckle their young just as humans do.'

'Indeed?' murmured Miss Posenby. 'It sounds as though you know a lot about them?'

Juliet's eyes danced. 'I do. I grew up with them.'

Miss Posenby's eyes lingered on that smile and then grew thoughtful. 'Hmm. Just a minute, I've thought of something that might do for you.'

She rose and went into the adjoining office and from the murmur of voices, Juliet knew she was consulting her assistant. Juliet relaxed with a sigh and thought about dolphins—and her stepfather, David Graham. In spite of the impression received by Miss Posenby, David Graham had been a fond, even doting father to Juliet. He had never officially adopted her after he married her mother, but that had been a decision made by Mary Graham, who had felt it would be a sort of denial of Juliet's real father.

It had been their recent death that had left Juliet without a home and needing a job. There had never been much money in spite of David Graham's position as one of the world's foremost scientists in the field of cetaceans—or, to the layman, porpoises, dolphins and whales. He preferred research to teaching and every cent he made, including the royalties from his books, had gone into financing that research. Nothing had been left over for a home or its trappings.

It had been his last book, *Dolphin People*, finished shortly before his death, that had made David Graham a nationally recognised authority in his field. Filled with marvellous photographs, it had been a warm, even loving account of the dolphin, presenting him as a happy friend and companion to man. It had been chosen as an alternative book of the month club selection and consequently, had been read by many people who knew nothing about the endangered species. David Graham had been credited with doing more to save the dolphin with that one book than all his scholarly articles and books had accomplished in the past.

Few people had any idea of the part that Juliet played in writing the book, but it had been she who had transferred his enthusiastic, but inarticulate, prose into the readable account it was. He had been honestly surprised by the book's popularity, by the royalties it had brought in. A scientist who was blindly devoted to his life's work, he was all too apt to take his wife and daughter for granted. When his will was read after his death, it was learned that he had left everything to the research station, which was really owned by the corporation that backed his experiments.

Mary, his wife, would not have wanted it any other way. She had been David's lab assistant, a young widow with a child, when she married him. Their common interest in their work had left little Juliet out. Growing up, she had listened wistfully, and hoped that some day she could do something to be part of their lives. An indifferent science student at the university, it wasn't until she hit upon taking a typing course after graduation that she found a way to assist her father.

Her parents' death had been sudden and unexpected. David had been diving from a ship anchored a few miles off the coast of San Salvador when he had got into difficulties and Mary had leaped overboard to try to save him. Both had drowned. The only thing that kept Juliet going in the days that followed was the certainty that they would have wanted to die together.

Miss Posenby came back into the room, looking at the file she held. 'I may have something,' she said briskly. 'Miss Short and I think this job will do nicely for you. We agree that your lack of business experience will not matter, although I—er—shall not mention that you were employed by your stepfather. I've been trying to get in touch with our client by phone, but it's rather difficult. There's no direct line, you see . . .' She looked doubtfully at Juliet. 'You'd have to live on an island, Miss Welborn.'

'An island!'

'Yes. And I must warn you, there's no access to the mainland except by boat or helicopter. Tamassee is not part of the West Indies, although it's in the path of the shipping lanes to the Bahamas. It's an island owned by an American citizen. Do you think you would be interested?'

'I might.' Juliet was intrigued in spite of herself. 'What's the job like?'

Miss Posenby consulted her notes. 'Apparently it's the same sort of thing you've been doing for your stepfather, helping in the collation and typing of a book of scientific research. The research is on underwater sea life, which is why I thought of you.' She read from her notes. 'No shorthand required but typing skill a must— and a love of the sea, plus an ability to use underwater breathing apparatus.' She looked up. 'I assume you qualify?'

'Yes,' Juliet said hesitantly. 'Can you tell me more about the island?'

'It is, as I said, owned by one person—Mark Bannerman. He will be your employer.' She watched Juliet closely. 'When Mr Bannerman is in residence, there's a daily mail drop by helicopter and a supply boat stops every week, so you wouldn't be altogether isolated. It's also a stopover for yachts cruising in those waters. There's even a small port town. But,' she warned, 'there's no social life and you may not find the townspeople congenial. There's no doctor, although there is a nurse and a first aid station, but your only contact with the outside world would be through the radio-phone.'

A fleeting smile touched Juliet's lips. 'You sound as though you're trying to warn me off!'

'I don't want you to expect too much,' replied Miss Posenby. 'I've supplied Mr Bannerman with temporary help before, and invariably they're disappointed after they've stayed on the island for a while. I thought about this job when you mentioned the dolphins, because it sound like what you've been used to. But we've had a hard time trying to fill the position. For one thing, most girls shy off when I mention the isolation without knowing another thing about it. And then the job is tempoary, Miss Welborn,' she added warningly. 'Six months at most, until Mr Bannerman finishes his book. To compensate, the salary would be good,' and she named a figure that made Juliet catch her breath. 'I'm sure, too, that the working conditions in the Bannerman household would be satisfactory.'

'If they're not, I can always leave,' Juliet said gravely, but her eyes were sparkling. 'You're right, Miss Posenby, it does sound like what I want. I'll take the job.'

Miss Posenby wondered fleetingly if Mark Bannerman's name had tipped the scales, then she acquitted this girl of having an ulterior motive. No, there had been no reaction to his name. Instead, the reaction had been to the salary figure, Miss Posenby thought dryly. It was a good one for an inexperienced typist—but then Mark Bannerman paid well. Most girls, of course, would have jumped at the opportunity to have a millionaire bachelor as a boss, which had been the reason Miss Posenby had kept his name out of previous interviews. Until now. It had made the vacancy a hard one to fill, but Mr Bannerman was too important a man for her to endanger her own position by sending him a money-hungry little 'groupie' who was dazzled by the publicity about him.

Miss Posenby then proceeded to explain about the helicopter. 'I'll get in touch with the airfield and make arrangements for the pilot to expect you tomorrow morning,' she volunteered. 'Meanwhile, I'll continue to try to reach the island through the radio-phone. If I don't get through before you arrive, you merely have to mention that I've sent you.'

After leaving the agency office, Juliet wandered along the sidewalk until the blinding glare made her dig her sunglasses out of her handbag and put them on. She was filled with an unaccustomed sense of accomplishment. Her first job! And the relief was so great that she felt giddy. True, it was only temporary, but if she made good at this, who knew where it might lead? Miss Posenby had hinted that there might be a place for her in the Bannerman Corporation when the book was finished, and Juliet, to whom the awesome name 'Bannerman's' meant nothing, could see that Miss Posenby thought this was an opportunity not to be missed.

Juliet was at the airfield early the next morning. Everything she owned, every memento of her parents and her childhood, was packed in her two battered suitcases plastered with the labels of a dozen world ports. Her parents had dived off the coasts of Australia and both Americas, and Juliet was conditioned to travelling light and never hanging on to possessions.

She had debated what to wear today, wondering if slacks might not be indicated for a helicopter ride. On the other hand, she would be meeting her boss for the first time, so she had compromised on a dress of coral polyester, cool and sleeveless. With it, she had carried a big straw hat that she had trimmed with a scarf of the same colour. The result was that she looked both elegant and expensive as she entered the dusty little waiting room and stopped at the main desk.

From there, she was directed to a little coffee shop at the rear of the building. From its windows, one looked out upon the landing field of the small private airfield. There was only one customer, leaning against the counter drinking a cup of coffee and flirting with a giggling waitress. He was dressed in a jumpsuit and had a pair of goggles dangling from a loop at his waist. He wore a cap pushed cockily to the back of his head. His face was good-humoured rather than good-looking, but there was something in the cynical eyes that watched her approach that gave her a prickle of warning. She came to a halt before him. 'Mr Tanner?'

He raised his eyebrows. 'Jack Tanner, sweetie, at your service. And I presume you're my passenger? Miss—Welborn, wasn't it? Mark's taste is improving all the time! Okay, honey,' he lifted his cup in a sort of toast, 'I congratulate you on beating the odds. You've managed to bum a ride to Tamassee.'

Juliet's brows knitted in a frown. This man talked a foreign language, so far as she was concerned. She was just about to tell him so when he added, 'I see you've brought a lot of luggage?' He nodded towards the two suitcases that had been placed beside the door.

'I'm sorry about that,' she apologised aloofly. 'Will it be too much? I'll be there for quite a while, after all, and I can't afford to store my things.'

He raised an eyebrow. 'Sweetie, anything you say goes, but I've taken Mark's popsies over and brought 'em back, and this is the first time I've met one with your confidence. Usually, they aren't quite sure of their welcome, but it's no act with you, is it? It simply hasn't occurred to you that he may throw you out. How well do you know him? He's known to be a moody guy, particularly when it comes to women.'

She stared at him blankly. 'What are you talking about?'

'Now, Miss Welborn—please, ma'am, don't try to pull an act on me. This is old Jack, remember? I've seen 'em come and I've seen 'em go, but if you try to tell me Mark invited you, I'll be tempted to call you a liar. Mark doesn't invite his women to Tamassee; they just come. It's his retreat and he likes to get away when he goes there.'

'I think you must be insane,' Juliet said icily. 'I'm going there to work, not to audition as one of Mr Bannerman's girl-friends! I'm being sent by the Posenby Employment Agency. I thought you knew all that!' she added irritably, 'but if you don't believe me, or object to taking me to Tamassee for some reason, I suggest that you go to that phone and talk to Miss Posenby

herself. She'll tell you whatever you want to know, I'm
sure.'

He looked startled. 'You mean it's on the level? They
did say at the desk that Posenby's was sending
someone—a typist, I think—but you don't look like a
typist. I thought, when I saw you, that it was just a new
angle you'd figured for getting to the island. Women
are doing it all the time to poor old Marks——'

'Yes, I know,' she said frostily. 'Mr Bannerman has
my sympathy. You've made it clear that he's been
harassed by women, and frankly, I find it pathetic. He
must be a very stupid man if he can't cope with his
private life any more efficiently than that.'

Jack Tanner looked rather shocked at that, but he
hurriedly paid for his coffee and joined her at the door.

During the ride, he did everything he could to regain
his lost status with his beautiful passenger.

He talked about the island they were approaching.
Tamassee was about twenty miles long and perhaps ten
miles wide at its widest part. It had fresh water and a
rich, loamy soil. The island had been unoccupied when
an early Bannerman ancestor had grabbed it, built an
ante-bellum mansion with the help of slaves, and
started growing sugar cane, also with the help of slaves.
Now, sugar cane was no longer as profitable and Mark
Bannerman, the head of the Bannerman Corporation,
lived in the States. However, he continued to return to
Tamassee and Bella Vista, the home of his ancestors,
and he had done much to help the people of the islands.
Mostly, it was a matter of finding ways to create jobs
for the population. But it was difficult. The young men
usually left home as soon as they could for the larger
islands where work was more plentiful. The ones who
stayed either worked for the Bannerman Corporation
or were the older people and the children.

Juliet listened, fascinated, and when finally, Jack
pointed out the island of Tamassee below them, she
gazed at it eagerly. It had had a romantic history and
from the air, it was beautiful. Lushly green, with a
white road that ran its length and from above, looked
like a ribbon, it glittered like a jewel in a field of

startling blue. At one end of the ribbon she saw the rooftop of a large house with several outbuildings—Bella Vista. At the other, was a cluster of rooftops of varying sizes and shapes. This must be the town, or village, that Jack had mentioned. She noted that it was located near a lagoon that curved gracefully inland, forming a perfect bay.

The helicopter hovered over a landing pad near the lagoon, then lowered itself like an awkward bird. The blades rotated slowly to a stop, and Juliet climbed out stiffly. The first thing that struck her was the smothering intensity of the heat. The sun, reflecting off the coarse white sand at her feet, was so blinding that the glare made her eyes hurt, even behind the dark glasses she wore. A dew of perspiration popped out on her upper lip and forehead and she fumbled in her purse for a handkerchief.

As she hesitated, gasping for breath, she gained a variety of quick impressions. The first was of the sweep of clean white sand, backed by a line of palm trees and creeping, jungle-like vegetation. A place had been cleared for a low block building with a tin roof that looked like some kind of warehouse. A long jetty ran out into the ocean and at the end of it, a cabin cruiser, sleek and well tended, rode the waves lightly at the end of its mooring lines. Behind the warehouse, a jeep was parked on the road. It was the only car in sight, but there were a number of bicycles also parked.

Suddenly, several men ran out of the warehouse towards them. Jack, who was busy pulling out her suitcases, began to briskly direct the unloading of the helicopter. As he joined Juliet, a short, dumpy figure emerged from the warehouse and came towards them. Jack watched its approach warily.

'Okay, Miss Welborn, honey,' he muttered out of the corner of his mouth. 'Uncle Jack has done everything he can for you. From now on, you're on your own!'

Juliet, assuming the figure was that of her boss, moved forward quickly, a tentative smile on her face, until she saw that it was a woman—a woman, moreover, without a trace of welcome in her homely, weatherbeaten face. She was dressed in jeans and was smoking a long black cigar, and she stumped towards them, anger in every line of her body.

'Hi, Cora!' Jack called nonchalantly.

She glared at him. 'Who the hell have you brought with you this time?' she demanded roughly. 'You know Mark said he'd fire you if you brought another woman to this island! He isn't going to like this one bit. You'd better hustle her right back into that thing and take her back to where she came from!'

'Now, wait a minute, Cora, it isn't like that at all,' Jack began feebly.

Cora turned on Juliet. 'How did you manage to persuade him to bring you?' she demanded furiously. 'When Mr Bannerman comes to Tamassee, it's for peace and quiet! He doesn't want his floozies following him here!'

'Now, wait a minute, Cora. Posenby's sent her.'

'Posenby's? The employment agency?' Cora was obviously incredulous. 'What for?' she asked suspiciously.

'She's here to do some typing for Mark.'

'I don't believe it!' Cora said flatly.

By this time, Juliet was fed up with being talked about as though she was not even present; of being insulted because she was a woman, and was suspected of chasing the licentious Mr Bannerman to his island hideaway. She was liking what she heard about him less and less. She wanted to do just as Cora suggested—get into the helicopter and return to Miss Posenby and tell her the job was impossible. But she could not afford the luxury of doing as she pleased. She had to hang on to her job if she could. That, and a sheer stubborn refusal to be intimidated, kept her from throwing the whole thing away before she had even started.

'You don't have to believe it,' she snapped, giving rudeness back for rudeness. 'I don't know who you are, but whether you like it or not, I've been hired to type for Mr Bannerman. I presume he didn't think it was necessary to ask your permission before he hired me, but if you think so, you're at liberty to check with him.'

A flush covered Cora's face, mottling the coarse complexion. 'For your information, I'm Cora Bannerman, a cousin of your boss, Miss High and Mighty!' she sneered. 'My job is to keep out undesirables and uninvited people! Besides, Mark has his own private secretaries, Paul Bradford and a typist named Miss Yeager. They're both at Bella Vista now. Why would he hire you?'

Juliet didn't hesitate. If Cora knew nothing about Mark Bannerman's book, she had no intention of satisfying her curiosity.

'I suggest you call and ask him,' she remarked. 'Or perhaps you would prefer to call Miss Posenby? If I'm not needed or wanted, then I can return with Mr Tanner. I'm merely acting on instructions.'

For the first time, Cora looked uncertain. 'That's all I'm doing,' she muttered. 'I can't be blamed when I've had no word from Miss Posenby.'

'She said she couldn't get through yesterday, while I was in the office, but she said she'd try again today.'

'Something was wrong with our phone yesterday, and I've been out of the office all morning,' Cora admitted grudgingly. 'I suppose it could have happened like that.'

Jack grinned. 'Then you're going to let her through, Cora?' he asked impudently.

Cora looked at him warily. Obviously, she would have preferred turning Juliet back, but hadn't quite the courage to do so without permission. 'I suppose she'd better stay. Posenby's would have sent her if it wasn't legitimate.'

'Right!' He turned his grin on Juliet. 'Well, honey, looks like you're all set.

He escorted her to the jeep where a driver was already installed, waiting. 'I'd wait around and see how you like your new job, but today's a busy day. I'll probably see you tomorrow or next day. Meantime, take it easy and don't work too hard.'

'Thank you, Mr Tanner. You've been very helpful.' Juliet climbed into the jeep.

'Jack, honey—Jack. And it was a pleasure. Won't

you please tell me your name? Miss Welborn seems so—so impersonal, somehow.'

A fleeting smile touched her lips. 'Juliet. Thank you again, Jack.'

The last sight she had of him, he was throwing his cap into the air, a delighted grin on his face.

The jeep did not go through the town but bypassed it to take a road that skirted the shoreline. After a few miles, the driver took a sharp inward turn and passed through a gate that led to a driveway overhung with branches trailing waving fronds of Spanish moss.

When the jeep finally pulled up with a flourish before a white-columned mansion that might have been lifted straight from the set of *Gone With the Wind*, Juliet felt the breath catch in her throat. Bella Vista lived up to its name—its view was beautiful, even magnificent. Through an open passageway that ran through the centre of the house, she glimpsed rolling breakers and sunwashed beaches, while on this side there was the contrast of smoothly manicured lawns and colourful flower beds beneath stately old trees.

The driver had parked before the front door and he climbed out, then helped her down. 'If you'll just have a chair on the porch, miss, I'll go see if I can find the housekeeper. Her name is Mai. She'll tell me where to take your luggage.'

The shady veranda held a glider and some old-fashioned rocking chairs covered with plump, chintzy cushions. Juliet sank gratefully into the nearest one and lifted her face to the breeze that stirred the trees. There was a restful atmosphere about this place that appealed to her. 'I'm going to like it here,' she exulted. For the first time since her parents' death, she began to feel at peace.

The scraping sound of footsteps brought her head sharply around. A man was coming from the corner of the house. He was dressed too carelessly to be a gardener, in a pair of cut-off blue jeans that hung low on his hips. That and a pair of ragged sneakers was all he wore. He had stopped short at the sight of her, and now he slowly ascended the steps.

'Who are you?' he demanded curtly.

Juliet elevated her chin, hoping her disapproving expression would show him what she thought of his mode of dress. He was tall without an ounce of surplus flesh and his rough blond hair shone with sun-streaks of gold. She could not read his eyes—they were rendered incognito by a pair of staring sunglasses—but the bunched muscles along his jawline showed that the firm, well-shaped lips were clenched with irritation. He was one of the handsomest men she had ever seen, with an aura of masculine sex-appeal that was accentuated by his half-naked appearance. Juliet was touched with a chord of instant antagonism. She bristled, acutely conscious of the bare muscular chest covered with a luxuriant growth of hair that tapered to the navel, then disappeared in the cut-off jeans. His lips curled sarcastically, and Juliet knew she had been staring. She looked away, flushing.

'I asked who the hell you were?'

She jumped, startled by the savagery of his rudeness. For the first time, it dawned on her that this must be her employer, the elusive Mr Bannerman. He had removed his glasses, and she saw that his eyes were grey—and as cold as ice.

'Are you—Mr—Bannerman?' she faltered.

His lips thinned. 'I am. And I'll ask you just once more—who are you?'

'Juliet Welborn. I'm here to work for you. I'm the typist you wanted.' The words came out in a nervous rush.

His eyes stripped her with insulting thoroughness. 'Are you trying to be funny?' he demanded coldly. 'Who really sent you? The local call-girl society?'

'Wh-what did you say?' she gasped.

'You heard me.' He put his sunglasses back on, and was at once dehumanised. He looked at her with the sort of chilling contemptuous appraisal that he might have given a worm crawling on the veranda rail. 'I suppose when they couldn't buy the island, the syndicate decided to try to soften me up by sending a woman to change my mind?'

'Th-the s-syndicate?' she stammered bewilderedly.

'Fat chance! You may be a cute little thing, but no woman changes my mind for me. You might tell your bosses that.'

'I—I don't know what you're talking about,' she whispered numbly.

His look sharpened. 'Maybe you don't, at that,' he said grudgingly. 'Maybe you were kept in ignorance. But you'll have to peddle your body somewhere else. If you like, you can leave your card on the way out and when I get back to the city, I'll give you a call. When I have more time.'

'Mr Bannerman,' she said slowly, 'I came here to work for you.'

'Indeed? And I tell you, I don't want you—working—for me,' he drawled, his voice making the verb a subtle insult. 'You've had your trip for nothing, so go back and get on the boat or whatever brought you, and tell your boss it's no go.'

Juliet looked at the jeep uncertainly, then back at him. 'Tell Miss Posenby?' she asked blankly.

His hand gripped her wrist in a paralysing hold, and she was jerked out of her chair and to her feet. 'Miss Posenby of the agency?' he growled.

'You're hurting me!' she gasped. She felt as though the bones in her wrist were breaking. 'Yes—yes!' she moaned as the grip tightened.

'So that's how you got past Cora!' he ground out between clenched lips. 'Your bosses certainly get around! So they found out I use Posenby's for casual labour? By the time we checked out your story, I suppose you intended to be successfully installed in my bed?'

He had dropped her arm, and instantly she threw herself down the steps and around to the far side of the jeep, where she stood trembling, ready to run if he moved an inch in her direction. 'You conceited beast!' she croaked. 'I think you and everyone on this island must be mad! I've had nothing but insults and insinuations from all of you ever since I walked into the airport and first met that pilot! Where do you and your henchmen get off, thinking that every girl who's looking for a job is also looking for a chance to jump into *your* bed? You must be some sort of egomaniac! I've got news for you, mister! You turn *me* off! Personally, I wouldn't work for you if you were the last man on earth!'

He hitched his thumbs in the pockets of his shorts and smiled sardonically, with a twist of the thin lips. 'Provocative as that statement is, it still doesn't tempt me to take you up on your challenge,' he drawled. 'I want you to get in that jeep and get out of here. And you'd better not come back. In case you don't understand simple English, that means I'm booting you off this island—for good! I hope your boss's boat is still hanging around somewhere, because if it isn't, you'll have to spend the night in the open.'

'It will be a pleasure!' she spat.

Just then the driver appeared in the doorway, followed by a tall, dignified woman with her hair wrapped in a turban and a spotless apron covering her flowing skirt.

'Sam! The lady is leaving. Return her to wherever you got her and dump her and her luggage. I'll call Miss Cora and let her know.'

'Yes, sir.'

'Bon voyage.' He gave Juliet a sardonic salute and turned purposefully towards the house.

The ride back was a wild one, Sam apparently reacting to the angry bite in his boss's voice. As he pulled the jeep into a parking position beside the shed, Juliet noticed the helicopter was gone. Her heart sank. Until then, she hadn't realised how much she had been relying on Jack's moral support, nor how lonely she felt at the sight of the deserted landing pad. She looked around for Cora and noticed that a depressing-looking boat, oil-stained and rusty, had joined the cabin cruiser at the end of the jetty.

At that moment Cora strode out of the shed. Without even bothering to greet Juliet, she called imperatively, 'Sam! Take that baggage to the *Lazy Lou*! Miss Welborn is leaving with Captain Smith.'

'Hey—wait!' Juliet made a grab for her luggage. 'Who says I am?'

Cora looked at her contemptuously. 'Mark just called and said he knew nothing about you. Your story about Miss Posenby is a lie. I don't know what you're trying to pull, Miss Welborn—or whatever your name is—but it won't work here. We're up to all the tricks used to get on this island. You're leaving by the first transportation out, and that happens to be the *Lazy Lou.* You're fortunate that Captain Smith has agreed to give you passage back to the mainland—otherwise you'd be spending the night on the beach.'

A scruffy-looking man wearing an undershirt and dirty duck trousers above his filthy bare feet strolled out of the shed. Grossly overweight, he had mean little eyes between thick folds of flesh. They opened wide when they saw Juliet. 'Is *this* my passenger?' He sounded stunned.

'Yep. Any objection?' Cora allowed a thin smile to crease her lips.

'Hell, no. It's better than I hoped for!' His eyes disappeared as he wheezed in what passed for a laugh. 'You an' I're goin' to have a good time, ain't we, baby?' he added, leering at Juliet.

She jerked away from the hot, foetid breath. 'I'm not going with you,' she said firmly. 'Where is the helicopter? I'll go back the way I came, with Mr Tanner.'

Cora's face darkened. 'The helicopter is Bannerman property and under *my* direction,' she said arrogantly. 'It's gone, and anyway, you're leaving before tomorrow morning, you snobbish little bitch!'

Her face was implacable and there was a gleam of triumph in her eyes that showed she was enjoying her power.

Juliet seated herself firmly on her larger suitcase. 'I'm staying right here,' she said determinedly. 'Does Mr Bannerman know what you're trying to do?'

Cora flushed angrily. 'He called and said you didn't belong here and I was to see that you got off the island! This happens to be the only way available! You may have to work for your passage,' she addded meaningly, 'but for a lady of your talents, that shouldn't pose any problem. You know,' she added viciously, 'you girls are all alike. You think because you have a pretty face and figure, you can kick an old warhorse like me around. I've been looking forward a long time for a chance to do a little kicking of my own, and it looks like it's here! Before you finally get home, you'll be sorry you ever tried to sneak on this island!'

'I was sent here by Posenby's,' Juliet said desperately.

Cora ignored her. 'Do you want to walk on board like a lady or do you want to be carried aboard by a couple of the boys here? It doesn't make any difference to me. In fact, I think I'd love to see you hauled aboard.'

Juliet stood up. 'I'll walk,' she said numbly.

She was shivering in spite of the heat, but, holding her head high, she walked down the jetty. As she drew closer to the *Lazy Lou*, she saw it was even more disreputable than it had appeared from a distance. The deck had rusted through in spots and was littered with a motley array of fishing gear, boxes, barrels, and finally, a bloody bait bucket crawling with bloated bottle flies. The only deckhand she saw was a half-naked sailor, who regarded her with a drooling, lopsided grin. Juliet stopped abruptly and turned to the gross man following closely on her heels.

'I am *not* going on that boat!'

Captain Smith blocked her way as she started to return. He stood with his bare feet splayed apart to keep his balance and lowered his head like a bull. His oily face glistened in the sunlight and Juliet recoiled at the hot, naked look of lust in the little mean eyes.

'Oh, yes, you are, girlie,' he said softly. 'Cora promised you to me. You ain't got no other place to go. It's either me or swim for it.'

'Very well, I'll swim for it,' Juliet replied bravely, clenching her fists. 'I don't intend to leave here with you. When I leave, it will be with Jack Tanner tomorrow. And if you or she put one hand on me or have any of your men do it, I'll see that all of you are clapped in prison for kidnapping!'

He drew back uneasily. 'I ain't forcin' you,' he scowled. 'It's Cora's doin', all the way.'

'Then you'd better move aside and leave me alone. I'm an American citizen and I have a right to refuse to accompany you. It's the law!' she added for good measure, suspecting that he lived on the thin edge of it, and had a healthy respect for the police.

'You 'n' Cora fight it out between you,' he muttered. 'Tell her I'll give her five minutes to convince you, then I'm leavin'.'

Breathing hard, Juliet walked steadily down the long jetty towards the island and met Sam on the way with her luggage. 'Turn around and take it back,' she commanded.

He rolled his eyes. The steely note in her voice apparently impressed him, for he hesitated, visibly uncertain, then finally dropped it where he stood and waited, watching Cora for directions.

Her face was flushed with rage by the time Juliet stood in front of her, but before she could say anything, Juliet spoke first.

'I've threatened Mr Smith with the law, and now I'm threatening you,' she said evenly. 'I am *not*—repeat, *not*—going to get on that boat. You know what kind of man that captain is and what will happen to me if I go with him. I can't believe that a man of Mr Bannerman's reputation would condone such a thing. He at least would know that I could charge all of you with a case of kidnapping if you put me on that boat forcibly, against my will. I intend to remain here until Jack Tanner comes tomorrow. At that time, I will most willingly leave this island, and I assure you, I will never return.'

'You'll have to sleep on the beach if you stay. I'll see to it that no one opens their door to you.'

Juliet looked at her contemptuously. 'I'll gladly sleep on the beach. I think all of you are a pack of maniacs, anyway, and I have no desire to be cooped up inside a house with any of you!'

They were interrupted by a hail from the shed. One of the workmen was waving at Cora.

'It's the phone, Miss Cora!'

Juliet motioned to Sam, who ran forward, grinning, carrying her luggage. He put the two bags down beside her. 'Where to, miss?'

'For now, right here. Then you go tell that—that Captain Smith——' she shuddered, 'to leave. I'm staying here tonight.'

'Yes, *ma'am*!' Sam's grin widened as he raced towards the moored boat. Obviously, it was a rare occurrence for anyone to get the best of Cora, and the measure of Sam's delight gave Juliet an inkling of Cora's popularity with her staff.

Juliet sat down quickly on the luggage before her legs gave out beneath her. She was cold and clammy in spite of the hot sunlight and felt sick and frightened as she contemplated her next move. She had meant what she said about leaving this island for ever. The people on it were all crazy, with their mania for privacy and Mark Bannerman's obsession with call-girls and gangsters and sex. She wondered how she could explain it to Miss Posenby, unbelievable as it was going to sound. Meantime, she had the problem of the next twenty-four hours, until Jack returned. Perhaps Sam could tell her somewhere she could go—if she could ask him without Cora knowing. Her stomach rumbled nervously as Cora emerged from the warehouse and strode towards her. Juliet stood up and willed herself to remain cool and controlled. The *Lazy Lou* had already left and there was nothing more Cora could threaten her with.

Cora's face was a study when she got to Juliet.

'Okay, you win,' she said abruptly. 'You're staying.'

'What?'

'That was Posenby's on the phone. She told me about your job. There's been a mistake,' she added defiantly. 'I'm not to be blamed for this mix-up. You're not supposed to work for Mark. You were supposed to work for his younger brother, James. Why didn't you tell me?' she added accusingly.

'Because I didn't know it myself,' Juliet replied

crisply. 'But all that's beside the point now. I'm not going to stay here and work for anyone. I'm leaving this place on the first safe transport out.'

'Oh, you're cleared,' Cora said grudgingly. 'I talked to James too. I don't think he'd even mentioned to Mark that he'd asked Miss Posenby to find him a typist. He's a scientist, you know, and slightly absentminded. Anyway, he's expecting you, so I'll send you and your luggage on down there by Sam.'

'Nothing doing! I told you I'm not staying and I mean it, Miss Bannerman! Mr Bannerman's brother can find himself another typist. I don't want any part of him or anyone on this island.'

'Suit yourself, of course,' Cora said mockingly. 'But I'm closing the warehouse in about five minutes.' She consulted the man's watch strapped to her broad freckled wrist. 'I go home to my lunch and siesta. Everything closes down for about two hours, and tonight everything gets locked up good and tight. This end of the island is as black as a pit. When you're lying here on the beach, hungry and thirsty, and trying to keep from freezing, just remember I offered you a place to go.'

'Why are you trying to blackmail me like this?' Juliet demanded. 'I should think you'd be tickled pink to see me go. God knows, you tried hard enough to get rid of me!'

'Personally, I would love to see the last of you, but James has talked to Miss Posenby and he's expecting you. Seems as though you've worked for some scientist he admires. If you don't show up, he'll demand to know the reason why, and unfortunately,' her lips twisted derisively, 'what James wants, James gets. Mark would try to give him the moon if he asked for it, so-o-o——' she stopped, shrugging.

'So—Mr Bannerman will blame you if I don't stay?' Juliet murmured comprehendingly. 'You should have been on duty to receive Miss Posenby's message, or at the very least, checked with her before sending me to Bella Vista! I believe you're scared,' she added shrewdly, and from Cora's flush, she knew she had hit upon the truth. 'Well, congratulations, you've succeeded in scaring *me*. I wouldn't work for Mr Bannerman's brother for a million dollars. I just don't want to be around that man.'

'You wouldn't be working for Mark,' Cora explained pleadingly. 'You'd probably never see him at all. James's place is a mile from Bella Vista. You see, he works with dolphins, and he hardly stirs out of his lab from one week to the next. How about it?' she added desperately. 'I promise you, if you don't like the set-up, I'll phone Jack Tanner to come for you at once.'

Juliet looked at her uncertainly. She equated Cora's promises about the same as she would Captain Smith's, but it was true that things sounded better now that she knew she wouldn't have to see anything of Mark Bannerman. Of course, James might be as bad as his brother, but Juliet doubted it. For one thing, he was a scientist, and they were a breed apart from macho-type tycoons.

But most importantly, he worked with dolphins, and Juliet *wanted* this job. She could hold her own in a job of this sort, and it would be a tremendous boost to her self-respect to succeed at it. She made a sudden decision.

'Very well, I'll go look the situation over.' And then, in case Cora thought she had scored a victory, she added warningly, 'Miss Posenby asked me to give it a trial, but if I don't like this job, I'll let *her* know.'

There was something oddly familiar about the low concrete structure built almost exactly on the same plan as her father's laboratory. There were the dolphin tanks, the observation platform, the catwalk out to the ocean—all so familiar! And there, stooping over one of the pens, was a man who could have been her father. Juliet began to feel reassured for the first time in that crazy, mixed-up day.

The man was thin and brown, and was wearing faded denim shorts and a loose shirt. He was making notes on a pad of paper, but at the sound of the jeep, he looked around quickly. The blue eyes peered uncertainly at her behind the hornrimmed glasses, a hank of light brown hair partly obscuring his vision. Juliet could not see any resemblance to his brother, except perhaps in colouring. As he strode towards her, his shirt tail flapped and she saw that every button on it was missing. In spite of her resentment at the way she had been treated today, she was touched; the odd scholarly figure was so much like her father.

'Miss Welborn!' He was beaming as he reached her and began to pump her hand almost before she could get out of the jeep. 'James Bannerman, at your sevice! You have no idea what a pleasure this is. It's most exciting to meet someone who's worked with David Graham!' Apparently Miss Posenby had not said anything about her being his daughter. 'I feel privileged to be able to find someone who can understand what I'm trying to accomplish here. I—I admired Dr Graham, and I know he trained you well.' His thin, brown face was alight with enthusiasm, 'And to think that you helped write *Dolphin People*! It—it's the most exciting thing that's happened yet!'

Juliet laughed—she couldn't help it. His welcome, after the rebuffs and insults she had received today, soothed her damaged self-respect.

'You've already said that,' she smiled. She was trying to crawl out of the jeep and regain her hand at the same time. She was used to these odd bursts of enthusiasm. Her father had been that way. He could be absolutely charming when he met someone whose interests were his, in spite of having no social small talk.

'Come along,' James bubbled. 'I want to show you my dolphins. I have four, and there's one in particular with whom I've made amazing progress in communication. You must see——'

'Later,' Juliet said indulgently, almost as though she was talking to a child. 'I want a wash and my lunch first. Surely you're hungry, too?'

He looked mildly surprised. 'I—don't think I am,' he said undertainly, 'although I do believe I haven't had my lunch.' He smiled. 'I'm sorry—you must excuse my discourtesy. I've allowed my enthusiasm to run away with me. You must put on something more suitable, anyway, before you visit the dolphins. Come on inside and meet Lallie—she's my housekeeper.'

Juliet's opinion of Lallie went down several notches as she entered the living room of the structure which apparently housed James's laboratory, too. She looked askance at the piles of books and periodicals stacked on every available surface, undusted and unkempt. A sliding pile of records were on the floor before a very good stereo in the corner. Dust was everywhere, plus an overflowing trash basket.

In contrast, the small, bright kitchen was spotless and filled with a delicious aroma that came from a bubbling pot on the stove. Lallie was middle-aged, and dressed trimly in a uniform. Her smile was reserved as she took Juliet's hand when they were introduced.

'Is lunch ready, Lallie?' James asked vaguely.

'It's been ready, Mr James. Don't you remember? I called you.'

'Oh. Yes, of course. Er—where did you put Miss Welborn?'

Lallie looked baffled. 'Not but one place to put her, and that's my room. Don't you remember? You said I could go home every night.'

James's face cleared. 'Oh, yes, that's right. You'll use Lallies room, Miss Welborn. She'll show you where.'

Juliet glanced at Lallie who stared back impassively. 'Come on, miss, I'll show you.'

She led Juliet to a room that fronted on to the ocean. It contained a plain neat set of bedroom furniture. The bed was covered with a white candlewick spread and a pair of gauzy curtains fluttered in the brisk ocean breeze. There was an adjoining bath with a shower. Everything was spotlessly clean.

'I cleared all the drawers and the closet for you,' Lallie remarked, opening the closet. 'And I put clean sheets and a clean spread on the bed, and fresh towels and soap in the bathroom. Mr James said you'd be here about six months.' When Juliet hesitated, she added quickly, 'The longer the better for me. My mother's been poorly lately and she needs me at home as much as possible.'

'It won't take any longer than that to complete the book, I suppose, but I haven't committed myself to staying yet,' Juliet explained. When Lallie looked astonished, she added defensively, 'There are a lot of questions to be cleared up first.'

'If you're worried about staying here alone with him, don't let *that* bother you!' Lallie said bluntly. 'He won't give you trouble that way. He doesn't sleep very well, and when he doesn't, he plays his records. And he has to be dragged in for meals, and won't let me touch his things, but otherwise, he's about the nicest person I know to work for, except maybe his brother, Mr Mark.'

Juliet stiffened. 'I hope I won't have any contact with *him*!'

Lallie's astonishment grew. 'Is that it?' she asked. 'Well, don't worry, you're not likely to see anything of Mr Mark. He does talk to his brother every day by phone, but he respects Mr James's privacy and leaves him alone. We just don't see all we'd like of Mr Mark. A pity, too,' she added firmly, in case Juliet misunderstood her feelings on the subject.

Juliet wasn't surprised to learn where Lallie's sympathies lay. Most of the people on the island would like Mark Bannerman, of course. He wouldn't treat them as he did an unwanted girl who arrived unexpectedly to invade his privacy. And if she was going to remain here, it would probably be wise to be more guarded in her remarks about Mark Bannerman. Her mother had always taught her to tread lightly over strange ground—at least at first.

She looked at the stack of luggage and diplomatically changed the subject.

'Well, no matter whether I go or stay, I shall need a shower and lunch. But I'll wait until I talk more with Mr Bannerman before I decide what I'm going to do.'

Lallie took the hint and Juliet gathered her things together, then went into the bathroom for her shower. The soap was fresh and unscented, and the water was very soft, making it necessary to stand under the shower and rinse for a while before she could remove the lather from her body. When she finally emerged from the bedroom, wearing a cream shirt and brown skirt, she felt like a new person. She had pulled her hair back into a ponytail and her skin glowed. Gone was that fragile look that made her look ill. James, glancing up as she entered, rose slowly to his feet, a startled look on his face.

Lallie was a better cook than a housekeeper. The meal was splendid—a fresh fruit salad, seafood gumbo and iced tea, followed by a blackberry cobbler covered with thick, rich cream—and Juliet felt replete when she had finished. She saw that it had been chosen deliberately as a meal that would not suffer from being held back indefinitely.

James did not talk while he was eating and Juliet, who was tired and hungry, preferred it that way. As he ate, he stared at her, but unlike his brother's James's stare was so absentminded that she felt he was working out some complex problem in his head. After lunch, however, he rose and, to her surprise, firmly took charge of the situation.

'I think we should discuss our business before we go any further, Miss Welborn,' he began crisply. 'To begin with, may I call you Juliet, and will you call me James? It makes it simpler since we'll be working closely together. Now, Lallie said you weren't sure you'd take this job?' A frown flitted across his thin forehead. 'I hope she's mistaken? I would like very much for you to stay on. My book is roughed out, but I need someone to take hold and put it in the right sort of order, and, of course, type it. You seem very suitable. I realise working conditions are not good, if that's your objection. Of course, the island is rather lonely, but Miss Posenby assured me you were used to working in these sort of conditions. Or is it something else you haven't mentioned?' he added anxiously.

Instead of replying to his question, Juliet asked one. 'When did you talk to Miss Posenby about me?'

'This morning. She called to find out if you were suitable. Imagine her surprise—and mine—when she learned that I hadn't had any word of you. She became quite agitated and insisted that I track you down immediately.'

'About Cora,' Juliet went on abruptly, 'would I ever have to have any contact with her?'

'Not at all.' He glanced at her shrewdly. She's supposed to be a supply clerk at the warehouse, and apparently she's efficient—at least, Mark seems to think so—but she certainly takes too much authority on herself.' The thin face hardened and Juliet was briefly reminded of his brother.

Yes, she did that all right, thought Juliet dryly. 'About the people at Bella Vista,' she added hesitantly, 'I wouldn't have to come in contact with them, would I?'

If he was surprised, he did not show it. An unsociable person himself, he probably thought she was the same. 'You may suit yourself,' he said seriously. 'If you don't care to socialise with anyone, that's all right with me. Neither do I. But I—er—suppose you'll want some time off for—er—shopping and things on the mainland occasionally?' he added doubtfully.

Juliet replied firmly that she would. She already saw the pattern of her days emerging if she allowed James to have his way. She would be working twenty hours a day, sleeping at odd intervals, eating only when it became necessary to refuel her body. That had been her father's way of working, but she was not going to allow James Bannerman to get away with it. She would start as she meant to go on. So she briskly provided for time off and they agreed on working hours, then, with that disposed of, James relievedly took her off to the dolphin tanks.

It was really one big tank with gates that could be lowered to divide the dolphins into separate pens. Right now, James was concentrating on one dolphin, a female whom he called Jo, with whom he was seeking to establish an artificial language by using a system that had been successful with chimpanzees. Carefully he lowered a magnetic blackboard into the water. It was marked with symbols—a triangle, a circle and a square.

Jo was to match the symbol with the one she had been given. As Juliet watched fascinatedly, Jo swam forward, pushing a metal circle with her nose, then carefully, she manoeuvred it into place with her grey snout. Afterwards, she smilingly received a fish for having performed correctly.

He told her that Jo and her classmates were adept already at cleaning up their tanks; answering questions by nudging a red ball for 'yes' and a blue one for 'no'; and showing off their built-in sonar by successfully evading an obstacle course while blindfolded. But he was a long way from actually conversing with them through an artificial language and wouldn't be, he admitted cheerfully, until he had taught them the concept of language itself.

'Do you expect to?' Juliet asked.

'Of course. I'm on the brink of a breakthrough,' he replied enthusiastically.

Privately, Juliet thought it was impossible. She had long ago come to the conclusion that the gurgles, sighs and squeaks that a dolphin uttered were just that—gurgles, sighs and squeaks. Her father had thought the same, although he had a high opinion of the dolphin's intelligence.

Whoever was right, dolphins were also lovable, Juliet admitted, watching them gather at the edge of the tank.

Only in a laboratory such as this could she continue working with them. She made up her mind. This was work she loved; she was good at it; so why shouldn't she stay and do it? At the same time, she wondered uneasily if she wasn't being foolish. She had been warned—if today's experiences could be called a warning—and at least two people, Mark and Cora Bannerman, did not want her here. Was she defying them merely for James's sake? James—who reminded her of David Graham? Was that why she was staying? She hoped not, but if so, she decided reluctantly, there must be more of her mother in her than she had thought.

# CHAPTER TWO

AFTER a couple of days, Juliet slipped into a routeine. She was doing work that she enjoyed and she liked James. Lallie had been right—he did not give her a moment's uneasiness when they were alone together at night. He was a pleasant, kind man and surprisingly amenable to any suggestion she made about his book. She soon found that unlike David Graham, whose love for his subject had shone through everything he wrote, James's writing was lifeless, stodgy and tedious, perhaps because his approach to the creatures was purely scientific. She wondered why he bothered to write the book and was not at all surprised to learn that it had been a brainwave of Mark Bannerman's. James had admitted it ruefully, and added that his brother had based his idea on *Dolphin People*, which he had read and liked.

On the other hand, James was assured about his experiments. He knew exactly what he wanted. He was using the notes for a future thesis which would get him his doctorate, and Juliet was surprised to learn that he was working under his old university chief, although the expenses of his project were being carried by the Bannerman Corporation. At times, he was glumly sure he would never accomplish his aims, and at others, he was buoyed with enthusiam. Juliet found that coping with his moods was a little difficult during the half days when she helped him with with the dolphins. She could never view them merely as subjects of an experiment. To her, they were warm, lovable creatures, each with its own distinct, different personality, and although James could not seem to view them that way, there was no question about his success in getting them to respond.

She had not told him that David Graham was her stepfather. He encouraged her to talk about Dr

32

Graham's experiments and theories, but was uninterested in David Graham, the man. Perhaps that was one reason Juliet did not mention her relationship to him. The other reason had something to do with James being a Bannerman, and a shrinking reluctance to enter into any discussion that might force her to talk about her parents' deaths.

The tragedy had left her with a crippling fear of diving. Since childhood, she had been a water baby, diving in strange oceans and the deepest waters with her parents and the members of the diving crew. She had become an experienced diver. But now, the mere thought of the deep, treacherous ocean filled her with dread. It had nothing to do with drowning, but was an irrational fear of the unknown. She was still confident of her breathing ability and took to the dolphin tanks like a pro, but she would not allow herself to think about the day when James might expect her to accompany him on a diving expedition.

On the personal side, Tamassee was good for her. Lallie's excellent food had put on a few needed pounds, and the brisk outdoor life was taking away the dark circles and bringing color back into her eyes and cheeks. She swam every day in the surf near the compound and took walks, but never very far. And in spite of her determination to keep her weekends for herself, she ended up working every one of them, and not venturing from the immediate vicinity of the compound.

Sam delivered their supplies every week and stopped by oftener than that for coffee with Lallie, who was his aunt. Lallie told her that Sam was the accepted taxi service to the village. One merely called Cora and asked for him. But Juliet shrank from doing so, and one day, Sam spoke to her about it.

'I hope you don't still blame me for what happened, ma'am,' he said gently. 'I was jus' following orders.'

'Oh, no, of course not, 'Juliet assured him. 'I understand.'

'Miss Cora is Mr Mark's cousin, and she's the boss. Like it or not, I has to follow her orders or I'll lose my job.'

'Then you're saying that putting me off the island the way she tried to do was his decision, not hers.'

He reflected quietly. 'I would say so, yes, ma'am. Though maybe he didn't expect her to use Cap'n Smith. He'a a fair man, Mr Mark is, an' he don't like the Cap'n—I know that for a fact.'

'But Cora told me she was following his instructions, so it sounds like he *did* know exactly what she planned to do,' she said bitterly.

Sam shrugged. 'You know best, ma'am. I just know *I* didn't like it. But I have to do Miss Cora's orders. You can understand that, can't you, ma'am?'

'Oh, yes, I understand.' And at his continued troubled look, she added more positively, 'I really do, Sam. But I don't think I'd better call you. It might interfere with a time when Mr Bannerman is using your services.'

He looked mildly surprised. 'Didn't you know, ma'am? Mr Mark is gone. He left the island the same day you came, late that afternoon.'

Juliet stared at him, relief, surprise and a dozen other emotions warring within her. 'No, I didn't know,' she said at last. 'Has he gone—for good?'

'For good?' Sam said slowly. 'Mr Mark never goes for good. Sometimes he stays away longer than other times, but sooner or later he comes back. No, ma'am, I'd say Mr Mark has gone for a while—but never *for good.*'

Whatever the mixed reactions she might have to Mark Bannerman's absence, Juliet knew that first and foremost, she felt relief. She knew now that she had been unconsciously expecting Mark to react to her presence by either anger or amusement, had she had been surprised and uneasy when he continued to ignore it. Her hesitancy to leave the compound and been a dread of meeting him. And her worry had been unnecessary! By the time he returned, she would be old news, and knowing James, and his egocentric preoccupation with his own problems, she doubted if it would ever occur to him to mention her in any of these daily phone calls Lallie said he had with his brother.

Mark might never find out that she was on the island.
The thought gave her an odd little feeling, almost of—
disappointment.

The next day, Juliet turned over a new leaf. Seizing
the broom as though it was a weapon, with a duster in
the other hand, she descended upon the living room and
dusted and swept and sorted. One of the things she had
organised for James had been a filing system of sorts,
with his papers in manilla folders. When filing them, it
was easy to see what should be kept and what could be
discarded. With Lallie watching, awed, she filled two
plastic bags with trash and hauled it outside and burned
it. Back inside, with an additional couple of dozen
folders added to the files, it was neater and cleaner, and
for the first time since Juliet came, Lallie was able to lay
the table in the dining room.

Naturally, James howled with dismay when he saw
what had happened, but Juliet appeased him by
showing him the files. However, he continued to
grumble that night and on into the next day, although
most of his grumbling had lost its steam. They were
outside the next morning, working with the dolphins,
when he returned to it. Patiently training the dolphins
to learn something new was hard work. It meant doing
it over and over. They were outside lying on air
mattresses at the edge of the pool, while James moved
the magnetic discs and Juliet took notes, when he
brought up the subject again.

'Sometimes I think you're worse than Mark. And he
treats me like I was about five years old.'

'Sometimes you act like you're about five years old,
James,' Juliet returned crisply. 'You need someone to
take care of you. Lallie doesn't feel she has the
authority to force you to eat your meals on time, or go
to bed when you should.'

'It looks like you're going to have to stay on.' He
glanced at her slyly. 'I'm going to be helpless when you
leave, Juliet. Have you ever thought about that? You've
succeeded in making me completely dependent upon
you. It's all your fault!'

'Oh, no, my lad, you don't lay that on me.' Her voice

was so dry that it was brittle. 'I didn't take this job to be your nanny. I suggest you get yourself a wife.'

James grinned. It was the first time he had made an attempt at humour, and Juliet was surprised at how engaging he could be when he tried. They were both flushed from hanging upside down, and his eyes gleamed behind his spectacles. 'Are you by any chance applying for the position?' he asked teasingly.

She laughed, 'You couldn't afford me!' Her voice was disastrously clear as it carried across the water. 'I'd be too expensive—even for a Bannerman—so leave me out of your calculations!' She flicked water into his laughing face.

'Does that mean if he meets your price you'd be interested, Miss Welborn?'

The voice, coming from above them, was coolly sardonic, and Juliet almost fell into the pool. She looked up with startled eyes and followed the lean length of Mark Bannerman's body from navy sneakers and neatly creased denims to a cold, unsmiling face. Scrambling to her feet, she felt at a disadvantage in her swimsuit. Although it was perfectly respectable, even modest, his cynical eyes made her feel she was clad in the most revealing of bikinis.

'Mark!' James leapt to his feet, grinning from ear to ear. 'This is wonderful! I didn't know you were expected home. And now you can meet my new assistant, Juliet Welborn. If you remember, I hired her just before you left?'

'I've already met Miss Welborn,' Mark replied grimly. Nevertheless, he held out his hand, taking Juliet by surprise and forcing her, by the rule of good manners, to accept it. She stared at it warily for a moment, then a twinkle came into her eyes.

'Excuse me,' she murmured politely. She had been holding a fish, a reward for the dolphin they were working with, and she dropped it into the bucket and gravely held out that hand.

But Mark Bannerman was equal to it. Without comment, he shook her hand, then dropped to a crouch and rinsed off in the pool.

'You'll stay for lunch, won't you, Mark?' James asked eagerly.

'With pleasure.' His brother rose easily to his feet. 'I never miss one of Lallie's meals if I can help it.'

'I'll tell her you're here—she'll be thrilled.'

'Still with us, I see, Miss Welborn?' Mark asked sardonically, watching James hurry off.

'Are you surprised?'

'I must say I am,' he said expressionlessly. 'The work is hard, the hours long, and the surroundings lonely. I expected to find you long gone when I got back. Now, if you were working for me—but James? Sorry, no, not a girl like you.'

Juliet's eyes glittered. 'Oh, I don't know,' she said coolly. 'I realised right away that for a girl like *me*, I was luckily working for the right Bannerman brother.'

His eyes narrowed. 'Indeed?'

'And even a girl like me can recognise what that means.' Her drawl itensified. 'We both know what you think about girls who come to Tamassee hoping for a chance at the Bannerman money. James, fortunately, has no such hang-ups. Now, if you'll excuse me,' she said sweetly, 'I'm really rather busy.' And picking up her air matress, she deliberately crossed over to the other side of the pool. It had been fun twisting the tiger's tail, but she shivered as she thought of the look in his eyes. Mark Bannerman had been angry, with the deadly intense anger of a man unused to having his will crossed. It had probably been good for him, she thought defiantly, dropping to her mattress.

By that time James had returned, and Juliet heard him say, 'Lallie is tickled to death to get a chance to show off her cooking. She's already planning to have your favourite dessert.'

'Bless Lallie,' said Mark, but his voice was absentminded. 'James, how do you like your new assistant?'

'She's great, Mark!' James enthused, with no idea that Juliet could hear him. 'As a matter of fact, she has more practical knowledge of my subject than I do.'

'Indeed?' Mark's voice was smooth, and Juliet had no

doubt that he knew she could hear every word. 'She sounds almost too good to be true. I find it difficult to believe that a beautiful girl with her—er—talents could be satisfied to settle down and play with dolphins.'

'Well, she is—she has!' James's voice was defensively sharp. 'If you think there's something phoney or wrong about Juliet, suppose you check her out at lunch? I think you'll find she's everything she says she is!'

'I intend to,' Mark replied grimly.

Juliet rose, not wanting to hear herself discussed any longer, and went inside. She found Lallie in the throes of an unaccustomed whirl. She had already set the table in the dining alcove, added flowers and place mats, and was now putting out drinks for a pre-luncheon cocktail.

Juliet eyed her preparations with a lifted eyebrow. 'If I didn't know better, I'd say we were having a party,' she remarked sarcastically.

Lallie stared at her, taken aback by the unaccustomed note of criticism in her voice. 'Mr Mark's staying for lunch,' she said in explanation.

'I'm already aware of that,' replied Juliet, swinging her wet towel. 'I just wondered why you bothered to go to so much trouble.'

'*I* happen to like Mr Mark and I don't mind the trouble!' Lallie said firmly. 'If you got any fight with him, you take it up with him personal—don't bring me into it! Now, if you don't mind,' she added with exaggerated patience, 'I've got work to do and you're holding me up. Mr Mark appreciates my meals, even if there's some around here who don't know what they're eating.'

Correctly reading this as a slap at James, Juliet went on into her room, to do as Lallie suggested and change her clothes.

She showered in a hurry and changed into jeans and a loose-fitting shirt. It did nothing for her, and after she had tied her hair into a ponytail, it did less. She looked like a clean, wholesome schoolgirl—which was exactly the effect she wanted. She was making no concessions to Mark Bannerman as a guest.

They were having cocktails as she entered the living room. James, too, had changed—into a pair of slacks and shirt—and he was listening amusedly as Mark teased Lallie about her cooking, using all that famous charm.

'But it looks like your housekeeping has improved.' He looked around solemnly. 'Last time I was here, you couldn't walk in this living room.'

'Oh, that's not my doing, Mr Mark! It's Juliet's. She has this part of the house clean every morning before I get here. James still won't let me in here with a duster.'

'Before you get here?' Mark was frowning slightly.

'I've been staying with my family at nights. Juliet has my bedroom,' Lallie added as Mark continued to look blank. 'I just come in during the day to work. That way, it works out just fine.'

'You know there are only two bedrooms in this place, Mark,' James reminded him.

'I did—but I'd forgotten.' Mark sounded reflective and the look he directed at Juliet was loaded with significance. However, he said nothing as he rose to get her a drink. 'What will you have, Miss Welborn?'

'Sherry, if you please.' She sank on to the couch beside James.

'Mark didn't know that you used to work for David Graham,' James commented. 'He was impressed, because he's read his book on dolphins and liked it very much.'

'He wrote many books on dolphins,' Juliet said coolly, 'but I presume you're referring to *Dolphin People*. It's the one that appealed the most to the general public.'

'That's the one.' Mark handed her the sherry. 'I tried to read one of the others, and found it a bore. He dedicated it to his wife, didn't he?'

Juliet fingered her glass. 'Yes.'

'Did she help him with it?'

'Some.' Juliet was noncommittal.

'You sound like you think he should have dedicated it to you?'

She tilted her chin. 'Do I? I don't intend to,' she said coolly.

'It's an amazing coincidence that you were available just when James started looking for someone to help him,' he remarked. 'How did you learn about this job?'

'Miss Posenby told me.'

'And you couldn't have chosen a man James admired more than Graham.'

'That's fortunate.'

'I overheard your conversation with James earlier, at the pool, and I wondered if you performed some of the same services for Graham? Let's see, what were they? Call him in for meals, put him to bed——'

'Mark!' James exclaimed, trying to laugh off his words and make a joke of them. 'David Graham was married, whereas I—Juliet and I——'

'Yes, I know,' his brother replied smoothly. 'But, from all accounts, she wasn't much of a homemaker. Did she mind sharing, Miss Wellman?'

Juliet paled with anger. Her fingers tightened on her glass stem as she fought to keep her voice under control. 'May I ask what all this has to do with my qualifications, Mr Bannerman?' she asked, with a tight little smile.

Her smile, her indifferent tone, apparently infuriated him, for his face darkened angrily. 'My God, you're a cool one! Didn't it bother you when Graham went overboard? Or did you *smile*, then, too?'

Juliet gaped at him, her cheeks paling with horror. 'How dare you?' she cried wildly. 'You—you're a *monster!*'

'Mark, I can't believe you'd be this cruel!' James looked from Juliet to his brother. 'Surely you didn't mean—to—imply——'

'Didn't I?' Mark queried smoothly. His glare was predatory.

Juliet rose and steadied herself against the back of the couch. 'At the risk of being rude, I must excuse myself, James. I don't want to eat at the same table with your brother!' she added violently.

James looked stunned. 'I—please—Juliet——'

'No, don't say any more.' Her eyes moved to James and softened slightly. 'I'd choke. Goodbye, Mr

Bannerman,' she added coldly. 'I hope I never have to see you again for the little time remaining to me on this island.'

Back in her room, she burst into tears. I'm not going to stay, she told herself violently. Not even for dear, bumbling James and the dolphins was she going to take this kind of punishment. She made up her mind right then. Tonight she was going to give James her two weeks' notice.

She had automatically locked her door, and she was thankful she had when there was a rap, followed by an agitated rattle of the knob.

'Juliet!' called James. 'Come out here! I won't allow Mark to speak to you that way! If he disturbs you, I'll ask him to go home!'

'No, please, James,' she begged. The last thing she wanted to do was cause trouble between the two brothers. 'I—I'm tired, and I'd rather stay in my room.'

'I don't believe you,' James said stubbornly. In her mind's eye she could see the obstinate set to his jaw. 'You're upset about Mark's insinuations, and I don't blame you. He means well, but he doesn't understand what a marvellous boost you've been for me—or how I've come to depend upon your opinions. I won't have him suggesting that you're an opportunist!'

With every word he spoke, James was digging her grave, she thought wearily. Didn't he know that was what was eating Mark—the fact that he had grown to depend upon her? Rather desperately, she repeated her excuses. Mark might be right outside there, listening to her, but she couldn't help that.

'I'm really tired, James. And I prefer to wait for a while before eating my lunch. I—I think I'll work a while on the book. Tell Lallie to put a tray aside for me and I'll be out presently, when I finish. Please, James, there's a dear.'

There was a long pause, while James evidently thought it over. He was used to working to the exclusion of forgetting all about his meals, so it didn't sound too illogical that she would want to do it. Finally he capitulated.

'All right, Juliet, I won't bother you any more. Come out when you feel like it.'

She worked for a while on the book, then slipped into her bikini, over which she put her shirt and jeans, gathered her towel and sunglasses and left the house. She had been slightly stung by Lallie's reference to her swimsuit, and this first wearing of her bikini was an act of defiance, a final cocking of the snook, as it were, before she left. And leave she would: she had made up her mind.

She went into the surf at her usual spot, a deserted stretch of the beach hidden from the dolphin compound by palm trees, and while she splashed, she went over her reasons for quitting again. For one thing, it wasn't fair to continue to use James as a substitute for her father. He wasn't her father, no matter how much he seemed like him, and sooner or later, one of them was going to get hurt. James had already begun to depend upon her too much. He hadn't been altogether kidding when he made that lighthearted proposal this morning. She felt the shadow of a change over what had been, until now, a perfect working relationship. But they were too close, the compound too small, for them to handle anything more personal and it *was* going to get more personal, now that Mark Bannerman had opened his can of worms. Which brought her to the real reason she was quitting—Mark Bannerman. Apparently he was convinced he had been right about her from the beginning, and she hadn't helped matters by making him think she was angling to be Mrs James Bannerman. It had been fun to mock him, but it had merely hardened his already bad opinion of her. And however much bowing and scraping the great man was used to from everyone else on this island, she thought fiercely, she had no intention of taking any more snide remarks from him!

Another ten minutes, and she came out, feeling better. Trotting towards her discarded clothes, she stopped halfway, staring. Mark Bannerman was waiting beside the little pile of clothing. The gold hair glistened under the sunlight, but the dark glasses effectively hid his expression as he watched her approach slowly.

'Waiting for me?' she quipped. Her voice was cool—and wary.

'As a matter of fact, yes,' he said slowly. 'We have to talk.'

'If you say so.'

She picked up her towel and began to rub herself dry as quickly as possible so that she could get into her jeans and shirt. She felt selfconscious in her bikini, although it was as respectable as anything worn on the beaches.

'How did you know I was here?' She was buttoning her shirt and she felt his eyes on her hips and thighs as she reached for her jeans. Squatting, she emptied her shoes of sand and pulled them on.

'Isn't it where you usually come for your afternoon swim?'

'Why, yes.' She looked puzzled. 'Did James tell you?'

'No. The man I set to watch you told me.'

'What?' The face she raised to his was blank. 'Do you mean someone has been *watching* me?'

'Since the first day you came to work for James,' he said matter-of-factly.

She shivered. 'But *why*?'

'I keep up with everyone and everything on this island, so doesn't it strike you that I'd make doubly sure of what's happening to my own brother? Particularly,' he added ironically, 'when he seems to have fallen into the hands of a scheming little bitch like you.'

Juliet gasped. She knew he disliked her, even was suspicious of her, but this—*this* was savagery—with a vengeance! He must really hate her. 'So you're convinced you know me like a book?' she asked sarcastically. Her mouth trembled and she firmed it angrily.

'Like a book—easy to read,' Mark agreed cheerfully. 'Are you sleeping with him yet?' he added abruptly.

Juliet's face flamed. 'Haven't your spies told you that yet?'

'I don't hire men to spy on my own brother,' he said

smoothly. 'That's why I dropped by today—to try to decide for myself what's going on.'

'I hope you weren't disappointed,' she drawled mockingly.

'If you mean in drawing some conclusions, I wasn't, but I don't know everything.'

'Really? I can't imagine you admitting you don't know all there is to know about women!'

'Did I say that?' he asked dryly. 'I know about women like you. It isn't hard, because your kind are all alike, interested in only one thing—money. In your case, by way of a marriage licence. But how you accomplish it isn't always clear—which brings me back to my original question. Are you and James lovers?'

'Ask him!' Juliet was breathing hard, her eyes glittering with rage. 'And when you do, I suggest you be prepared to defend your accusations! James won't like you insulting me that way.'

'Which is exactly why I won't ask him. Besides, James would lie to me,' he added calmly, 'out of a mistaken sense of chivalry. He's got a thing about you. I will give you credit for being a fast worker—all things to all men. When you arrived, you looked like my kind of woman, classy and cool, then today, lo! there's a transformation. You came to lunch looking like a freshman co-ed, squeaky clean and innocent. That appeals to a man like James. It makes him feel protective and wise. It makes him want to fight for your honour, even against his own brother. But you haven't neglected the sex appeal, either, in case you haven't yet reached the primitive man. You go around all morning wearing a swimsuit to remind him of your curves.'

'That does it!' Juliet stood up and brushed the sand from the damp seat of her jeans. 'I'm getting out of here! I've had all I can take from you! Cora said she'd send me home the instant I wanted to go. I presume you have no objection if I ask her to phone for the helicopter?' she added sarcastically.

He reached for her arm almost casually and jerked her back to the sand beside him. His strength made her feel puny as she flopped into an ungainly, struggling heap. 'You're not going anywhere.' He retained his grip on her wrist. 'Do you think I'd let you fly off in a huff and jeopardise my relationship with my brother?'

'I don't care about your relationship with your brother!' she raged, clawing ineffectually at his restraining fingers. 'You can't stop me from leaving! You may be the big cheese around here, but you don't own me, and I don't intend to work here or anywhere else where I might see or hear of you! You pollute the air I'm trying to breathe!'

'You're not going anywhere.' He regarded her efforts to free herself with amusement. 'You're stupid if you didn't know I would anticipate your reaction to what I said. I had a long talk with Miss Posenby today,' he added, with seeming irrelevance. 'I told her how pleased James was with you and how well you were doing. She told me that you'd written to her that you liked your job, too, so I suggested that we sign a contract for six months—or until the book was finished. It would protect both you and James—and she was happy to agree. As your agent. When she learned the salary I was prepared to offer, she said she knew you'd be thrilled,' he added sardonically. 'So you're signed, sealed and delivered, Miss Welborn, and if you try to break your contract, I'll sue you for your reputation and reliability. You'll have difficulty recovering from the mud I'll sling on you before I'm through.'

'You wouldn't!' she gasped.

'Try me and see,' he said calmly.

'You really are a nasty bill of goods,' she said clearly. 'What a foul, devious mind you have, to think up a twist like that! I should have followed my first instincts and got out of this place at once.'

'Perhaps you should have. But it's too late now,' he warned. He seemed unmoved by her words. 'I don't intend for you to leave until James changes his mind about you. Right now, he thinks you're wonderful, that he can't get along without you. Maybe he can't; I presume you're as good as he says you are. Anyway, you are staying—but on my terms. For one thing, this will be a nine-to-five job. You're not remaining alone in the house with him.'

Juliet started. 'So that's what this is all about!' She laughed harshly. 'Big brother Mark has appointed himself guardian of his little brother's morals! And because we're unchaperoned, you've automatically assumed I'm corrupting him? How—how *quaint*! I suppose you think the instant Lallie leaves, I hop into his bed, just as you once insinuated I wanted to do to yours?'

'I don't know. Do you?' he asked sardonically. 'James is a mere man, after all, with little experience of your type of female. It would be easy to use sex to tie him up with a wedding ring.'

Her eyes darkened with rage. She drew a shaky breath. 'You seem to have an inflated idea of your worth, Mr Bannerman. There are a lot of women in this world who aren't dying to sleep with a Bannerman—or even marry one!'

'I haven't run across one,' he drawled dryly. 'Sorry, Miss Welborn, but Miss Posenby was a fount of information. Oh, she presented a touching picture of you as an orphan, without a home or a job. I could almost hear the violins in the background.' His laughter was unpleasant. 'But you came through as a girl with an eye to the main chance. When did you hear about this job, and realise you were tailor-made for it? Before or after you left the Graham project? It was easy for a bright girl like you, wasn't it? When you learned of it, you knew your special qualifications would get you hired. If not, a little play for sympathy and Miss Posenby's soft heart was touched.'

Juliet drew a deep breath. She was too angry to speak sensibly. She certainly had no intention of defending herself to Mark Bannerman! He wasn't her boss, she reminded herself fiercely, and she wasn't accountable to *him* for anything! Anyway, why try to explain? It was useless to protest that she hadn't known anything about this job, because his mind had been made up before he even talked to Miss Posenby. Everything she said merely strengthened his prejudice against her, because he *wanted* to think badly of her! He was contemptuous of all women, even those whom he made love to, except someone like his cousin Cora, and that was because her type was no threat to him.

He waited, watching the play of emotions on her expressive face. 'Have I managed to shut you up at last?' he asked mockingly.

'You're doing the talking,' she said bitterly. 'Go ahead and finish, so I can remove myself from your presence. I feel dirty, just sitting here and listening to you!'

His mouth thinned. 'That's a pity,' he said softly, 'because we'll be seeing quite a lot of each other from now on.'

'What do you mean?'

'Don't you remember? I said you aren't living with James any longer. You will be living at Bella Vista until that book is finished. I'll see to it that you're driven down to the compound every morning and picked up after lunch every afternoon. You'll work on the book at Bella Vista.'

'I won't!'

'Oh, yes, you will. And don't bother to go running to James, thinking he'll back you. When I tell him how you're endangering your reputation by staying with him, he'll be the first person to agree with me that this is best. James is a gentleman, you see.'

Stung by the bleak relentlessness of his words, Juliet burst into furious speech. 'You mocking devil, you're crazy if you think I'll live at your house!' she choked. 'I don't intend to have to look at your face every day for the next six months!'

'Then finish the book early and you'll be free to go,' he remarked humorously. 'I'll do everything I can to make it easy for you. And don't think you'll make me angry by calling me names, my dear. Frankly, it's a relief to know you hate me enough so you won't change your tactics and try to get your money-grabbing little paws on me.'

'You're safe, I assure you,' she said in a frozen little voice. 'And whether you believe me or not, so is James. Not even the pleasure of spending the Bannerman millions would reconcile me to the prospect of having you as my brother-in-law!'

Juliet moved out that same afternoon. James did not try to stop her, although he was reluctant to see her go.

'If Juliet really feels she must——' he offered grudgingly.

'Come on, old man, you know how people talk, especially in the tight little communities on these islands.' Mark laughed easily, as though he had nothing in mind but the protection of Juliet's good reputation. 'She's a dishy little female and you're a Bannerman, and anything a Bannerman does is news.'

'Of course I know how people talk,' James said impatiently. 'But Juliet knows I wouldn't——'

'Juliet wants to go,' Mark said firmly, and that seemed to be that.

Later, when Juliet was packing, James came to her room.

'I wish this wasn't necessary,' he said wretchedly. 'It's going to be inconvenient, having you working on the book at Bella Vista and only here in the mornings. Besides, I'm going to miss you terribly.'

'Why don't you move to Bella Vista, then, James?'

He looked surprised. 'Well, naturally, I couldn't leave the dolphins! Surely you know that? The dolphins are more important than my feelings or any inconvenience your absence may cause.'

'That's all right, James,' said Juliet, blindly folding a blouse and tucking her shoes into odd corners. 'Just be a dear and don't go on about it, please. It doesn't suit me, either, this move, but it seems I'm being given no choice.'

'Don't go, then,' he said eagerly. 'Mark won't force you to go if you refuse. And I—I've been thinking of a way around things——'

'Almost ready?' Mark asked coolly from the doorway.

James flushed embarrassedly, and with the mumbled excuse of having to feed the dolphins, disappeared.

Mark was furious. 'He's going back to that

conversation, and next time I expect you to stop him cold,' he snapped. 'I'm warning you right now that you'd better find a way to make James understand that you're not returning here in any circumstances. If you don't, I'll do it for you, and I won't be kind about it!'

Juliet looked at him defiantly. 'Go to hell, Mark Bannerman! If you don't want your brother asking me to stay then go tell him yourself. Don't threaten me—I'm not going to take any more of your abuse!'

'You'll take what I dish out and keep your mouth shut about it.' He bit off the words with chilly emphasis. 'Don't cross swords with me, my dear. If you do, you'll get hurt. Now, get your things together and let's get out of here before you have that poor fool in worse shape than he is already.'

Juliet snapped the catches shut on her suitcase and faced him, her face frozen in a mask of dislike. 'I'm ready to go when you are.'

Mark didn't say anything more to her until they reached Bella Vista. Parking the jeep before the front entrance, he hopped out, remarking, 'Go on in. I'll have your luggage taken up. They're expecting you.'

For the first time, Juliet remembered Mai's warning and wondered if this could be some elaborate plot. Had Mark Bannerman brought her here because he wanted her, as Mai had hinted he might? But no. Remembering that cold, pitiless face and eyes, she knew that he despised her. She was in no danger of his trying to make love to her.

In the well-lighted hallway, she was greeted by a woman with a plain, weatherbeaten face, a charming smile and a pair of kind eyes. She greeted Juliet warmly.

'Hullo there! You must be Juliet Welborn? I'm Daisy Yeager.'

'Oh! You're the typist, aren't you?'

Daisy's smile widened. 'Is that what you were told? By Cora Bannerman, I expect?'

'Isn't it true?'

'Oh, yes, I type.' Her eyes danced as though she found Cora amusing.

'Have you been making Daisy's acquaintance, Miss

Welborn?' It was Mark, who had come in right behind her. He laid an affectionate arm across the older woman's shoulders. 'Shall we call the girl Juliet, Daisy?' he asked sweetly. 'After all, she'll be with us for a while, and we want her to feel at home. Daisy is my indispensable right hand, Juliet,' he added, his eyes glinting as they met hers. 'I think one calls a person like her a private secretary. I just know the Bannerman Corporation would grind to a halt if I lost her. She worked for my father and taught me everything I know, although she's training young Paul now to take over some of her duties.' Juliet, who was astounded by the change in Mark Bannerman, mumbled something indistinguishable. 'Speaking of Paul, where is he, Daisy?'

Daisy looked mischievous. 'Oh, he's around, but never fear, he'll show up when he gets a look at Juliet.'

Mark looked taken aback. 'Indeed?' He frowned slightly. 'Will you show Juliet to her room, Daisy? It's the Blue Room. Make sure she has everything she wants and tell her about the dinner hour and that sort of thing. Meantime, I'll find Paul.'

Daisy nodded and led the way up the stairs. Juliet, following her, was able for the first time to take a good look at her surroundings. She saw that the house was gracefully proportioned, and its furnishings including some priceless antiques of the period. Nothing she saw agreed with her impression of Mark Bannerman, and although the house was richly furnished, nothing gave her the cloying feeling the luxurious cottage had done.'

'This is a beautiful old place,' she murmured.

'Oh, yes,' Daisy agreed cheerfully. 'It has a colourful history, too. It was built by an ancestor of Mark's who was a pirate, one of Elizabeth the First's buccaneers. He saw the island on his wanderings and fell in love with it. When he married, he brought his wife here to live and built Bella Vista for her. She was a Spanish lady who was crossing the ocean to marry a man her parents had chosen for her when Thomas Bannerman raided the ship, stole its gold and the lady.'

'It sounds like the plot of a pirate movie,' Juliet commented sceptically.

'Except that it happens to be true. There they are—Thomas and Carlotta.'

Juliet and Daisy paused before two ancient portraits, side by side. They had obviously been painted by the same artist. One was of a swashbuckling gentleman in silk and lace, wearing a blond perruke, his hand resting on the hilt of a sword at his side. He had the look of a pirate, arrogant, dangerous, someone who took what he wanted and be damned to the rest. His lady was a beautiful girl, with dark, gentle eyes and a serene smile beneath her lace mantilla.

'She doesn't look unhappy,' Juliet ventured.

'She wasn't. She was very much in love with him. It's said that when he died, she went into deep mourning and never left the island again.'

'There's a look of Mark Bannerman about him, but he doesn't resemble James at all,' Juliet went on thoughtfully.

'Of course not. James isn't a Bannerman.'

Juliet stared at her, shocked. At the same time, it answered a lot of questions that had been puzzling her all along. The difference in the brothers, for instance. James was gentle, with an obstinacy that held nothing of Mark Bannerman's forcefulness of character. James was also kind and considerate, and Mark was tough and cruel. 'I can't say I'm surprised,' she said dryly.

Daisy looked at her thoughtfully. 'James was adopted by Stephen, Mark's father, when he was a boy. Caroline had died when Mark was ten and Stephen married James's mother, Lisa, for one reason—to have a mother for his son.' She drew a sharp breath. 'It was a disaster. At that time, Mark was twelve and James about four. Lisa shirked her responsibility from the beginning. Stephen and Lisa were killed in a car crash when Mark was in his first year at Harvard and it left him with James to raise—an awesome burden for an eighteen-year-old boy. Of course, Stephen left the Bannerman money to Mark, which was only fair, but James has taken advantage of it to lean on Mark rather too much at times. He can be quite a handful. He's drawn to the wrong women, for instance.'

Juliet stared. Daisy must be crazy! James—and the wrong woman? Why, he would be like a sacrificial lamb!

'I can see you don't believe me,' Daisy grinned reluctantly. 'It isn't exactly James's fault, but he *has* got into some scrapes with women. He seems to be a patsy for any female who comes along and sees him as an easy route to the Bannerman money through marriage. Mark has had to rescue him more than once.'

Juliet continued to stare at her blankly. It didn't sound like James, but she had to concede reluctantly that Mark Bannerman might have a point there when he worried about her possible effect on James. Apparently he was highly susceptible to feminine influence, but, unlike Mark, who thought it was sex, Juliet knew better. She had lived alone with James for a month, and he had never made a sexual advance towards her. Whatever his brother might think, James was not a womaniser—but he *had* responded to her interest in his work. And if Mark Bannerman thought he could stop *that*, he didn't know James!

'There's this thing he's involved with right now,' Daisy was talking on. 'Very much against Mark's better judgment, he agreed for James to withdraw from his university training and take up this project with the dolphins. He approved only if James agreed to spend no more than two years on the theory he's trying to prove. But it worries him.'

'Mr Bannerman takes himself seriously,' Juliet said dryly.

'He has to. Most of the time, James is either in a scrape or getting over one, and Mark thinks people take advantage of him.'

'Women?' Juliet asked solemnly.

But Daisy saw the smile she was suppressing and was put on the defensive. 'All right, laugh! I know you think it sounds ridiculous, but James can be a pack of trouble. And if Mark snarls at people sometimes, it's because he's trying to cut trouble off at the pass before it makes headway. Take my word for it.' By this time they were at the door of Juliet's bedroom. 'How do you like it?' she added, abruptly changing the subject.

The Blue Room derived its name from the touches of blue in its furnishings and that of the adjoining private bath, and it was very luxurious. The windows, with their own balcony, overlooked a well-tended rose garden, complete with fountain and statuary. Juliet was pleasantly surprised. In Mark Bannerman's present mood, she had expected to be given something like an attic bedroom.

'It's very beautiful,' she said admiringly.

'It's one of the most beautiful rooms in the house.'

'Isn't yours the same?'

'One of the nice things about Mark,' Daisy said obliquely, 'is that he insists that his employees must be as comfortable as he is. It's his guests who are assigned small rooms with hall baths. But this particular room is reserved for Mark's—favoured guests. It adjoins his, you see,' she added blandly.

Juliet looked at her sharply, a little disquieted by her expression.

'Do you mind my asking a question, Juliet? I hope you don't think I'm getting out of line, but I prefer to deal in straight facts, so I won't goof.' As Juliet continued to look blank, Daisy added coolly, 'Does Mark have a yen for you? That silly story about your reputation is just an excuse to bring you here, surely? No one pays any attention to things like that any more.'

Juliet hesitated, then took the plunge. 'I'm here because Mark Bannerman is afraid I'll compromise James into a marriage proposal if I stay,' she said evenly.

'You can't be serious!' Daisy was openly disbelieving, but one look at Juliet's face convinced her. 'That's absurd! Why should he object to James getting married? He's often said it would be the best thing that could happen to him.'

'But not to someone like me! You see, he's implied that I'm a gold-digger, a man-chaser and some other equally unpleasant things. In other words, I deliberately formulated a campaign to marry James by applying for this job, knowing that Miss Posenby couldn't help but think me suitable when she learned of my qualifications. You see, I used to work with a scientist whose field was dolphins. According to Mark, when I learned that James was looking for a typist, I quit and decided to come here so I could marry him.'

She stopped because Daisy had collapsed into a chair, laughing. 'Now *that* does sound like a movie! One of those corny old musicals about gold-diggers!' She wiped her eyes. 'Mark isn't crazy and he certainly isn't stupid! Are you trying to tell me he really believes all that nonsense?'

'I assure you he does.' Juliet eyed her bitterly. 'If he isn't crazy or stupid, then what's wrong with him? He seems to have the idea that every female who sets foot on this island is trying to capture a Bannerman, matrimonially or otherwise!'

Daisy sighed. 'Unfortunately, it happens all too often that way. We have a lot of gate-crashers, even here, where we should be reasonably safe from intrusion. In the city, Mark has had to hire a bodyguard at times. Oh, it's partially due to the publicity he gets, for the scandal sheets have a heyday every time he dates someone new. But there are some women who simply can't resist a challenge.' She sighed again. 'I'm sorry, Juliet, you seem to have got the backlash. Ordinarily, Mark's eyes are wide open, but he recently had a very bad experience. A teenaged girl bribed a servant to get her into Mark's bedroom. She threatened to claim rape, drugs, the whole sordid story, if he didn't either pay or keep her. Her mother was behind it all, but it was a mess! And she was only fifteen!'

Juliet shuddered. 'But what have I done to make him think I'm like that?'

'Probably nothing. You did say he was acting for James, didn't you? He's protective of James, partly because the lad is such a wide-eyed innocent, and partly because he's been responsible for him most of James's life. If he thought you were tampering with James's happiness, or a threat to it, he'd be down on you like a ton of bricks. You see, James's mother——' she stopped, hesitating.

'Go on!' Juliet said resentfully. 'You can't get that far and then stop. What has James's mother to do with it?'

'She was—like that. Like you've described. Stephen Bannerman fell in love with a woman he thought would love him and his son, and all the other things he cared for—quiet things like coming here to Tamassee. She wasn't like that at all. She married him for his money, and it wasn't long before he knew it. She didn't even care about her own child very much. There were other men, and that just about broke Stephen, for he was a proud man. I'm afraid Mark got a distorted view of marriage from her. It was particularly bad since Lisa Bannerman was the one who was driving the car that plunged over the cliff and killed them both. She was drunk.'

Juliet was silent, digesting what she had been told. In spite of herself, she felt a twist of pity for Mark Bannerman. Perhaps he was merely acting out of love for James, however misguided his intentions were. . . . She herself knew how easy it was to feel protective towards James.

When she looked up, Daisy was watching her uneasily.

'What's the matter?' Juliet was rueful. 'Wishing you hadn't told me the family secrets? For what it's worth, I promise you I won't blab what I've been told in confidence.'

'No, I don't think you will,' admitted Daisy, 'but I *am* wishing I hadn't told you about Mark's childhood. It's made you feel sorry for him, hasn't it?'

'Yes. Wasn't that why you did it?'

'I suppose so—but it was stupid of me. You're a beautiful girl, and also very vulnerable about people. So long as you hated Mark, you were armoured against him. Remember what I said about this room? It's usually occupied by his favoured guest? Substitute current love interest, and you'll have it. I'm not sure if that's what he has in mind, but I'm afraid, Juliet—for you. He's hard,' she warned. 'And he's not above using you mercilessly and discarding you rather ruthlessly when it's over. Don't allow yourself to feel pity for him or he'll use it. Don't be vulnerable—he'll take advantage of that, too. I love him as I would a son if I had one, but I'm not blind to his faults. He'll break you, Juliet, if you yield one inch to him. Please don't.'

Juliet smiled. Whatever gave Daisy the idea that Mark Bannerman had such powers? She must bring out the protective instinct in the older woman. Right now, Daisy was looking like an anxious hound dog with her forehead set in a thousand wrinkles as she watched Juliet with woeful eyes. But she meant well, even if she was totally wrong about Mark Bannerman's powers of persuasion.

'Don't worry, Daisy,' she assured her gently. 'I won't fall in love with Mark Bannerman—I promise you, he's not my type. But I'm glad you told me what you did, because perhaps now I won't have to hate him so much. I don't like to hate people—it makes me ill. And, Daisy,' she added smilingly, 'I meant what I said. There's not a chance in a million I'd *ever* fall in love with Mark Bannerman!'

# CHAPTER THREE

THAT night, Juliet wore something that had seen service at many a faculty cocktail party, a slim, oyster-coloured skirt topped by a long-sleeved silk blouse. Unfortunately, it missed the restrained appearance she was striving for. Nothing could subdue the glow carried by golden skin or blue-black hair. No make-up, however discreetly applied, could have equalled the black-lashed violet eyes, moistly pink lips or the tinge of natural colour on her cheekbones. Looking at herself in the mirror, she was vaguely dissatisfied. She had wanted to look sedate and dignified, but there was nothing she could do about the sparkle of anticipation in her dark eyes. It had nothing to do with make-up and everything to do with the conflict between herself and Mark Bannerman. Dispassionately, she thought about what she had learned that afternoon. She didn't need Daisy's warning to know that she would be headed straight for disaster if she allowed herself to be taken in by his charm. But there was no danger of that so long as there was this strong mutual hatred of each other. And that, she reminded herself grimly, wasn't likely to change. Mark Bannerman was an arrogant bastard, and nothing could ever sweeten his personality so that she found it palatable.

Downstairs, she found Daisy and a young man having cocktails. Daisy introduced him as Paul Bradford, Mark's secretary. Mark, she explained, was tied up right now with a business acquaintance who had arrived unexpectedly this afternoon with his wife, and who wanted Mark to invest some money in his business.

'Mr Alexander has Mark cornered in the study right now, but he might as well save his breath. He hasn't a prayer of persuading Mark,' Daisy said dryly.

'Does Mr Bannerman like disappointing people?'
Juliet queried sweetly.

'Wait until you meet the Alexanders before you
defend them,' Daisy warned sharply. 'Mark has a
reputation for honesty in business circles, but Alexander
hasn't. Also, they gatecrashed by hiring a pilot to fly
them in, then somehow bluffed their way past Cora.
Mark is sending them home first thing tomorrow. He
doesn't like people who invite themselves to Tamassee.'

'Too bad,' Juliet said blandly. 'Is he going to make
them sleep on the beach?'

'What?'

'Never mind.' She took a sip of her cocktail and
smiled at Paul. 'This tastes good. What is it?'

'A local drink that's made with the local rum. Most
ladies like it because it's concocted with fruit and mint.
But beware, it's lethal—two of them and you're flat on
your face!' He grinned. 'It's a speciality of the house
down at the hotel.'

'Hotel? What hotel?'

Paul and Daisy looked at one another and laughed.
It was Daisy who answered. 'You don't know about the
hotel? It's a relic, of course, an antique. You'd have to
see it to believe it.'

'Really, is it an operating hotel? On Tamassee?'

'I believe there are a couple of rooms equipped to
handle guests,' Daisy chuckled. 'And the cook *can* serve
extra meals—if he's notified in advance. Actually, his
baked swordfish is delicious.'

Juliet was stunned. A hotel! There had been one here
all along when Cora, acting on Mark Bannerman's
orders, had threatened to force her to sleep on the
beach! It was another little pinprick, another score to
add to the growing list against both of them.

'Daisy! This girl thinks you're talking about a *real*
hotel!' Paul chuckled at the look on Juliet's face. 'Take
it from me, Juliet, this one bears no resemblance to the
real thing. It was built in the early 1900's, and hasn't
been touched since. The rooms have ceiling fans,
hanging flypaper, iron beds, no electricity, and the one
bath is down the hall—a clawfoot tub and antiquated

plumbing. The public rooms are electrified by a generator—and there's a bar, of sorts. One long, unbroken piece of Honduras mahogany with a brass rail. Get the picture?'

'I think so,' she laughed.

'Would you like to go there for dinner tomorrow night?' he asked diffidently.

Before she could reply, Mark Bannerman entered with his guests. Juliet knew that he had overheard Paul's invitation and she sensed his disapproval. He was looking very handsome tonight—disturbingly so—his tanned blond looks accentuated by a dark dinner jacket and white ruffled shirt front, but beneath the suave surface, Juliet knew he was angry and irritable and spoiling for a fight. It was an oddly exhilarating thought.

Juliet disliked his guests on sight and saw no reason to be polite once they had snubbed her. John Alexander was a cold, calculating business man and his wife, Stella, a bored blonde with hard blue eyes, was wearing a chic black dress that showed off an astounding amount of her thin, tanned body. Two pairs of cold eyes summed up her faculty dress as beneath their notice.

It was a relief to Juliet, as it meant she could concentrate on Paul, who was entertaining and fun. He took her outside to show the part of the grounds that was lit at night, and she stayed as long as possible. When they returned, she lingered near the door, listening as Paul talked eagerly, unaware that Mark Bannerman was watching them disapprovingly. She put off the moment of return as long as possible, not noticing how often he looked their way, his face growing darker every time they laughed or Paul bent his head solicitously towards her.

Finally he broke up the lively twosome with a harshly voiced command.

'Paul! We need you over here!'

The interruption sounded over-loud in the quiet room and Juliet, glancing up in surprise, met an icy glare of disapproval. Surely Mark Bannerman didn't object to her talking to his secretary? It should have had him cheering—anything to keep her away from James!—but he was acting like a Victorian chaperone. Good grief, the man was impossible!

Paul, stopped in the middle of a sentence, looked slightly disconcerted, but he rose at once, obedient to his master's voice. 'Don't go away,' he whispered before he hurried over to join Mark and the Alexanders.

But he didn't come back. Mark kept him at his side until dinner, and then Juliet found herself pinned firmly between her host and John Alexander. The seating was casual, and obviously Alexander hadn't got what he was after, but that didn't keep him from dominating the table with talk of business. His conversation excluded his wife as well as Juliet, but that did not help, since Stella was set upon a course of ignoring Juliet. Altogether, it was the most uncomfortable dinner she had ever endured, and by the time it was over she was simmering with indignation.

As they left the dining room, Paul caught her eye and grinned ruefully.

'Looks like it just isn't my night! Nor tomorrow night, either. Mark wants me to accompany them to the airport tomorrow morning and see them off. I won't get back.'

The indignation that Juliet had been nursing throughout dinner burst its bounds. 'I didn't know your duties included baby-sitting,' she remarked sarcastically.

Paul flushed with embarrassment. 'I do whatever I'm asked to do,' he said stiffly. 'I'm lucky to have an opportunity to work for Mark Bannerman and I wouldn't do anything to jeopardise my position. I'm sorry it means that *our* plans will be changed, b-but——'

By that time Juliet was feeling guilty. 'I'm sorry,' she said quickly. 'It's all right, we'll do it another time.'

'Look,' he said eagerly, 'how about this? Could you get off and go with me? We could stay overnight, have dinner, go dancing. What about it?'

It sounded wonderful and Juliet longed to get away, but she hesitated. Paul asked quickly, 'Aren't you allowed weekends off?'

'Yes, of course—James agreed to that. It's just that——' It was just that she couldn't afford the price of a hotel room, not during tourist season, and although Paul Bradford might have thought she would be sharing his, she had every intention of paying her own way. She decided to be frank. 'Look, I'd love to go, but I can't afford a hotel room. Another time, when I can pay my own way——'

He interrupted eagerly. 'Oh, if that's all, I'll lend you the money.'

'I couldn't possibly let you do that,' she said firmly.

'Nonsense! Daisy and I borrow from one another all the time. She's always running out of cigarette money.'

Juliet laughed. 'We're talking about slightly more than cigarette money!'

'Having financial difficulties, Juliet?' The drawl was loaded with meaning.

She whirled around. 'Not at all,' she said crisply. 'Nothing I can't handle, at any rate.'

'I'm trying to persuade Juliet to accept a loan,' Paul explained ingenuously.

The hooded eyes surveyed her thoughtfully. 'And you object, Juliet?'

Paul, who was oblivious to cross-currents, spoke up enthusiastically. 'I know what we can do! My married sister lives in the Keys. She'll be glad to put you up. I'll call her as soon as we get there. How does that sound?'

'It sounds wonderful. I'm dying to get away from here.' An imp of mischief made Juliet turn to Mark and ask sweetly, 'Don't you agree, Mr Bannerman?'

'That you're dying to get away from here?' he asked sardonically. 'Yes, I expected that sooner or later the façade would crack. You're not the sort of girl to last long on Tamassee.'

She was stung, but she couldn't allow herself the luxury of a reply until the bridge players had left the room. When they did, she stopped him.

'Just a moment—if you please, Mr Bannerman! I think I'm entitled to an explanation and an apology!'

He raised his eyebrows. 'An apology?' he drawled. 'For what act of mine do I owe you an apology, Juliet?'

Her anger exploded. 'Yes, you're right—you insult me so frequently that it *is* hard to pinpoint one instance! But you owe me an explanation for your objectionable behaviour while I was talking to Paul Bradford!'

He looked at her impassively. 'I have no objection to you talking to Paul Bradford so long as you keep it impersonal. But I won't have you tampering with his feelings. Like James, he's a vulnerable young man. I won't have you using him merely to tease me. He's too susceptible.'

'To *tease* you!' she gasped, horrified. 'How dare you suggest such a thing?'

'Because it's obvious that's what you're doing.' His drawl was bored. 'You'll go to any lengths to punish me for breaking up your little plot to get James. And, incidentally, to try to bring yourself to my attention. But it won't work, my dear. I haven't the slightest interest in you, either as my mistress or a sometime playmate.' His eyes raked her coolly, then he smiled. 'You're not my type.'

Juliet felt as though the top of her head was coming off. It was the smile that did it. With icy deliberation, she controlled her fury. It was a fight to the finish, and she was going to have to keep her wits about her if she was going to win. So, slowly, coolly, she smiled back.

'Do please give me credit for knowing that from the beginning,' she murmured languorously. 'But you must admit, Paul is a good catch.' His eyes narrowed. 'He told me all about himself while we were in the garden. Personable, well off, the son of a wealthy real estate man in Miami—oh, he's such a g-o-o-o-d catch!' she cooed. 'And he's already very impressed with me! It would be so easy this weekend to put him—shall we say—under obligation to me. It means working fast, but then I don't have that much time. If I don't move in on him while I have the chance, some other girl might come along and beat me to the prize. Of course, his income isn't up to the Bannerman millions,' she added casually, with a sidelong glance at Mark's darkened face, 'but then, with you so critical, it might be wiser to drop James altogether and concentrate on someone like Paul.'

Almost she quailed before the look in his eyes. But he merely asked harshly, 'Are you daring to defy me?'

'Why not? Do you really think you can stop me?' Her heart was beating fast. This living dangerously was scary, but it gave her a heady triumph to realise she had angered him to the point of almost losing control.

'I can try.'

'Perhaps. But if you issue a direct order, telling Paul to stay away from me, he's going to want to know why. And if you tell him, I don't think he'll believe you. Not everyone sees me as the monster you do. Even Daisy thinks you're prejudiced! Anyway, it will be interesting to see which one of us wins, won't it?'

Mark did not reply. The grey eyes were watching her with an oddly appreciative expression in their depths.

Supremely confident in her powers at having stopped him at last, Juliet went on mockingly, 'Paul is really a rather refreshing innocent, don't you agree? Not like my usual conquests, of course, but then I like a change occasionally.' She studied her nails and patted back a languid yawn. 'I haven't made up my mind yet if I should take a hotel room or accept the invitation to his sister's house. It *would* put a crimp in my plans but then, respectability *is* the keynote, when one is angling for a marriage licence, isn't it?' she added, with honeyed innocence.

'I think you'd better dismiss Paul from your plans.' He seemed to have recovered his good humour: there was even a hint of amusement lurking in his eyes. 'I've changed my mind. Paul won't be going; Daisy will see the Alexanders off. If you like, of course, you may go to town with Daisy, but I warn you, she isn't much for night life.'

Juliet stared at him. For God's sake, she thought blankly, does he really think I'm serious? I've been babbling nonsense for the past five minutes, but he must think I mean it! How long could he expect to keep her from Paul, if she was really interested in dating him? Not that she was, except as an excuse to get off his

island and away from that oppressive atmosphere.
Perhaps she could even find a job while she was gone.

She shrugged wearily. 'I haven't the money to go with
Daisy and you know it. You pay my salary, so you
must know it's due. And I suppose now that you know
I'm broke, you'll take a mean pleasure in withholding it?'

He did not reply and she looked up to find him
watching her calculatingly.

'Why did you leave after Graham died?' he asked
abruptly.

'I wanted a change,' she said shortly.

'A change? Because you were knocked for a loop by
his death?'

'Is that so impossible to believe?' Her voice was bitter
with ice.

'Impossible? No, but it could be most objectionable,
in certain circumstances.'

'Objectionable? Why? In what circumstances?'

Instead of explaining, he added, 'I looked up the
records of Graham's laboratory. In case you wonder
how: a subsidiary of Bannerman's financed Graham,
and the financial records were open to me. I found you
were Graham's protégée, green, untrained, without any
scientific background. Your salary came out of
Graham's pocket. In other words, he was keeping you.
Everyone else on that team was a professional,' he went
on grimly, 'including Graham's wife. They all stood
high in their fields. You were the only amateur there.
So I'm asking you again, Miss Welborn—why?'

'Suppose you tell me,' she said shakily. 'I'm sure your
devious little mind has come up with a brilliant
deduction.'

'If you like,' he drawled. 'I think you were Graham's
mistress.'

The shock hit her like a blow, staggering her with its
unexpectedness. It was the last thing she expected to
hear. She had thought he was going to tell her that he
knew she was David Graham's daughter. She gave a
sharp cry of rage and glared at him, her teeth clenched,
her hands doubled in fists. How did one deny such an
obscene charge?

'How dare you? You—you're vile! You're unspeakable! I—he—he *loved* his wife! There was never anyone else for either of them!'

Mark was watching her without the slightest trace of remorse, his cold grey eyes registering her shock and horror.

'Very well, it wasn't Graham,' he said bluntly. 'But it was someone—or something else—that's knocked the stuffing out of you. And don't try to tell me it's my imagination. You flinch every time I mention Graham or that diving trip.'

His eyes were like searchlights, trying to read her mind. Juliet glared back, her eyes hating him, her cheeks burning as though they were afire. That was the way she felt, as though she had been exposed to a hot blast. She shuddered at the thought of telling him anything about herself or her parents. Whatever he learned, he would use it somehow against her—any small scrap of fact, any small straying register of emotion. She would never tell him anything, *never*, *never*!

'Go to hell!' Her voice was virulent with hatred.

He smiled, a slow smile full of anticipation. 'I may,' he drawled. 'Or we may together. At any rate, keep your secrets. I'm not overly concerned with your past—or the men in it. From now on, I propose to be the only man in your future. You wondered what I meant by saying I found your grief for Graham objectionable? I don't like to share, particularly not with a dead man.'

She stared at him, shocked, unsure that she had heard right, and a slow tide of red blood crept up her throat and across her face. 'You—you're crazy! You hated me five minutes ago!'

His eyes glinted with amusement. 'And then I learned that I wanted you,' he said smoothly. 'While you were spinning that fairytale about Paul. I like a woman with a sense of humour.'

'You know, you're dangerous, Mr Bannerman! All this because you want to separate me from James?' she gulped.

His face darkened. 'Leave James out of it. It has nothing to do with him.'

'My God, the lengths you'll go to to protect him!'

He frowned. 'My motives are obscure even to me, but I assure you, protection of James is not one of them. I'm not as altruistic as you seem to think. I have no intention of allowing Paul Bradford or James to have you. You're mine.'

Juliet raised her hands to her hot cheeks. 'J-just what are you trying to say?'

'You want a weekend on the mainland, right? I'm offering you one.'

'Why—how?'

'By paying lavishly for the pleasure of your company.'

'I—I don't know what you mean,' she said shakily.

'Surely I've made myself clear? I've said I want you, and I know you're not precisely indifferent to me. This weekend would be an enjoyable interlude for both of us while we—er—explore our feelings for one another. And who knows? If we find our pleasure a mutual thing, as I suspect we will, we might turn it into something more permanent.'

She drew a long shaky breath. She was calmer now, although her heart was beating so rapidly she felt choked. 'Are you asking me to marry you, Mr Bannerman, or to be your mistress?'

He raised his eyebrows. 'I certainly am not asking you to marry me, Miss Welborn,' he said dryly. 'But if you put security above all else, may I remind you that money carries its own security? And I can be very generous to someone who gives me pleasure. I promise you, you won't be disappointed.'

Juliet flushed, humiliated by the contemptuous indifference in his voice. She was a fool. She had got in above her head, merely because her hot temper made her want to score one on Mark Bannerman. She shook with the intensity of her hatred, and when she spoke, she didn't even recognise her own voice.

'Sorry, it wouldn't work, Mr Bannerman.' Her smile was a grotesque parody of itself. 'I think you really must accept the fact that not even the pleasure of spending your money can sweeten the aversion I feel for you.'

'Are you trying to be provocative?' he asked slowly.

'In plain English, I'm trying to get myself thrown off this island by telling you a few home truths about yourself!'

'Do you allow me the same privilege?'

'What do you mean?'

'What you feel right now isn't aversion, I assure you.' He smiled wolfishly.

Juliet slapped him then, an act of desperation, and knew instantly that it was the wrong thing to have done when she saw his eyes light with a look of unholy satisfaction.

'I never refuse a challenge,' he said deeply.

He pulled her into his arms as though she was a doll. She struck him again, frantically this time, but he was ready for her. His fingers tightened cruelly, paralysing her with pain until she went limp. She cried out shrilly with rage, but the cry was choked off as his mouth closed over hers. It was a brutal kiss, a violation, a punishment, as though she was a woman whom he had bought for the night and from whom he intended to have his pleasure. Flattening his hands across her hips, he jerked her forward with brutal insolence, allowing her to feel the thrusting hardness of his thighs, jamming her soft breasts against the rocklike muscles of his chest. She fought wildly, trying to avoid the rough caresses he was forcing on her unwilling body, but eventually it betrayed her, reacting with swelling breasts and deep, shivering tremors. As she capitulated, her lips softening beneath his, the kiss grew more insistent as he received the response he was seeking. His mouth left hers and he tilted her head back, tightening the line of her throat until it was a taut, pure column that he proceeded to line with a row of hot, greedy kisses.

Juliet was dazed, mindless. floating on a sea of sensation. She heard a series of hoarse gasps and realised to her shocked horror that it was her breathing. Suddenly he put her violently aside, and the physical parting was so searing that she felt as though she had lost a limb.

She opened her eyes slowly. Mark was staring at her,

a reddened tinge on his cheekbones, his eyes brightly
turbulent, his chest rising and falling with quick
breaths. But he was in control. Juliet stared un-
comprehendingly at herself. Her blouse was partially
unbuttoned, exposing an embarrassing amount of
cleavage, and her taut nipples were vividly outlined by
the clinging silk.

'Next time, don't dare me,' he said harshly.

She blushed, and dragged a trembling hand across
her mouth. 'How could you?' she asked shakily. 'I—I'm
leaving here—tomorrow! I don't care what you do—
I'm not staying another day!'

'You're not quitting,' he said flatly.

'I am! I—I'll leave if I h-have to swim!'

'If you leave, you'll never work another place again, I
promise you that.' His voice was implacable.

She sounded stunned. 'I don't believe you!'

'You'd better believe me. I'll ruin you.'

Juliet drew a long, shaky breath. 'You're bluffing,'
she said scornfully.

'I never bluff.'

She tightened her lips. 'Very well, I'll stay. But only
because I don't want to leave James in the lurch.'

His mouth twisted sardonically. 'James is out of this.
You're staying because I say so.'

She hesitated. 'Only if you promise never to kiss me
like that again.'

The hard look faded and his eyes glinted with
amusement. 'Okay,' he said derisively, 'I promise—I
won't kiss you *that* way again. That is, so long as you
don't provoke me.'

She flung him a look of burning hatred and thrust
past him to go towards the stairs. In the safety of her
own room, she locked the door and sank upon the bed
to try to pull herself together. Gradually her breathing
steadied and her pounding pulse settled down to a
normal rate, although she could still feel the pressure of
his mouth on hers and her body still tingled from the
caresses he forced upon it. And, unbelievingly at first,
her dazed mind began to accept what had happened:
she was the girl Mark Bannerman had marked as his.

She had meant it today when she told Daisy she had no intention of falling in love with Mark. She was not a fool and she knew that loving a man like that would be disastrous, a heartbreak it would take a girl a lifetime to recover from. She hadn't changed her mind about it either, but now she was vulnerable. And frightened. She was aware of him in a strange new way and she was no longer in control of her own destiny. It's not love, she told herself fiercely. It's just plain, old-fashioned lust. But not even telling herself that could prevent the pulse from fluttering madly in her throat nor the surge of shamed blood to her cheeks.

Flight would be the best thing, but if that was denied her, then the next best thing was to finish James's book as quickly as possible and get out of here.

Just before she fell asleep, she wondered why he had been so angry when she had accused him of wanting her because of James.

# CHAPTER FOUR

JULIET came down to breakfast to find Daisy sitting alone. She was in a tizzy because she had just learned she was accompanying the Alexanders to the airport. She had also been given additional orders to make a reservation for Paul on a commercial flight to New York the following day.

'Why?' Juliet asked bluntly.

Daisy shrugged. 'Mark's orders. He's in a bad mood this morning. It's like walking through a minefield to cross him. First he screws up all the arrangements by sending me instead of Paul, then he tells me to get back here as soon as possible.'

So much for his suggestion that Juliet spend a swinging weekend in town with Daisy! Not that she intended to, but . . . 'Why is he sending Paul away?' she insisted.

'Mine not to reason why,' Daisy quipped, but she avoided Juliet's eyes. 'But I do know why I'm to come back tonight.'

'Really? Why?'

'To be your chaperone, of course. Fine thing it would be for him to snatch you away from James for lack of a chaperone, then fail to provide one here.' Chaperone, ha! thought Juliet scornfully. What, she wondered, would Daisy say if she knew what had *really* happened last night? Meanwhile, Daisy rose and prepared to leave. 'I've got to run. Not that I'm looking forward to *this* job.' She made a face. 'They'll be disappointed and consequently nasty. That woman is a fool and too stupid to see that that big play she made for Mark just turned him off her and her husband—in fact, the whole business. You're not working today, are you?' she added. 'Why don't you get a lift into town—or call Sam? There's not much to see there, as you learned last night, but there's a general merchandise store that sells everything, including a nice supply of native goods. And you can buy a soda at the hotel.'

Up in her room, Juliet felt restless and at a loose end. She was not in the mood to work on James's book, and although as a general rule a day of sunshine combined with the surf and sand would have been enough to send her spirits soaring sky-high, she couldn't work up much enthusiasm today. She remembered Daisy's words and wondered if the general store would have material and thread. Last night had taught her that she was going to have to augment her meagre wardrobe for evenings, and since she had a flair for sewing, she could make herself a couple of simple long skirts if she could find some suitable material. With blouses, that would see her through until she could afford to buy something on the mainland. Or until she could leave.

If she hurried, she might catch Daisy before they left and get a lift in with them. If not, she could call for Sam—although she didn't relish the idea of begging a favour from Cora. Hurrying, she slid her feet into sandals, clapped a straw hat on her head and ran downstairs, her footsteps light on the carpeted stairs. The door to the study was opening as she passed and she literally bumped into Mark, who was coming out at the same time. Behind him, she could see Paul bent over the desk, studying some papers.

'Where are you going?' asked Mark, giving her a slow, appraising look.

'To town.' She started moving away—fast. He sounded casual, but she was taking no chances. She intended staying out of his way in future.

'Walking?' He was keeping up with her.

'Why not?'

'Surely you're kidding? It *is* fourteen miles. I'll take you in the jeep—I want to talk to you, anyway.'

Before she could inform him that the desire was not mutual, he was gone, and a couple of minutes later she heard a horn honking from the front drive. She went out reluctantly and climbed into the jeep, glancing at him from beneath lowered lashes. He was dressed in jeans and an open shirt that showed a triangle of bronzed throat and chest. There was a hint of stubbornness about his jaw that made Juliet's stomach flip-flop with nervousness.

'Well, aren't you going to ask me what I want?' He directed a teasing look at her. He was waiting, one hand on the gear shift, the jeep idling noisily in the driveway.

'What *do* you want?' she asked bluntly.

His grin flashed and the jeep started moving. 'I wanted to apologise for last night—I have this nasty habit of teasing when I see it riles someone. Anyway,' he added casually, 'I'm sorry. I got out of line.'

Sheer surprise held her motionless, her tongue stilled. The last thing she had expected from him was an apology, and frankly, she *had* thought he had meant what he said last night.

'You'll be working and living here for months to come,' he went on, changing gears to pull into the road. 'The last thing either of us wants is *that* kind of complication. It's much better to get it all out in the open, accept each other's motives for what they are.'

She stared at him blankly. It was total capitulation— or was it? Her thoughts raced suspiciously.

'Do you mean you've changed your mind about my motives for coming here? You've accepted my explanation?' she asked warily.

Mark hesitated. 'Your motives are your own business,' he said finally. 'I have no right to question them, particularly since you're already here, you're efficient and good for James. No, I meant that I got out of line when I kissed you last night,' he added, by way of explanation.

Julient flushed angrily. Nothing had changed. He was merely apologising for a kiss that might make her seriously think about leaving. And of course, he didn't want that, because she was 'good for James'. Or—or— her mind did a rapid double-take—was it possible that he was also thinking she might take advantage of the fact that he had kissed her? A woman like her, like he *thought* she was, might become a nuisance on the basis of one kiss! She might take it as encouragement. Well! Her lips tightened and her eyes sent off angry sparks. He had a damned nerve!

'Aren't you really saying *you* don't want that kind of complication?' she snapped.

'Surely neither of us does?' he asked, in a patient, reasonable tone. 'You've made it clear how you feel about me, and naturally I——'

'Naturally you're scared to death that I'll turn my greedy little claws on you now that you've slipped up and kissed me?' she broke in furiously. 'Well, forget it, Mr Bannerman! You haven't a thing to worry about! I wouldn't touch you if you came plated with gold!'

'Looks like I can't do anything right,' he said sadly. 'I try to apologise and——'

'You call *that* an apology?' she cried, in a goaded voice. 'As an apology, it hit an all-time low, even for you! All the time you were making it, you were hoping I'd get the message that I wasn't to get serious about you! Well, I have news for you, Mr Bannerman! Even a moron would know better than that!'

'Then we're to remain enemies?' His face was straight, but he sounded suspiciously as though he was doing his best to keep from laughing.

'We are!' she asserted recklessly. 'You know, you really are something! First, I'm a gangster's girl-friend, then a man-trap for James, then—then you accuse me of having a love affair with my—with the finest, most dedicated man——' Her voice shook and she paused. 'And then, on the basis of a half-hearted apology, I'm supposed to forget that you kissed me and asked me to spend the weekend with you!'

Mark's hands tightened on the wheel. 'It does sound as though our relationship is doomed.' His voice was choked and Juliet peered at him suspiciously. She was right—he *was* laughing at her! Damn him, she raged. *She* wasn't joking, she was deadly serious! 'I'm beginning to think we're fated to always quarrel. Our emotions seem to run too deep for a cool, calm friendship. Perhaps we *had* better remain enemies.'

'That suits me fine,' she said frigidly.

And just what did he mean by enemies? she fumed. Was it possible to know one's enemies better than one's friends? She barely knew Mark Bannerman—how many

times had she even spoken to him?—yet she sensed
when he came into the room, even if her back was
turned; she knew when he was angry, with that deadly,
icy anger that was all coldly implacable on the surface.
Perhaps she did it by thought waves or something
through her skin ... Just like right now, she knew he
was sitting over there trying to suppress his amusement,
whereas he probably knew she was seething with fury
herself. Sometimes he scared her to death, but she had
never felt so exhilarated and alive before in her life.

She was momentarily distracted by the fact that the
jeep had slowed to a crawl as they approached the first
scattered shacks on the edge of town. Children and
livestock walked freely in the road. They were greeted
on all sides as Mark was recognised and waved in
return. Juliet noticed that everyone looked happy and
well fed, in spite of the tumbledown condition of the
houses. And so far as that went, most of the gardens
boasted a vegetable patch of some sort behind a fence,
and the houses were decorated with passionflower and
bougainvillaea running riot, providing rich splashes of
colour against the unpainted boards.

The trip hadn't taken long, but it was certainly too
far to walk, but Juliet didn't want to depend on Mark
Bannerman every time she needed transportation.

'There isn't a taxi or something I can hire, is there?'
she asked lightly.

He shot her a quick look. 'This jeep is usually
available,' he said dryly. 'Cora has another for business
use, and the Commodore has the only other car on the
island.'

'The Commodore?' she queried.

'He manages the hotel.'

Juliet frowned, remembering Cora's threat to make
her sleep out if she wouldn't leave on the *Lazy Lou*.

Mark glanced at her. 'What's the matter?'

'Are strangers allowed to stay at the hotel?'

'Allowed? That's an odd way to put it. Naturally the
hotel takes in strangers.'

'Even if it's—someone—you don't want on the
island?'

'The Commodore is the manager. It would be his decision, although he would try to consider my wishes. However, you can ask him about his policy when you see him. Why do you ask?'

She shrugged. She had no intention of telling him. By this time they were in town, which was nothing more than a few unpainted, weatherbeaten stores sprawled along the length of the hard-packed oyster-bed road. There was a general store, a bar, a first aid station, a church and the hotel. The only building that had two stories, the hotel, flaunted a first and second floor porch, complete with rocking chairs. Across the street was a park. Its one water tap seemed to be the hub of the town's social activity, for a group of laughing, talking housewives were lined up with buckets and pails, awaiting their turn to draw water. But most astonishing of all was that the little park also contained an abandoned miniature golf course and roundabout. Juliet watched delightedly as shrieking children ran and played between the wooden horses with their faded, peeling paint and chased one another through the obstacles of the abandoned course.

She turned towards Mark, her eyes sparkling, but he was looking at a man who was running towards them from the direction of the lagoon. The jeep, which had almost slowed to a stop, took off with a roar, the tyres spurting dust and shell. Juliet's head bounced as Mark screeched to a halt and called, 'What's up?'

'Man, Mist' Mark!' The rest was lost as the jeep roared again, taking the curving road towards the lagoon on two wheels before pulling up with a jolt behind the warehouse. Juliet saw that a group of fishermen were bringing someone out of the water and were bending over the body.

Horrified pictures surfaced in her mind, of mangled flesh, torn limbs, shark bites. But she saw no blood, and to her relief, she noticed that the man was moving. In fact, his movements were violent, as though he was in a convulsion.

Mark leaped out of the jeep and ran towards the group of fishermen, and Juliet, following him, noticed that Cora was also approaching on a run from the warehouse.

'What is it?' Juliet cried.

He did not reply. He was bent over the body, the movements of his hands deft and sure. He ignored her frantically voiced question but put his hand in his pocket and threw a set of keys at Cora.

'You know what we need!' he said briefly. 'Hurry!'

'What is it?' Juliet begged again. This time she was asking Cora, but that lady ignored her and proceeded to start the jeep and drive off without a single look at her. It was Mark who answered her question.

'Sting ray.' He flung it over his shoulder. 'It got him while he was fishing. Cora will bring something to help until we can get him to a doctor, but we've got to hurry. Unfortunately,' he added savagely, 'the helicopter's gone, taking those damned people to the airport.' He rose and gave quick orders. Six of the men had picked up the writhing body and Juliet saw he was just a boy, with wide pain-filled eyes. They shambled towards the jetty, Mark leading the way. Juliet followed helplessly, wanting to help but not knowing what to do.

'I—I didn't know sting rays could be fatal,' she said.

'Not usually, but the poison in the nervous system can send the victim into shock. And if he happens to be allergic——' his voice trailed off.

'Isn't there a nurse? I thought there was a nurse.'

'She's on leave, damn it!' he muttered. 'This boy has to go to hospital! I'll have to take him on the *Sea Witch* and hope I can make it in time.'

Once aboard the trim white cruiser, Mark led the men down to the cabin salon, where a cushioned seat ran under the portholes. They lowered the boy gently to it. By this time Cora had arrived with the first aid box and while she and Juliet watched, Mark broke open a vial and carefully drew the contents into a needle.

'Shall I come with you?' Cora asked importantly.

'No. I need you here to notify the hospital we're on the way. Have an ambulance waiting for us.' He looked up and his eyes settled on Juliet. 'Can you give an injection?'

'Yes,' she said calmly.

'I mean—really give one? Without doing the wrong thing? He may need another one before we get to the hospital.'

'My mother was an insulin diabetic,' she told him.

'Good. You'll be useful, then. I'll take her,' he added to Cora.

Cora submitted with ill grace, but she followed Mark and the other men up the stairs, leaving Juliet with the patient and an elderly man who identified himself as the boy's grandfather. His wrinkled old hands trembled as he smoothed the hair back from the sweating brow. He began to croon to the boy, a sort of sing-song in West Indian dialect. At first Juliet thought it was a lullaby, but as she listened, fascinated, she realised he was scolding the boy softly.

'He got no pappy—his mammy, she dead. He a good boy—do as I said. I tell him be careful, stay out of bay. But he go fishing, meet sting ray.' He added sadly, 'He no listen to old man.'

But apparently the boy was listening, because he seemed to grow quiet under the old man's hands. The deck began to throb under their feet as the engines started, and Juliet, peering out of the porthole, saw that the boat was moving gently out of the lagoon. Once it was beyond the reef, the engines increased their tempo and she saw the island disappearing quickly behind them.

Meantime, the boy had fallen into a deep sleep. His muscles had continued to jerk, but he seemed to be stupefied. Juliet put a hand on his forehead and found it icy cold and clammy to her touch. Apparently the grandfather had not noticed anything wrong, so moving quietly without alarming him, she made her way down the passageway towards the bedrooms. There she would find blankets.

There were two bedrooms. A cursory glance into each showed that they were very luxurious, with shag carpet underfoot, sunray blinds at the portholes, large, comfortable beds, and each with its own bathroom. A search of the larger bedroom with the king-sized bed

brought forth blankets and pillows, and she carried a
pile back to the main salon where the boy was. She
piled blankets on him and tucked them around
securely.

'Miss, is my grandson going to be all right?' the old
man asked fearfully.

'Of course.' She smiled confidently. 'Just keep him
warm and quiet. I'm going up on deck to see what Mr
Bannerman has to say about when we'll get there.'

In the control room, Mark was gazing with frowning
concentration as the bow of the *Sea Witch* cleaved the
water into two dazzling arcs of spray. He shot her a
quick look as she halted beside him.

'What's the matter?'

'I—I don't know for sure. He's cold and—well, he
may be in shock.'

Mark withdrew a thin, dark cigar from his pocket
and lighted it thoughtfully. 'It's the pain that's sent him
into shock, unless he's allergic—and then we have
another whole set of problems that only a hospital can
cope with.' His teeth clenched on the cigar. 'Do the best
you can, and try not to let the old man sense your
worry.'

It was odd, standing here with him like this, what an
extraordinary sense of security she felt. No tension, no
tightening of nerves, merely a soothing matter-of-
factness that did wonders for her own morale.

'I just wish the nurse had been available,' she said
worriedly.

He withdrew his cigar and looked at it carefully.
'And there, unfortunately, I *can* accept the blame. I
insisted upon her taking her leave at this time.'

'Well, I'm sure you didn't anticipate this would
happen,' Juliet said tartly, and moved to go back
downstairs.

The boy was still asleep, and still cold, but the shivers
had stopped with the blankets. There was really little that
Juliet could do except sit and watch for signs that he was
coming around, or his condition was changing. She
learned from the old man that the boy's name was Carlos
and his was Beebo Johnson. Beebo seemed to have a

need to talk and she let him ramble on. Carlos had never known his father; he had been illegitimate; his mother, Beebo's daughter, had left her baby with her parents while she went to Trinidad to work. Her parents knew that her work meant a job as a singer in a sordid bar, with prostitution on the side. She had done it before—and she knew what she was going back to. They had not heard from her since then, and the old man preferred to believe that she was dead. Since then, the boy had become the centre of the old people's existence. 'Mist' Mark knows all about it—how much Carlos means to me 'n' Lucy.' Juliet knew intuitively that this was what had been eating Mark when he savagely referred to the helicopter being out of reach.

Carlos was still unconscious when they arrived at the mainland, but he was hanging on by a tenuous thread to life. Mark accompanied the boy's grandfather in the ambulance while Juliet followed in a taxi that was also waiting. By the time she got to the hospital, the boy was in the Emergency Room, the magic name of Bannerman having provided a standby team of doctors and nurses.

Juliet and Beebo Johnson sat outside the Emergency Room cubicle and watched the scurrying to and fro with wide, uncomprehending eyes. The bench was hard and they were getting restless when someone put coffee into their hands. They were drinking it when Mark joined them.

'Have you been told anything?' he asked.

'Not a word!'

'I understand he's responding to the drug they gave him and has fallen into a natural sleep. I've been in the office arranging for a private room. Wait, I'll see what I can find out.'

Mark went into the cubicle and soon came out again. He placed a hand on old Beebo's shoulder. 'They're moving Carlos upstairs to a private room. There's nothing you can do here and I know you're both tired. I've made arrangements for you to stay at the Key Palms Hotel. Come.'

But the old man proved unexpectedly stubborn. He had no intention of leaving the hospital until his grandson awakened and he could see for himself that he was going to be all right.

'Very well,' Mark said wryly. 'It looks like there'll be two of us sitting up tonight. I'll take Miss Welborn to the hotel and come back here.'

Juliet stood up uncertainly. She had only a small clasp purse that contained a few dollars plus a lipstick and comb. She had never felt so unprepared in her life.

'Don't worry,' Mark's look was ironical, 'there won't be any charge. I own a suite in the hotel.'

As they were going down in the elevator, she asked weakly, 'Is the old man really going to sit up all night?'

'I'll have a cot put up in the boy's room. I've already made arrangements for a tray to be sent up to him. I should have known he wouldn't want to leave the boy,' he added ruefully. 'After tonight, it will depend on what Lucy—his wife—decides.'

Juliet looked up, 'I believe you really do think Carlos is going to be all right?'

He looked surprised. 'Sure—why not? He's young and healthy and barring unforeseen complications, he should be all right by tomorrow or the next day. The shock was brought on by an allergic reaction, as I suspected,' he added in explanation.

By this time they were at the Emergency room exit and Juliet saw that it was late afternoon. It was much cooler and there were long shadows beneath the palm trees that ornamented the parking lot. The perk-up from her coffee had long since disappeared, leaving a dragging weariness, and she realised to her surprise that she had had nothing since breakfast. Mark evidently had the same thought.

'Hungry?' he asked.

'Very,' she admitted.

'I'll arrange for you to have dinner when we get to the hotel.'

Juliet's ears pricked, catching the offhand implication that she would be dining alone, but she said nothing. The situation was too delicate for thoughtless words. She knew she could not return to the island today, and she certainly couldn't sleep alone on the boat. She had not liked the idea of staying in Mark Bannerman's suite at the hotel, but on the other hand, he had implied that he would not be staying there. Much better, she thought, to play it by ear, wait and see, before she made a fool of herself with a lot of stupid objections.

The taxi driver was waiting for them, smoking a cigarette while he leaned against the hood of his cab. Juliet remembered that she hadn't paid him, but he hadn't followed her into the hospital, demanding his money. When he saw Mark, he jumped smartly to attention and opened the door, after grinding the cigarette under his heel.

'Where to, Mr Bannerman?'

'The Key Palms.' Mark helped Juliet into the cab.

The Key Palms was about what Juliet had expected, a luxury hotel surrounded by plenty of palm trees. The lobby was like something out of the Arabian Nights, with its multi-storied vaulted ceiling and the enormous hanging clusters of globes that served as chandeliers. Mark did not pause at the desk but proceeded directly to the bank of elevators, where he punched the Penthouse button. For that at least Juliet was thankful, for she felt conspicuous enough in her wrinkled clothes, without lingering among the elegantly clad men and women passing through the vast lobby. Mark, wearing denims and sneakers, looked perfectly self-assured, and from the deferential way he was bowed to an open elevator by the bell captain, she saw that he had been recognised.

Inside the suite, which was marked by a discreetly gold-lettered 'one' on the door, Mark looked around uninterestedly.

'I think you'll find everything in order. Take any bedroom you want. I don't know much about this place, except that it has several bedrooms and each has its own bath. It's used mostly by business guests—that sort of thing.' He picked up the phone. 'I'm going to have them send up a menu. Would you like a drink?'

Juliet stood in the middle of the floor, clutching her purse and said, politely, 'No, thank you.'

He spoke in the phone, then replaced it in the cradle.

'They'll be up shortly. Order anything you like—it will automatically be charged to this suite. You'll find an extra key in that drawer over there, if you want to go downstairs. The boutique in the lobby will be open until ten if you need something for tonight and tomorrow. Just charge it to the suite.' He walked over to the door. 'I'm going back now. Anything you want to ask before I go?'

'D-did you tell James where I was?'

He raised his eyebrows. 'No. But he can find out easily enough. Anything else?' he asked impatiently. Juliet shook her head and he said briskly, 'Right, then I'll see you in the morning.'

Even if there had been other questions, he was in a big hurry to be gone. Juliet felt a little blank as she stared at the closed door. Whatever she had expected, it hadn't been that bored brush-off, as though she was a nuisance to be settled somewhere as quickly and painlessly as possible. Did he have another apartment somewhere, that wasn't for the benefit of 'business guests'? Or was he going back to the boat? Or was he really going to sit up all night merely to keep a frightened old man company? It didn't sound like what she knew of Mark Bannerman—the Mark Bannerman who wanted to send her out on Smith's boat and, later, wanted to seduce her practically under his brother's nose.

She looked around cautiously. The room was furnished with all the impersonality of the usual hotel room, although the decor was luxurious, even ostentatious. It even had a sort of kitchenette at one end of the enormous sitting room, with a wet bar with bar stools under, it, and behind the wet bar a refrigerator and micro-wave oven. Several bedroom doors opened off the short hallway, and Juliet chose the first one she came to. By the time the waiter arrived with the menu, she had already investigated the contents of the bathroom and found everything she would need for tonight, including a new toothbrush.

She chose a steak, and while she was waiting for it, checked out the other bedrooms—there were two—and found them exactly like hers. All had big, fluffy towels in the bathroom, all had adequate reading light plus the latest best-sellers beside the bed—and all were completely impersonal. It was as Mark had said—a place to house business guests who for one reason or another were not coming to Tamassee.

The sound of clinking dishes brought her back to the sitting room. Her meal must have been given top priority, considering the speed with which it was produced. The waiter was hovering behind a chair which he pushed in before pouring the wine she had ordered. He did not remain after he served her food.

'Just push the cart outside when you finish, miss, and I'll pick it up later.'

Juliet had not ordered coffee, although after last night she didn't think she would have any trouble falling asleep. The wine, on an empty stomach, went straight to her head, and by the time she had eaten her steak she was feeling pleasantly fuzzy. She took her last glass into the bedroom and sipped from it as she prepared for her bath. Drying herself afterwards, it dawned on her that she didn't have anything to wear to bed. For some reason, that struck her as funny, and she was still giggling about it as she downed the last of the wine. She could wear her undies, of course, or she could wear a towel, or. . . . Finally, feeling delightfully sinful, she slipped into bed naked and promptly fell sound asleep.

# CHAPTER FIVE

JULIET was awakened by the sound of the closing door. She opened her eyes cautiously, frowning as she tried to capture an elusive memory of hearing a door close earlier. As memory returned, her eyes sprang open and she saw Mark Bannerman standing beside the bed, a cup of coffee in his hand. He was clean-shaven and his hair was still damp from the shower. He wore a wide-awake, alert look on his face.

'Wake up, Sleeping Beauty.' She groaned and he grinned. 'If it's a hangover, I must admit you deserve it—I noticed the inroads you made on that bottle of wine!'

Juliet groaned again and propped herself on one elbow before she remembered she was nude under the sheet. Flushing, she anchored it hastily under her arms, then had to watch helplessly as his eyes travelled deliberately from her bare shoulders down the length of her body, clearly outlined by the clinging sheet.

'Don't worry,' the grin widened, 'you look beautiful.'

She ignored that. 'How did you get in? I distinctly remember putting the night latch on the door.'

'Yes, I know,' he said soothingly. 'But you didn't notice there was a service door beside the refrigerator. Lucky for me, too. Carlos was so much better by four this morning that I came on back here to get some sleep.'

'I see.' She waited, then said patiently, 'I hate to rush you, but if you'll put the coffee on the table, I'll drink it as soon as you leave.'

'Better drink it now, while it's hot.' He smiled at her innocently.

'*Please!*' she snapped. 'I want to get dressed.'

'I'm not stopping you.'

'Don't be ridiculous! You know perfectly well I can't get up until you leave this room.'

'I don't see why not. I wouldn't see anything I haven't seen before.'

She stared at him speechlessly.

'I got a good view when I came in this morning about dawn,' he drawled lazily. 'Do you always sleep in the nude?'

Juliet's face flamed. Her mind leaped at the memory of a door closing some time in the early morning hours, and she was goaded into speech. 'You've got a nerve, spying on me like that while I'm asleep!'

'Did you know you hug a pillow when you sleep?' He put the coffee down, then sat on the side of her bed. 'Doctors say it's a sign of insecurity. Perhaps you need someone to sleep with, hmm?' He paused provocatively. 'That's a thought that gives rise to some interesting possibilities.'

She glared at him fiercely but said nothing. She knew he had no intention of leaving until he was ready and that he would love to see her humble herself and beg. But she was not going to do it. She was just going to lie there and ignore his baiting until he got tired and left.

Mark smiled as though he read her mind and, leaning forward, lazily trailed a finger across her shoulder to the edge of the sheet, where it was pulled tautly across her breasts. Her skin rippled in response and she shivered. The hot colour flooded her face, and she clenched her teeth to keep from speaking.

His mouth twitched and he added softly, watching her reaction, 'Suppose we try an experiment, eh?'

Juliet's eyes flew open and her mouth parted in surprise. She watched unbelievingly as he reached for the sheet and began to pull it downward. At the same time, he leaned forward and planted a light kiss on her shoulder. Her hands flew in two places at once and the sheet slid over her breasts.

'Stop!' Her voice was shocked. 'Stop right now or I— I'll scream!'

'Do you have a pretty scream?' he whispered.

'Y-y-you ca-can't!' She grabbed frantically at the slipping sheet and turned a horrified face towards him.

'I already have.' By that time, the sheet was around

her hips, and, spanning her waist with his palms, he pulled her towards him. Her breasts met his chest and the tips hardened at the contact. Juliet went into frenzied action. Pressing her hands against his chest, she shoved and, at the same time, flung herself to the other side of the bed. But Mark pulled her back with indolent ease. Bending over her, he let her feel the weight of his body while he gauged her reactions. With narrowed eyes, he watched the hectic blood flood her cheeks, staining them crimson. Her eyes were wide and shocked, the violet hue deepening until they were almost black.

Her throat grew dry with panic and she tried to fight clear, but her hands were caught beneath his chest, her legs immobilised by his thighs. Like a bird beating its wings against a cage, she struggled frantically, with each struggle growing progressively weaker. Her breath was coming in hoarse, laboured gasps now, and for the first time in her life, she knew what it was to be utterly helpless.

Suddenly she realised that he was speaking, that he has been speaking to her for some time in a soothing voice. 'Don't struggle so—I'm not going to hurt you. I'm just going to kiss you.'

Juliet didn't know why that thought sent her into a tailspin of panic. 'No!' she whimpered. 'Please——'

'I'm not going to do a thing to you against your will, but if you keep fighting me, you'll make me angry.'

'No, no,' she sobbed. Her voice rose. 'Stop! I don't want——'

'Damn you—be still! I *am* going to kiss you!'

The harsh-voiced command touched off a deep, primitive fear and she froze, gazing at him with terrified eyes. It didn't occur to her to disobey him. She watched helplessly as the angry face descended and the hard, ruthless mouth took hers. He was pitiless, giving no quarter, allowing no retreat, forcing her to acknowledge his dominance. She shuddered as he carelessly plundered her lips. When he finally raised his head, she could taste the salty tang of blood within her swollen mouth.

Mark studied her with acute interest, easily reading the fear on her expressive face. Raising himself slightly, he released her hands and taking them between his, placed them around his neck. Still watching her closely, he touched her breasts gently, trying not to alarm her, cupping them between his palms. She stiffened, her eyes flying open, but he soothed her by murmuring into her ear, running his tongue around the outer lobe and finally into the soft inner curl. He resumed caressing her breasts, the slow, sensuous movements of his hands unbearably tantalising as he teased their smooth fullness into throbbing peaks. Juliet shuddered and he drew back and looked at her again, his hands motionless.

'Kiss me,' he said deliberately.

Her eyes flew to his and she caught her breath on a long, shuddering sob. He smiled gently.

'Kiss me,' he repeated, and his thumb moved across her mouth, easing it open.

She moaned and he covered her face with little kisses, each one an erotic experience as his lips travelled over her eyelids, cheeks and paused to drink deeply at her mouth. Her fingers moved restlessly, threading through his hair, and her body arched convulsively. This time her mouth was as hungry as his as they exchanged a deep, passionate kiss that left her gasping with pleasure. The hot blood raced through her veins like a runaway forest fire. When Mark finally drew away, she was shaking and her eyes were glazed.

He eyed her with satisfaction, then put her from him abruptly and stood up. 'I wonder what James or Paul would think if they could see you now?' he asked ironically.

She stared at him dazedly. He was watching her with cool, impersonal eyes. A humiliating tide of colour washed over her heated skin and she groped for the sheet. She wanted to crawl under a rock and die, but summoning up every facet of her acting ability, she shrugged and forced her voice to light mockery.

'Probably nothing. After all, what's happened? A few kisses—a little heavy petting, that's all.'

His eyes narrowed. 'Are you trying to say you were unmoved?'

She avoided his eyes. 'Do you deny you had to force me?' she demanded, instinctively sensing that the best defence was attack. Inside, she was shaking all over, but by a supreme effort of will she forced herself to remain calm.

Mark's face hardened. 'Force you?' His voice was cutting. 'Not after the first thirty seconds! In fact, you were boringly easy! But why lie to yourself? You know you would have been begging me to take you in another minute!'

She felt nauseated, and wanted to shrink back into the pillows, hiding herself. She caught her breath on a sob and closed her eyes wearily. 'All right, you've had your say,' she whispered. 'Now get out of here and leave me alone.'

He didn't move. 'Not until you admit that you want me.'

She stared at him bitterly. 'If I admit it, will you get out of my room?

'Must I show you again?'

Juliet flinched and dragged her arm across her eyes, hiding their flickering depths from his scrutiny. 'Very well, you've made your point, Mark,' she said thickly. 'I admit it. Now, will you please leave me alone?'

He leaned over and jerking her arm away, glared into her eyes. 'You've admitted nothing, you little cheat, but you will! You and I are going to make love sooner or later and you know it, so stop playing hard to get! I don't know what you want of me, but if it's security, I told you once before I don't mind paying a high price for my pleasure!' He stared at her frowningly, his eyes moving from the trembling lips to the shadow-filled eyes. His voice was ragged with frustration as he continued, 'If you're angling for a positive declaration from me, I admit that I want you—badly! I have from the beginning, and when I learned that you were going to work for James, I decided I was going to have you. As long ago as then! You gave me a couple of uneasy moments with him, but now that I know you better, I can see he'd never interest a girl like you.'

'A girl like *me*!' Her voice was choked with self-loathing. 'Is that supposed to make me feel better, to know that I'm a pushover when you start applying the sex-appeal? Anyway, how can you talk about your brother like that, as though he was a—a—nothing! He's worth a dozen like you!'

'And you, too, sweetheart. We're two of a kind, you and me.' Mark grinned narrowly. 'James's lovemaking would bore you to tears within minutes—and you, my sweet, would scare him to death. That cool little smile hides a raging torrent, and it would send him running for cover if he unleashed it! He prefers to worship his goddesses from afar.'

'But not you?'

'Not me, Juliet. I prefer a flesh and blood woman in my arms, as you'll discover when we become lovers.'

'Never! Not in a million years!'

'But yes, my darling, and before I'm through, the world will know it,' he said softly. 'Struggle all you like, it will only make the ending that much sweeter. Do you understand?' He shook her slightly. 'Do you?'

She stared at him confusedly. 'You're crazy! I don't care if you are the rich and powerful Mark Bannerman, you can't *make* me become your mistress! You're insane! Before I'd give in to your demands, I'd disappear where you'd never find me again!'

'You're not going anywhere,' he said in a chilly voice. 'We've been over this before, and I assure you, if you leave, I'll find you if I have to hire detectives in every city in the country. And when I do, I'll make you sorry.'

'You're a raving maniac!'

'And you're frightened.' His cold smile sent shivers down her spine. 'You're frightened because you know I'm going to win.'

Her fear made her sick, but she flung back her head and glared at him defiantly. 'Win? I'll see you in hell first!'

'Heaven, Juliet,' he corrected her smilingly. 'Heaven, my darling. My bed—where you will learn the pleasures of the flesh. You'll be an eager pupil, whether you believe it or not. And I shall enjoy teaching you, for I can see that your former teacher must have been singularly insensitive to your needs.'

'What d-do you mean?' she whispered.

'Your former lover, darling. The one you've been so mysterious about. He must have been a clumsy clod. Your responses tell me you're a novice in the art of making love—although it's a talent that you'll acquire quickly.'

Her first impulse was to deny the existence of a former lover or lovers, and if she had thought he would believe her, and it would accomplish what she wanted, she would have done it. But she sensed that he would listen with disbelief, even a certain degree of sardonic amusement, then conclude she was lying for her own devious purposes.

He strolled towards the door. 'By the way, your breakfast will be waiting for you by the time you get dressed.'

As soon as the door had closed behind him, Juliet jumped out of bed and began to dress. Clumsy with haste, her eyes on the door, she was nevertheless through in record time, and emerged from the bedroom to find Mark at his most businesslike on the telephone. The waiter had brought up their breakfast, and was busy plugging in the coffee carafe.

The telephone call finished abruptly, and Mark dismissed the waiter. He seemed to be in a good humour, and as he helped himself to bacon and eggs, he asked Juliet casually, 'Well, what shall we do today after we visit the hospital?'

'Return to Tamassee!'

'Sorry. Tomorrow.'

'*Tomorrow!* But why? Isn't Carlos better?'

'You wanted a holiday in the city, didn't you?' he asked mockingly. A twinkle lurked in the corner of his eye. 'Besides, the boat is out of commission. When Lucy got here during the early morning hours, she told me emphatically that she had no intention of staying in the hotel. She wanted to stay on the boat. Just as I expected,' he added, with a grin.

'But—then that means Jack is here, too! Why can't he take me to Tamassee?'

'The helicopter and its pilot operates at my covenience, not as a shuttle bus for passengers,' Mark returned coolly. 'I'm afraid you're going to have to settle down like a good girl and enjoy your holiday in the city.'

'But I haven't anything to wear!' she cried in dismay. 'And——'

'The everlasting cry of woman!' The grin returned. 'If that's all that's worrying you, there's a boutique downstairs. You may charge whatever you like to this suite, and if she doesn't have what you want, she'll get it for you.'

'I will not!' she snapped. 'Where's Paul? she added, with some idea of appealing to him by telephone for help.

'Paul?' He looked deliberately at his watch. 'Hmm, he should be over Georgia now on the way to the New York office. Anything else you want to know?' he added silkily.

'No. I just want to return to the island! I—I have a job there!'

'I didn't realise you were so conscientious,' he said dryly. 'Very well, you may return tomorrow, but we stay tonight.'

'I'm not sharing this—this place with you!' she cried. 'If you think——'

'I do—and I have,' he said sardonically. 'I'll be sharing the boat with Lucy and Beebo. You'll stay here.' He held out his cup. 'Now, pour me some coffee, like a good girl.'

Juliet poured his coffee, then another cup for herself, and sipped it while she thought about what he had said, and searched it for hidden flaws. 'No,' she said finally, '*I'll* stay on the boat. You stay here.'

Mark shrugged. 'Suit yourself.'

She frowned, her eyes sharp with suspicion. Was this what he had wanted her to say all the time? In spite of herself, she found herself asking, 'What, no protests?

No more vows that you're going to seduce me? Are you giving up so easily?'

He shrugged again. 'Why waste my energy? Everyone in the hotel already believes I have. It will get out. Before the day is over someone will drop a hint to a gossip columnist that Mark Bannerman has a new lady.'

Juliet paled. 'How could they? You didn't sleep here last night!'

He looked amused. 'I came in at four. It's now— nine-thirty. Plenty of time for a full-scale seduction scene.'

'But the hospital——'

'Ah, yes, the hospital. If they ask there, they can find out what happened yesterday. But will they ask? I doubt it.'

'You're hateful!' she cried. 'I really believe you think all this is amusing!'

'My reactions are mixed,' he said oddly. 'But I learned long ago not to concern myself with things I can't change—and that includes gossip columnists. No one cares these days about who's sleeping with whom. It will be forgotten tomorrow—or at the latest, next week.'

'*I* care.' Juliet rose and pushed back her chair. 'If I'm to stay another day, I'll have to get some pyjamas. Did you say the shop was in the lobby downstairs?'

'Yes.'

'James owes me a month's salary,' she added crisply. 'He told me you would pay it. Will you?'

'I'll write a cheque.' Mark rose and went to the desk in the corner. Unlocking one of the drawers, he withdrew a chequebook and wrote in it.

'Is this right?'

To her surprise, it was for the correct amount of her salary. 'Yes. I'll go now.'

'Wait for me downstairs. We'll go to the hospital together.'

The attractive girl who ran the boutique was unlocking the doors as Juliet walked up.

'Something in pyjamas? Yes, madam, I have something in your size.'

She was curious but not unduly so as she idly glanced at the cheap, wrinkled sundress Juliet was wearing. Her eyes lingered on the taut, vulnerable mouth and the beautiful shadowed eyes.

'Here you are.' She flipped a pair of tailored satin pyjamas on to the counter, then bent down. 'And then, if you like, I have something like this.' She withdrew a pair of sheer bikini pyjamas, loosely tied in front with a couple of satin bows. 'Or would you prefer a nightgown?'

Juliet blushed. 'No, thank you, these will be fine.' She was about to ask to see lingerie when she noticed the price. She touched her fingertips to the satin pyjamas. 'Just these. Can you cash a cheque?'

The girl's eyes widened when she saw the signature on the cheque. 'If you like, I can charge these to Mr Bannerman's account,' she suggested eagerly. Her eyes were avid now, as they lingered on Juliet's face and put a mental price tag on her clothes.

Juliet's eyes hardened. 'I want to pay for them myself, if you please,' she said frostily.

'I'll have to cash the cheque at the desk,' the girl said reluctantly. She glanced beyond Juliet and her face broke into a wide smile. 'Good morning, Mr Bannerman,' she gushed. 'Shall I charge madam's purchase to your account?'

A warm hand slid around the nape of Juliet's neck and a husky voice breathed in her ear. 'Darling, don't you know your money is no good here? Put it away and we'll go shopping later.'

Juliet's face burned and she jerked out of his gasp. 'Forget the pyjamas!' she snapped at the hapless girl. 'I'll get them somewhere else!'

Her face was stormy as she flew out of the shop and through the lobby doors. Outside, she came to a halt on the sidewalk, her eyes blinded by the sunlight as it reflected off the white concrete. She fumbled in her bag for sunglasses and surreptitiously checked its contents again. It was still there—about five dollars and her salary cheque. Providentially, a taxi slid to a halt beside her and she reached for the door.

'Can you take me to the nearest bank?' she asked.

Mark slid into the seat after her. 'By all means, we'll stop off at a bank on our way to the hospital.' He gave directions to the driver, then handed her a bag labelled with the boutique's name. 'Your pyjamas. You embarrassed the salesgirl by storming out like that.'

But he sounded amused, and Juliet gritted her teeth in frustration as she took the bag, knowing he was capable of embarrassing her further if she didn't. His eyes were dancing with pleasure at her anger, and her heart missed a beat before picking up its normal rhythm. Deliberately, she turned and looked out the opposite window, shocked by a terrifying realisation. Beneath the bright plastic bag in her lap, her nails dug sharply into her palms. 'Dear God,' she breathed to herself, 'not that! Please—not that!'

Mark looked out the other window, whistling soundlessly to himself, and Juliet was given a brief moment of grace in which to recover her poise. She needed it. Her thoughts were in a state of confusion, her emotions a mingling of pleasure and pain. She breathed carefully, every instinct alert for the slightest change in him that would indicate that he had guessed her secret. She knew now that she was in love with him. It would be fatal if he guessed. He already had few enough scruples about taking her, and if he knew she loved him, nothing in the world could stop him. So far as he was concerned, she was nothing more than a pawn in a game he was determined to win. Right now, his hunting instincts were aroused by her reluctance, but with assuagement of desire would come satiation and eventually boredom; then on to newer game. And the price she would pay would be months, even years, of nagging heartache. She was fiercely determined not to become his plaything for the brief interval he would want her. No matter if at times the longing to give herself over to the hot beat of her blood was overwhelming!

Her defences were so pitifully few that she knew she couldn't hold out against a determined campaign by Mark. For instance, tonight. She suspected that he intended to move while she was in a vulnerable position, reasoning that once they had made love she would not be able to resist him thereafter. So she had better do something about getting back to Tamassee, she thought grimly.

She had such a little money—and it would be folly for her, a lone woman, to hire a boat. Perhaps she could get help from someone. Lucy Johnson, perhaps? A lot depended upon how well entrenched Mark was with the family.

She shivered slightly and he asked, 'Cold?'

'No. Just thinking of how much I hate you,' she returned tartly.

He laughed, but by then the taxi had stopped at the bank. They both cashed cheques, then went on to the hospital. Juliet got out with her face averted, still reluctant to look directly at Mark. Inside, the air-conditioned coolness was a relief on her hot cheeks. One thing about a hospital, it was a great leveller. In the hotel, she had been acutely conscious of her clothes: in the hospital, no one cared. They all had troubles of their own.

Carlos was sitting up in bed with a wide grin on his face, his grandparents on either side of him. His bed was littered with wrapping paper and boxes. His grandmother had gone out early and, with Mark's connivance, bought new clothes to replace the ones Mark had ruined when he slit them.

Juliet stood beside the window in the crowded room and watched Mark with the Johnsons. He was very good with them and he kidded Carlos in the hip vernacular of the teenager. Relaxed and charming, he couldn't be faulted in his performance, and as Juliet watched, she realised something that surprised her—he liked people. She found she was glad—she would have hated for Mark Bannerman to be unworthy of her love.

Lucy was built on massive lines. She was wearing a voluminous muu-muu, and a number of necklaces and bracelets. Her laughter was rich and hearty. Juliet noticed at once a resemblance to Mai, Mark's housekeeper, then learned that they were twin sisters,

Lucy being the elder by ten minutes. She looked capable of chasing Mark, or anyone else, away with a mop if he invaded the *Sea Witch*—but still Juliet was uneasy. *Would* she really defy Mark, if he made an issue of staying on the *Sea Witch* tonight?

Finally Mark straightened from his casual stance against the wall and said, 'We've got to be going. Okay if Juliet takes the other bedroom on the *Sea Witch* tonight, Lucy?'

'Sure thing, Mark.' The old woman's bright eyes moved to Juliet. 'You like jambalaya, Julie?'

'I—I don't know. I've never tasted it.'

'What? Never tasted no jambalaya?' The old woman acted astonished. 'I make the best.' She smacked her lips. 'Tonight I cook you best dinner you ever had in your life? Okay? Mark knows how good I cook, hey, Mark?'

'Does that mean I'm invited, too?' he grinned.

'You want to come—you invited. Hey, you bring wine and we have a party. Okay?'

'Can I come, Gran?' asked Carlos.

She laughed. 'You one silly boy, you know you too young to drink wine! You wait—I bring you jambalaya tomorrow for your dinner, in place of this hospital food.' She made a face. 'I get sick myself, I have to eat this stuff.'

'Okay, Lucy, we'll be there tonight—with the wine.' Mark held the door open for Juliet to precede him out of the room.

Outside the room, she saw Jack Tanner lounging at the nurses' station, deep in conversation with a beautiful redhaired young woman in a nurse's uniform. He saw them at the same time, and murmuring something in his companion's ear, strolled toward them, his arm under her elbow.

'How did you find Carlos, boss?' he asked.

Mark did not reply, and Juliet looked at him in surprise. His face wore a tight, controlled expression, and he barely moved his lips as he introduced Juliet to the woman, who was Serena Cadwell, the island nurse. Serena glanced briefly at Juliet, then turned to Mark, a tentative smile on her lips.

# GIVE YOUR HEART TO HARLEQUIN®

**FREE!**

*Mail this heart today!*

# AND WE'LL GIVE YOU
# 4 FREE BOOKS, AND A
# FREE MYSTERY GIFT!

SEE INSIDE!

# ⋆∘ IT'S A ∘⋆
# HARLEQUIN HONEYMOON
# A SWEETHEART
# OF A FREE OFFER!

## FOUR NEW "HARLEQUIN ROMANCES"–FREE!

Take a "Harlequin Honeymoon" with four exciting romances—yours FREE from Harlequin Reader Service. Each of these hot-off-the-presses novels brings you all the passion and tenderness of today's greatest love stories… your free passports to bright new worlds of love and foreign adventure!

But wait…there's <u>even more</u> to this great offer!

## SPECIAL EXTRAS–FREE!

You'll get our free monthly newsletter, packed with news on your favorite writers, upcoming books, and more. Four times a year, you'll receive our members' magazine, Harlequin Romance Digest! <u>Best of all, you'll periodically receive our special-edition "Harlequin Bestsellers," yours to preview for ten days without charge!</u>

## MONEY-SAVING HOME DELIVERY!

Join Harlequin Reader Service and enjoy the <u>convenience</u> of previewing six new books every month, delivered right to your home. Each book is yours for only $1.50— <u>25¢ less per book</u> than what you pay in stores! Great savings plus total convenience add up to a sweetheart of a deal for y<u>ou</u>!

## START YOUR HARLEQUIN HONEYMOON TODAY– JUST COMPLETE, DETACH & MAIL YOUR FREE OFFER CARD!

## HARLEQUIN READER SERVICE "NO-RISK" GUARANTEE

- There's no obligation to buy—and the free books and gifts remain yours to keep.
- You pay the lowest price possible and receive books before they appear in stores.
- You may end your subscription anytime—just write and let us know.

# HARLEQUIN READER SERVICE
## ⋙ FREE OFFER CARD ⋘

**PLACE HEART STICKER HERE**

**4 FREE BOOKS**

**PLUS AN EXTRA BONUS "MYSTERY GIFT"!**

**FREE HOME DELIVERY**

☐ YES! Please send me my four HARLEQUIN ROMANCES® books, free, along with my free Mystery Gift! Then send me six new HARLEQUIN ROMANCES books every month, as they come off the presses, and bill me at just $1.50 per book (25¢ less than retail), with no extra charges for shipping and handling. If I am not completely satisfied, I may return a shipment and cancel at any time. The free books and Mystery Gift remain mine to keep!

116 CIR EAXF

FIRST NAME_____LAST NAME_____
(PLEASE PRINT)

ADDRESS_____APT._____

CITY_____

PROV./STATE_____POSTAL CODE/ZIP_____

PRINTED IN U.S.A.

"Offer limited to one per household and not valid for present subscribers. Prices subject to change."

Limited Time Offer!

Make sure you get this great FREE OFFER- act today!

BUSINESS REPLY CARD

First Class    Permit No. 70    Tempe, AZ

Postage will be paid by addressee

NO POSTAGE
NECESSARY
IF MAILED
IN THE
UNITED STATES

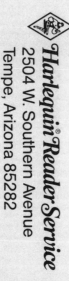
*Harlequin Reader Service*

2504 W. Southern Avenue
Tempe, Arizona 85282

No one had prepared Juliet for the woman's beauty. She had a stunning figure, the kind of smoothly tanned complexion that some redheads, if they are fortunate, have, and widely spaced green eyes. They were fixed nervously on Mark now.

'Hello, darling, surprised to see me?'

He didn't bother to answer. 'What are you doing here?' he asked harshly. 'Aren't you supposed to be on leave—or something?'

'Or something!' She laughed and made a little face. 'I was, sweetie, but when I heard about the boy, naturally I returned immediately.'

'Why?' he asked bluntly. 'The hospital has a very efficient nursing staff.'

A faint blush reddened her cheeks. 'Really, Mark! I feel he's *my* patient!'

'Do you?' His lids hooded the expression in his eyes. 'Who told you he was here, anyway?'

'One of my—one of the nurses here at the hospital. A—a friend of mine.'

'And you returned all the way from wherever you'd gone to nurse your patient?' he drawled. 'Your loyalty does you credit.'

'Of course not, darling!' Serena said gaily. 'I was here all the time. I didn't leave Florida.' She lowered her voice. 'Surely you knew I wouldn't?'

'No. I thought I made it clear that I expected you to.'

'C-can't we talk about it—in private?' Serena coaxed, slipping an arm under his elbow.

Mark hesitated, then turned to Jack. 'I have to run downstairs to the office for a few minutes. Look after Juliet for me, will you?'

'Sure.' Jack was rather pale, and Juliet wondered if he was ill. He turned sharply towards her. 'Coffee, love?'

She followed him to the coffee machine as Mark and Serena started towards the elevator. Serena had dropped his arm, apparently from a lack of response, but there was something triumphant about her back as she moved swiftly behind him. When they had been swallowed up in the elevator, Juliet turned to Jack.

'What was that all about?'

Jack looked cynical. 'Simple, my sweet,' he said ironically, handing her her coffee. 'The boss tried to give the lady a polite brush-off with a three months' paid vacation, hoping she'd used the time to get another job. But the lady refused to accept the hint and continued to hang around Key West, with every intention of going back to work when her time was up. This thing with Carlos has given her her excuse.'

Juliet listened frowningly. 'I don't understand. You mean he fired her? I'm sorry, Jack, but I find it hard to believe that Mark Bannerman has any difficulty getting rid of an employee when he wants to.'

'Yes, I heard about your experience with him,' he said sympathetically. 'Sorry about it, pet. It was partly my fault—I should have cleared you with Posenby's before I brought you out. Sorry you saw our boss at his worst.'

'Well, I've seen him at his best, too,' she remarked thoughtfully. 'He did everything right when Carlos was stricken.'

'Oh, I'm sure he did. He has a great flair for organisation.'

She was struck by a sudden thought. 'Jack, can you take me back to Tammassee today?'

'Sure. When?'

'Right now.'

He looked startled. 'But Mark said you were to wait.'

'Oh, he was just going to see me to the hotel,' she said casually. 'He'll be relieved to find I've been taken care of. And I really do have a lot to do, Jack.'

If he was sceptical, he did not show it. 'Okay. But mind you, you accept the blame if Mark doesn't like it.'

'Oh, I'll take the responsibility alright,' she said grimly. She threw her cup in a waste bin. 'Let's go!'

Juliet arrived at Bella Vista before lunch. Daisy was sitting on the veranda when Sam dropped her off, and she rose and stared at her with lively curiosity.

'What on earth are you doing back here without Mark?'

'I do have a job to do, you know,' Juliet replied shortly, avoiding her eyes.

'Girls who go off with Mark Bannerman don't usually think about their jobs,' Daisy twinkled. 'How's the boy?'

'Better.' Good manners forced Juliet to pause and answer Daisy's questions, giving her a rundown on what had happened.

'Where did you stay last night?' Daisy asked finally.

Juliet flushed but answered truthfully. Daisy's eyebrows rose at the news, but she said nothing, and finally Juliet excused herself. 'I'm going to shower and get into some clean clothes before lunch.'

At lunch, she had no appetite, but rather than attract a caustic remark from Daisy, she made an effort to eat. They were on dessert when Mai came in and stood with folded hands.

'Cora just called,' she said reprovingly. 'She said Mark rang up and wanted to know if you were here. He was too late to talk to Mr Tanner, but he was angry. He said when he left you, he expected you to wait, but when he got back, you had disappeared.'

Daisy looked up with dancing yes. 'Aha! What happened? Did you run out on Mark?'

Juliet felt sick. 'Nothing of the sort! I—I had a chance to come back here with Jack and I took it, that's all! Why shouldn't I return? I had nothing to do there and there was plenty of work for me here!'

'Well, James will certainly concur with *that* idea!' Daisy agreed dryly. 'He was over here last night, complaining that you'd left the island and your work. He didn't like it at all. Didn't you have an arrangement with him to have your weekends free?' she added.

Mai went on as though no one had spoken. 'Mark says he'll be returning as soon as Mr Tanner gets back with the helicopter.'

'Indeed? Well, he certainly won't find me waiting around here to be scolded as though I was a child!' snapped Juliet, leaping to her feet. 'I'm going to see James, in case anyone is interested!'

She regretted her outburst almost at once. What

happened in Key West was not Daisy's or Mai's fault, but she could not rid herself of the knowledge that they were first and foremost Mark Bannerman's employees and friends. Now they were really going to wonder what had really happened last night. Moreover, by seeing James, she was breaking her own rule—that of not working at weekends. And that, she told herself, was a tactical error. She almost turned around and went back, but stubbornness drove her on.

She was glad she hadn't when she saw the state of the house. Lallie was still away at night, which meant that James had been alone all weekend. It had taken him just that long to undo all her good work. In spite of Lallie having left plenty of food in the refrigerator, he had apparently eaten nothing but bread, butter and watery tea. At some time he had spilt tea on his desk and the papers were a soggy mess. At some other time he had been into the files and they had undergone an upheaval. Papers, files, and catalogues were scattered all over the room. It would take Juliet days of hard work just getting things back to where they were, with no guarantee that they would stay that way.

She found James outside, feeding the dolphins. He didn't look up until she stood beside him and then he muttered sullenly, 'Where have you been?'

'Key West. Weren't you told?'

'Oh, I was told all right.' He glared at her. 'Daisy took a great deal of pleasure in telling me.'

'I don't believe that, James.'

'Why did you go away with Mark, Juliet?' His lower lip jutted like a small sulky boy's. 'If you're falling for him, it isn't going to do you any good,' he added spitefully. 'He already has a girl here on Tamassee.'

'James,' she cried angrily, 'I went to Key West to take care of a sick boy. No matter what you might think, I was the only person available!'

'I don't believe that, Juliet,' he mimicked savagely.

She compressed her lips. 'Very well, you force me to be blunt. It isn't any of your business what I do. If you can't accept that and want me to leave, I'll oblige you. Perhaps your next secretary will allow you to run her life!'

His expression changed drastically. '*No!* Please, Juliet, forgive me. I don't want you to leave. I know I'm a selfish bastard. I—I'm jealous, I guess. Mark always spoils things for me. I knew he wanted you that first day, and I knew he was going to try to take you away from me. And it isn't fair!' It was the wail of a spoiled child.

'That's foolish, James. He doesn't want me.' Juliet swallowed. 'And even if he did, he isn't getting me!'

'Oh, you don't know Mark. He'll find a way—he always gets what he wants. Women, money, power come easy to him. And everyone thinks he's wonderful. Haven't you found out by now how people on this island feel about him?' he added miserably. 'He's successful with people and scores with women—not like me. Oh, I know I'm jealous, but you were mine before you were his.'

'I'm not his, James!' she reminded him sharply.

'But you will be,' he insisted. 'For no other reason but that he's trying to part us. I don't want you to become just another name on his list of available girls, Juliet.'

'I'm not on his list, and I'm not available,' Juliet said coldly, and hoped it was true.

'Have you had anything to eat?' she asked. They were walking back to the house.

'Nothing but bread and tea.'

He sounded injured, as though it was her fault—or Lallie's—that he had been forced to starve the whole weekend. Juliet ignored his grumbling and led him into the kitchen, where she made casual conversation while she heated a frozen dinner Lallie had left and made coffee. After he had eaten and she had washed the dishes, they went into the living room to try to restore order. James helped, and didn't seem very concerned as he shook out wet tea and spread papers on the floor to dry. His selfishness was a revelation to Juliet. She would be glad to finish and leave Tamassee. The Bannerman brothers had brought her nothing but heartache, and there was more yet to come.

She left at ten o'clock. It did not occur to James to

offer to accompany her, but Juliet was not afraid. There was nothing on Tamassee to fear and there was a full moon that made everything as clear as day. A fresh breeze was blowing across the island, bringing with it the thousand and one scents of the night—rotting woodland mingled with the tangy salt of the sea, and the smell of the wild, growing things that abounded in the woods.

The muted boom of the surf was a fit accompaniment to her thoughts. The tide was going out, so she took off her shoes and walked on the hard, damp sand. It was firm and cool beneath her bare feet. The receding tide was leaving behind a crest of foam that glittered in the moonlight like jewelled lace. Apparently the moon had a soothing effect on the ocean's turbulence, because it was relatively calm, with only an occasional whitecap breaking far out to sea. White on black.

Juliet walked slowly and as she approached Bella Vista, she was suprised to see that every light was on. She wondered what sort of reception she was going to get from Mark. Would patching up his quarrel with Serena cause him to abandon his pursuit for her? *Had she lost him?* When she realised the path in which her thoughts were leading her, she shivered. She had to think of someone—something else. She readily admitted she was becoming obsessed with Mark. It wasn't an overnight thing, either; he had been in her thoughts ever since that first day. It was becoming a sick fantasy, this dream of him, and she was weak to continue to indulge it.

'Where have you been?'

The question, flung out of the quiet darkness, startled her into an outcry. It held a deep savage anger barely held in check, and chill bumps rose on Juliet's neck. A glowing cigar made a perfect arc as he tossed it into the damp grass, then she saw a shadow move.

'What are you doing here?' she gasped.

'Waiting for you.'

'That was kind of you,' she said nervously. 'But it was unnecessary.'

'I didn't do it to be kind.' The shadow moved again and strong fingers gripped her upper arms. 'I could kill you for putting me through hell today,' he said tonelessly. His hands shook with the force of his anger. 'The next time I tell you to wait, you'd better not move until I come back for you. How do you think Lucy felt when I told her you'd walked out on her dinner invitation?'

Juliet glared at him defiantly. 'I'm sorry I had to be rude to Lucy, but I had no choice! I wasn't going to stay there and let you try to seduce me!'

There was a brief pause, then, 'But we both know I don't have to try very hard, don't we, Miss Welborn?' Mark asked silkily.

She felt as though she had been slapped. 'If it's an easy seduction you want, go back to Serena Cadwell!' she stormed. 'She's coming back to the island, isn't she?' She could have bitten out her tongue as soon as the words were out, but it was too late.

He froze. 'Who told you about her?'

She laughed harshly. 'Is it a secret? If so, I'm afraid it's out. Even James knows about you and Serena!'

'Go to bed,' he said levelly, loosening his grip on her arms. 'Right now, I have an overwhelming desire to punish you as you deserve, but no love affair should begin by using sex as a weapon. Just be thankful I don't show you how easy *your* seduction would be.' She flinched and he added, 'Wait.'

'Yes?' Juliet was so tired and shaken she was visibly trembling.

Mark studied her, frowning, but he made no comment on her appearance. 'I had to make some excuse to Lucy,' he said slowly. 'So I told her you had to return to Tamassee because James needed you for some extra work. So she renewed her invitation for Thursday when, I hope, she'll be back home and Carlos will be out of the hospital. I accepted for both of us.'

'Thursday?' she faltered.

'Yes. And this time, Juliet, you'd better be there,' he added with soft menace.

After that, Juliet avoided him whenever possible. She became adroit at making herself scarce when he was around. Fortunately, there was her work—she was very busy for long hours in her room. And there were the others—they were unconscious allies in her campaign. Of course, Mark saw through her ruse and she knew it angered him, although he made no effort to change the situation.

Monday, Carlos came home and Serena returned to Tamassee. Jack, too, was ordered back to take up residence in Bella Vista. The usual practice of having the helicopter based at the airfield was reversed. Now Jack flew out for the mail and returned, all because, he told Juliet, Mark hadn't been very happy about their isolation when Carlos was ill. But Jack, who enjoyed city night life, didn't seem too concerned about the new arrangement. 'It won't last for ever,' he told Juliet lightheartedly. Meantime, he spent a lot of time loafing in town, either at the hotel or with Serena.

There was a certain look on his face when he spoke of Serena that made Juliet wonder if he was in love with her. It would explain a great deal. For one thing, his earlier brashness towards Juliet had disappeared, and he treated her more or less the way he did Daisy. Daisy would have liked to think he was falling in love with Juliet, but no one in their right mind could make anything lover-like out of Jack's brotherly approach.

Serena's arrogance in the face of Mark's indifference was astounding. She seemed supremely confident of her ultimate success. She gave orders to Mai in her cool little voice as though she was mistress of the house, and she ignored Daisy and Juliet. Her breakfast was carried to the cottage every morning on a tray and she had the services of one of the maids for her exclusive use. Obviously, this was the way it had always been, and since Mark gave no counter-orders, it went on that way.

Her ploys with Mark seemed to be working, too. On Monday, he warmed slightly; Tuesday, he was warmer and by Wednesday he was responding with flattering attention. Serena was flushed and brilliantly witty with success. After dinner, he accompanied her to the cottage and so far as Juliet knew, he stayed on.

Juliet lay awake that night in her bed and faced the bitter realisation of what she meant to Mark. No more than a night's casual sex, the cheap response of her body to his sensual expertise—in other words, a pushover! She couldn't even delude herself that she meant something special to him, for he had turned too easily back to his other lady. She tossed and turned, trying to purge her memory of his kisses and caresses, but it was impossible. The truth was he had captured her heart without even trying, without caring, and as a result she had bought herself months of unhappiness. But, thank God, she hadn't the most humiliating memory of all to cope with! She had held out, even though he had decided in the most contemptuous manner possible to abandon the pursuit.

She wondered if he had forgotten about Lucy's dinner. Would he cancel it or take Serena? Lucy would probably prefer Serena. As the island nurse, she was popular and she, Juliet, was just passing through.

The next day, Serena made no pretence of going to work. When Juliet got back to the house at noon, she was lying beside the pool in a lounging chair, talking to Jack. She joined them for lunch wearing her bikini covered by a thigh-length matching coat. Mark came in late, and although Serena exerted herself, he was morose and brusque in his replies. When he finished lunch, he lingered a moment to give Daisy some orders about some letters he had put on the recorder.

Serena yawned daintily. 'Surely you aren't going to work through the siesta hour, darling?' she pouted provocatively. 'I intend to have a cool shower and stretch out on my bed with a good book.' Her words were a not-so-subtle invitation.

In the silence that followed, while everyone's minds dwelt on the image of Serena in bed with a good book, Juliet threaded her napkin carefully through its holder. If Serena had expected Mark to react, she was disappointed. He didn't bother to answer, but left the room without a word. It took Daisy's common sense to bring things back into focus.

'Sounds good to me,' she said briskly. 'I might do the same thing after I've finished those letters.' She turned to Juliet. 'Mark asked me to remind you to be ready by six.'

'Oh! Y-yes, all right,' Juliet stammered.

'Good,' Daisy said briefly, and hurried off towards the study.

Serena's narrowed eyes were cold. 'Do you have a date with Mark tonight?'

'Yes—for dinner.'

'I'd like to talk to you,' Serena went on in a hard voice. 'In the library, if you please. Will you excuse us, Jack?'

He watched thoughtfully as Serena led the way towards the library. She shut the door, then turned disdainfully to Juliet.

'In case you're under the delusion that Mark is available, I want you to know that he isn't, and won't be,' she said coolly. 'He may have been last week—or when he made that arrangement with you—but things have changed, as you may have noticed. We had a quarrel a month ago and split up. During that time he apparently noticed you. But we've made up our quarrel. It took some humbling on my part, I admit, because Mark Bannerman doesn't crawl to any woman. But I did it, and it was worth it. I have him, and I intend to keep him. So, if you imagine holding him to this dinner engagement is going to accomplish a miracle for you, I can assure you it won't.'

'He doesn't have to keep the dinner engagement,' Juliet said stiffly. 'I can go alone.'

'Oh, he'll keep it. Mark is nothing less than a gentleman,' Serena drawled. 'He may be bored stiff and wish he was somewhere else, but you'll never know it. He's that way. I've seen him treat some fat old wife of one of his vice-presidents as though she was a beauty queen, and she loved it! He won't cancel your dinner date.'

'What do you expect me to do?' Juliet demanded. A slight flush had stained her cheekbones, for she had taken Serena's inference.

Serena shrugged. 'I suppose nothing—if you don't mind knowing you're merely tolerated from politeness. Personally, I'd want to get out of it, but I'm sure you're eager to hold him to his promise. I just wanted to let you know what his thoughts on the subject will be.'

'Has he mentioned them to you?' Juliet asked quietly.

Serena hesitated, but apparently thought better of lying. 'No,' she admitted. 'He wouldn't want to make me feel uncomfortable because I wasn't going.'

'Well, whatever you say,' Juliet said bleakly, 'I'm not cancelling my part of it. I don't intend to disappoint Lucy a second time.'

'Lucy?' Serena asked sharply.

'Lucy Johnson—Carlos' grandmother.'

'Oh, I see,' Serena said thoughtfully.

Back in her room, Juliet slammed papers and folders about for fully five minutes before she could concentrate on her work. Whether Serena went tonight or not, she was sure of one thing—her pleasure in Lucy's dinner party had evaporated. The thought of being considered a bore and a duty was never pleasurable, and now she had begun to wonder if Lucy really wanted her; if she didn't want Serena in her place. She was sure of it when she finally made her way downstairs about six o'clock. Knowing that she was probably going to one of the shanties in town, she had dressed simply, but not wanting to insult Lucy by dressing down for her party, she had put on one of her prettiest summer dresses. It was apple green, trimmed in bright yellow, and she wore large plastic yellow hoops in her ears and a pair of high-heeled sandals.

Downstairs, she discovered Serena waiting with every intention of accompanying them to the party. But she had dressed to the hilt, in a long cotton frock of white splashed with lavender and green tropical flowers. The back was superbly cut to show off her beautiful tanned shoulders and most of her back. But no dime-store earrings for her! She wore amethyst earrings in her ears, and a matching amethyst necklace nestled between her breasts.

'Hullo,' she murmured indifferently. 'Mark just would insist that I go, too. Hope it doesn't spoil your plans, but I was told on good authority that Lucy would be tremendously hurt if I didn't show up.' She

raised her eyebrows at Juliet's dress. 'But the last thing
I'd do is hurt poor old Lucy's feelings by showing up
for her party dressed like a teenager! She'll expect to
show us all off to her neighbours.'

Mark walked in in the midst of the dead silence that
followed that remark. He was wearing dark brown
slacks and a chocolate brown shirt that was open to
reveal an unnerving wedge of bronzed chest. The
narrowed grey eyes were noncommittal as he noticed
the difference in the two girls' dresses, but he said
nothing beyond an impersonal, 'Hello, you two. Ready
to go?'

Lucy's little house was filled to bursting. Neighbours,
relatives, friends—they were all there. Apparently
Serena had been right—Lucy did expect to show them
off. Juliet held back shyly, painfully embarrassed, but
Lucy, who had met them at the door wearing a red silk
dress and apron, wasn't having that. Clasping her to
her bosom in a bear-hug, she pulled her into the centre
of the room and announced to all the guests at large,
'Meet Miss Julie, Mr Mark's lady.'

Juliet blushed and glanced quickly at Mark, but
apparently he had heard nothing, for he was looking
the other way.

Lucy's greeting to Serena, 'Glad you could make it,
Miss Cadwell,' didn't indicate that her dinner would be
a total failure without her. However, Serena made
herself at home, playing the part of Mark's gracious
assistant. He had brought the wine—enough to go
around—and she stayed close, helping him pour and
distribute it in paper cups. She knew everyone there and
spoke to each as she moved around the room.

Meanwhile, Juliet had shyly found herself a corner
and sat down while the talk swirled around her. The
voices were soft and musical, all talking at once in the
West Indian dialect that slurred some words and
dropped others. As the wine was passed around again,
the voices rose and fell happily—and loudly.

The jambalaya was everything Lucy had promised—
and more. The wine Mark had selected for the dinner was
a perfect complement to it. Dessert was a fresh fruit cup.

And Lucy seemed bent on linking Mark and Juliet. She blandly inferred that Serena was present only because she had been Carlos' nurse. 'This nurse of Carlos, she one fine nurse, all the time popping in and out while he was in the hospital.' The assumption was that there hadn't been as much popping since. And then, as they were climbing into the car—Serena manoeuvred things so that Juliet sat in the back seat as she had coming there—Lucy called out in her full, rich voice from the doorway, 'You take good care of Julie, Mark! She is one shy little girl, not pushy at all like some of those modern girls!'

The jeep exhaust roared, then throttled down, and Juliet caught the tag end of a sentence delivered in Serena's soft husky voice, '—sweet old thing, but she's getting rather senile. How old is she, anyway, Mark?'

'Not old enough to take that from you, Serena,' he said crisply. 'I hope you don't hint anything like that to her.'

'Of course not, darling! What do you take me for? But she is just the merest tiniest bit—tactless—don't you think?'

'No, I don't,' he said bluntly.

That disposed of that, and Serena was quieted, at least until they got home. Juliet went directly to her room, having no desire to watch the bitter sight of Mark escorting Serena to her cottage—and staying.

Upstairs, she was restless, on edge and too unhappy to sleep. She thought of the pool. It would be empty this time of night—Mark still retained his habit of swimming at dawn, one of the reasons she had stopped—so he would not be there, and being on the other side of the house from the cottage, he wouldn't see her if he returned early. She slipped into her bikini, slid her feet into thongs and picking up a large towel from the bathroom, went downstairs. The foyer was lighted, but the rest of the house was in darkness and Juliet didn't turn on a light in the library as she slipped through the glass doors that led outside to the pool.

She swam briskly at first before tiring, then drew herself out and sat in the lounging chair, the same one that had held Serena's luscious body earlier today. Thinking of Serena—which she had been trying determinedly not to do—brought on a wave of depression and loneliness that Juliet hadn't experienced since the death of her parents. Before she knew it, she was crying. She tried to stop, but couldn't: her tears were a cleansing relief that wouldn't be halted. She used her towel repeatedly as a handkerchief, drying her eyes only to have them refill and overflow again.

Finally her tears slowed enough for her to become aware of other things—night things like the soft rustling breeze that struck chill on her arms and legs and the pattern of light on the water. Then, abruptly, she knew she was being watched. She looked up. Mark had halted before her and stood absolutely still, as though shocked by what he saw. She could see the gleam of light on bare skin, but his expression was hidden from her. He was just a black shadow looming up against the shifting light on the pool.

'I—I'm s-sorry,' she stammered, swinging her feet to the ground and standing up at the same time. 'I—thought you were in bed or—or——'

'In bed is the operative word, I think.' His mockery was harsh, derisive. 'No, I was in the library when you sneaked past and I thought I'd join you for a swim. I didn't know I'd be interrupting an orgy of tears.'

'T-tears?'

For answer, he reached out and gently smudged a tear that was even then rolling down her cheek. 'Does a moonlight swim do this to you? Or was it the wine? Or perhaps you misled me and there *is* a man somewhere in the background whom you're missing?'

Conscious of his hand, which had slid down and was resting against her throat, Juliet said shakily, 'No—man. I was just missing—my parents.'

A vagrant glint of moonlight illuminated his face briefly and she saw that he was frowning. 'Your parents?' he asked questioningly.

'They—they died recently. They were drowned.'

'My God,' he said quietly. The hand at her throat cupped the nape of her neck and he drew her forward insistently. She leaned against him, her cheek resting against the springy curls of his chest, and her breath fanned them slightly against her nose. He had drawn her into his arms in a gesture of sympathy she felt nothing but an extraordinary sense of peace and comfort. 'I'm sorry.'

His hand gently stroked the back of her head and her shoulder. He put the other arm, the one that had been holding his towel, around her, too, and she snuggled closer. For a long time, it seemed, they stood like that, then subtly, the feeling changed. Juliet became acutely conscious of Mark's body and realised that the caresses had become erotic instead of comforting, as his hands crept lower and fanned out along her waist and hips. Wild signals of alarm and warning raced to her brain, carried directly from the nerve endings of her body. Her breathing quickened until she almost choked.

She drew away. 'Don't!'

'Don't?' he murmured, on an upward inflection.

'Don't use my weakness as a way to force me again! It's—wicked!'

She looked up and met his smile, narrow and hard with a glitter of dislike. He held her away from him deliberately and she shivered as his eyes cynically stripped the bikini from her body. 'But then I *am* wicked, my dear,' he said softly. 'Don't you know that by now?'

Juliet started to move, but his mouth swooped, arrogant in its cruelty. She knew she should resist, but it had been too long; she was hungry for his kisses. Her lips parted eagerly and shaped themselves to his mouth. She shuddered convulsively, pressing closer, winding her arms around his neck. Somewhere, in the dazed, unreachable areas of her mind, she was aware that what she was doing was dangerous—insane—but she could no more stop herself from responding to him than she could have stopped the rise and fall of the tide. He moulded her half-naked body to his, and she felt the unmistakable thrust of his desire. With a swiftness that startled her, he lifted her into his arms and carried her into the library. There he laid her upon the sofa, while his hands fumbled briefly with the minute scraps of material that were her only clothing. She felt him remove them, then he lay down beside her.

From that moment time stood still, crystallised into its own moment of eternity by the upbeat singing of her blood. All her scared objections fell away as though they had never existed. Nothing mattered any more but the feel of Mark's hard, taut body next to hers; the touch of his hands stroking her, making erotic traceries on her flushed skin as he murmured things like, 'Darling, sweet, I want you. I need you . . .' His kisses had increased in intensity, and her senses swam as a feverish heat licked through her veins.

She cradled his head on her breast, and a warm mouth fastened on a rosy nipple. His tongue teased it into a hardened peak, creating an unbearable ache in her loins. Her heart lurched and the sensation flowered into a gnawing, burning *need* that grew until she thought she would die unless it was assuaged. Then his lips closed hungrily over hers, and as though he felt the surrender implicit in her trembling responses, his caresses grew more leisurely and his hands grew bolder in their exploration of the heretofore uncharted regions of her body.

'Mark,' she groaned. 'Darling—love me. Love me now——' Without bitterness, she had already reckoned the costs of this night's passion, and they did not count against the wild clamour of her senses and this sweet abandonment of self.

He drew away. 'If you really mean that,' he said tautly, 'then I suggest we move upstairs to my bed where we'll be more comfortable.'

Juliet opened her eyes dazedly. 'I—what did I say?' she whispered hoarsely.

'You asked me to make love to you.'

She closed her eyes and a tear squeezed out between the long lashes fanning her cheeks. 'I—oh, God—no!' she moaned. 'I didn't mean it. Oh, Mark, please be merciful! I don't want you to make love to me.'

'I thought not,' he replied grimly.

He didn't say anything else for a long time. She

couldn't look at him, her shame was too great. She had buried her face in her hands, fighting to hold back the tears that threatened to well to the surface.

Finally, 'What's with you, Juliet?' he asked coolly. 'You blow hot and then cold. Is it because you've only had one lover, or is it merely because you're a tease?'

'Not a tease!' she protested brokenly.

'Not a tease?' he offered reflectively. 'No, I don't think so, either. I could have had you if I hadn't mentioned going upstairs. You were ready. But once that little brain started working, you turned me off. What do you want? Is it marriage you're after?' he added contemptuously. 'Is that what you're holding out for?'

'*No!*' She took her hands away and lifted her ravaged face. 'I'm not a fool. Do you think I'd want marriage with a man who had to be cajoled into it? Do you think I want the heartbreak that would follow when you tired of me?' He said nothing and she looked around helplessly. 'Where are my clothes? I must get to my room.'

He helped her gather them together, then handed her the towel that had been bunched up beneath them. She didn't bother to try to put on her bikini, but wrapped the towel around her body, mummy fashion. Then she stood up.

'It was all my fault for responding to you, but I can't keep my emotions in deep-freeze,' she went on tiredly. 'I don't want to have a love affair with you, Mark, so from now on, please leave me alone so I can get over you in my own way.'

'Then you admit there is something there between us?' he asked harshly.

'Oh, yes,' she admitted drearily. Her face was taut and white with pain. 'You've made your impact on me, all right. But that still doesn't mean I'm going to bed with you. So—just leave me alone.' And fleeing from the room as though from the devil itself, she ran blindly up the stairs.

## CHAPTER SIX

JULIET came downstairs the following morning looking
so pale and ill that Daisy was shocked. She stopped her
as she was crossing the hall and asked, 'What's
happened to you?'

'I'll be all right, Daisy, if I can get off the island
today. Do you think Jack will take me?' she asked
desperately. 'This job is no good—I'm going to have to
quit.'

'Honey, that's impossible. They've all gone.'

'Gone?'

'Yes—early this morning. Mark got me up about
six o'clock and gave me some instructions, then he
and Jack took off at seven. I'm afraid the supply boat
will be our only dependable transport until they get
back.'

Juliet's eyes flickered. 'When will that be?'

'I don't know. Mark said to expect him in a week or
two, but since he didn't give me any idea why he was
leaving, I can't say.' She waited, trying to pretend she
hadn't noticed the almost stupefied look of relief on
Juliet's face. 'Guess Madam is going to be slightly
disappointed.'

'Serena?'

'Yes. She wasn't asked to go along, so apparently she
isn't as firmly entrenched as she'd like to believe. Guess
we'll have to put up with her during meals, though. But
don't worry, she won't stay long. She'll be off to
Florida and that new car of hers if Mark stays away
long.'

'How will she go?' asked Juliet.

'The supply boat stops on Monday. But surely you
don't intend to leave now, when you're so nearly
through?' Daisy asked anxiously. 'Juliet, stick with it!
Things will get better before long, and you know you
want to see the book to the end!'

'Yes,' Juliet said thoughtfully, 'I would like to finish the book before I leave.'

'Good! I'll help you,' Daisy offered generously. 'I'm a fast typist and I can make things move. Between the two of us, we'll have that thing licked by the time Mark gets back—maybe.'

Juliet's pinched face brightened and Daisy marvelled at how quickly she had recovered. Even half dead with worry and lack of sleep, the girl was still beautiful. *Damn* Mark Bannerman, anyway!

'Meantime,' she went on briskly, 'you're going to take some time off for a little holiday. Just this weekend,' she added hastily, as Juliet's face shadowed. 'It's time you saw our little town and met somebody besides James! Today's Friday. Tonight we're going in for one of the hotel's famous seafood dinners. With any luck, a boatload of tourists will have stopped and there'll be dancing. The Commodore has a load of big-band records.'

At noon, Daisy had a violent quarrel with Serena, although the quarrelling was mostly conducted by Serena. Juliet overheard it because she came home early from James's. Before Serena finished, she had dragged Juliet and Mai into it.

She had made a late appearance after a leisurely breakfast in bed, and headed for the pool. Apparently the atmosphere of desertion had struck her for the first time, and she came into the house, looking for an explanation, and ran into Daisy.

'Where is everyone?' she demanded.

'Oh, Mark and Jack have gone to Florida. If you're really interested, Juliet's working—No, here she is now. Juliet, Serena was asking for you,' Daisy added pertly.

'V-e-erry funny!' snapped Serena. She was wearing a new ice blue bikini and she slipped into her bathcoat since there was no one to impress with a dazzling display of flesh. 'When will he be back?'

'Who?'

'Who do you think? Mark, of course!'

'Oh, *him*! He won't be coming back,' Daisy said innocently.

Serena paled. 'What do you mean?'

'Just what I said. I have no idea of his whereabouts or when he'll return.'

'You're lying!' Serena shrilled. 'Of course you know! I demand that you tell me at once!'

'Sorry, I can't tell you what I don't know,' Daisy said breezily. 'Could be he didn't tell *me* because he was afraid I'd blab it to you.'

'How dare you?' gasped Serena. 'He would want me to know! In fact, he probably left me a message—When did he leave? What did he say?' she half screeched the last words.

Mai came in from the kitchen door, attracted by the noise, and stood beside Juliet, watching impassively.

'He left about seven, and he said a lot of things. But not where he was going.'

'You're lying, you crafty old bitch, and I know it! What's more, I know why!' Serena's eyes fell on Juliet. 'It's to pave the way for that scrounging little slut! Oh, don't think I haven't seen you with your heads together, plotting against me!' She turned back to Daisy. 'You're his private secretary—you have to be able to reach him in case something happens. You know you're keeping it from me! If you don't tell me at once, I'll have you fired when Mark gets back!'

Daisy looked at her mockingly. 'Even if I knew, I wouldn't tell you after that,' she informed the wildly angry woman. 'And it will do you no good to rant and rave and threaten me, because I shan't change my mind. But I just might tell Mark about this conversation!'

Serena subsided abruptly, shuddering as she apparently realised that she had been indiscreet. 'Very well,' she said thinly, 'we'll call it a day. If you try to lie about me, I'll retaliate, I promise you! I'm not going to eat another meal in this house if I have to sit at the same table with you two!' She turned to Mai. 'I'll be served in the living room. You can clear that small table by the window.'

'That makes extra work,' Mai said evenly. 'We've never served but one meal at a time in this house. No one, not even Mark, ever asked me to do it differently.'

'Aw, come on, Mai, have a heart!' Daisy pleaded audaciously. 'We don't want to sit with her any more than she does with us!'

Mai smiled slightly. 'Very well, Miss Daisy, seeing it's you, I'll do it. I wouldn't like to see you and Julie put off your food because you had to look at a scowling face every meal.'

'Oh!' Serena whirled and dashed out of the room, her sandal heels clacking on the bare floor. At dinner time, she was driven out by hunger to make an appearance, only to be disconcerted to find that she had the table to herself after all. Since Daisy and Juliet were away most of the weekend, they did not see her again, although Daisy reported that she had apparently rummaged through Mark's desk Friday night in search of some clue as to his whereabouts. On Monday she bought a passage on the supply boat and went back to Florida.

That Friday night Juliet and Daisy dined at the hotel, where Juliet met a charming group of elderly fuddy-duddies, housed in the hotel, who had retreated, for one reason or another, to this little island paradise, and now they considered themselves islanders: they had put down roots and had a vested interest in seeing that Tamassee stayed alive. Barring Cora, they were mostly retirees, and they had a real fondness for their decaying Victorian home.

Among their number was an elderly schoolteacher whom Mark had hired to teach in the little one-room schoolhouse and gave the children a chance to pick up the basics of reading, writing and arithmetic. Of course, any child who wanted a higher education had to go to another island, and two had done so, with Mark paying for their tuition. Her school, and the guidance of the children, were now the most important things in Miss Foster's life, and she was eager to tell Juliet all about it.

Then there were the Commodore and Mrs Elliott, who ran the hotel. He was also retired, and had discovered the hotel on a fishing trip, then made a proposition to Mark that he re-open it. It was the only place on the island that operated in the black, but they had a gifted cook, the Commodore was his own barman

and desk man and Mrs Elliott was an extremely
efficient housekeeper and extra cook. And the island
was gaining a reputation as a good place to stop over
for an excellent dinner.

All of this Juliet learned gradually. She and Daisy got
in the habit of dropping in often, and told old dears
were thrilled to tell her about their town. She learned
that it had no mayor or city council; the town meetings
were social affairs; the fire department and school were
subsidised by Mark Bannerman—and yet, somehow
everyone managed to muddle along. On the plus side,
there was no crime, no taxes, no politics and no social
problems, but the island lost all its young men. There
was no television, no movies, and the radio reception
wasn't all that good. However, the islanders had
learned to make their own entertainment and in the
hotel, at least, there was usually a brisk game of bridge
or chess going all the time.

During the ten days that Mark was away, Juliet and
Daisy visited the hotel often and Juliet grew very fond
of her new friends. She would miss them when she left
Tamassee, she thought wistfully. She had already made
up her mind that she would probably be gone by the
time Mark returned. She had made such progress on
the book that one, or possibly two, more days of hard
work would see it finished. Then, if James wanted to
hack it to pieces, he could. And from what she had seen
so far, that might easily happen.

James had done a hatchet job on it a week earlier.
Having given Juliet freedom to write it up as she
pleased, he had suddenly decided to change the whole
format and had gone through with a blue pencil,
slashing right and left.

Daisy, grimly surveying the wreckage, had said,
'What does he expect you to do with this mess? What
does he want—page after page of statistics and
experiment results? You had an interesting, free-flowing
narrative there—which he's destroyed! What are you
going to do?'

Juliet, who was stacking pages, looked at her blindly.
'What he says, of course,' she replied tautly.

'But he's sabotaging his own book! Don't ask me
why. It could be he's getting cold feet about it now that
it's so near completion, or it could be that he sees
you're almost finished, and he wants to keep you here!
What do you think?'

'You tell me.'

'A little of both, but more of the latter. How do you
feel about him, Juliet?'

'Friendship, a little pity, but nothing else. You should
know that, Daisy!' Juliet added bitterly. Although no
word had been said about it, she was aware that Daisy
knew how she felt about Mark.

Daisy avoided her eyes. 'Then you'd better find a way
to cool things between you,' she said bluntly. 'He
already can't bear the thought of you leaving him, and
he's going to get worse. And I'm getting tired of re-
typing pages,' she added wryly.

Juliet was struck with remorse. She had already
learned the reason why Mark had begun grooming Paul
Bradford to take Daisy's place—she had a heart
condition and Mark was determined that she was going
to let up.

'That settles it—you're quitting,' declared Juliet.

'I am not! I *need* to work! Besides, I want this book
finished so you can be free to go if you like!'

Something in Daisy's face—pity, sympathy—touched
Juliet so that her eyes filled with tears. 'Oh, Daisy, I—
know,' she murmured wretchedly.

'Cut the tears,' Daisy said gruffly. 'I can't stand 'em.
Let's concentrate on what we can do about James and
his book. He has a right to mess it up if he wants to,
but it would be a darned good book if he'd leave it
alone.'

'Yes,' Juliet nodded. 'I'll talk to him, make him
understand. But about the other. If you're right, Daisy,
I should let him know there's no use pinning his hopes
on my staying—or feeling anything more than I already
do. How can you let a man know you don't love him
when he hasn't mentioned a word to you about it?'

Daisy looked baffled. 'Better let me handle it,' she
said finally. 'I'll tell him he's complicating things for

you and that Mark will be angry if you don't finish the book on schedule. Or ahead of schedule. By the time I finish scolding him, he'll feel so guilty he won't touch the manuscript again. About cooling it,' she added, with a grin, 'I haven't any experience to draw on to tell you how to do that—I'm an old maid, remember? But I do have an idea. When he comes tomorrow night, we just won't be here. We'll be having dinner at the hotel. And next weekend, when James expects you to be free to spend all your time with him, we'll be out with the Commodore on his boat, fishing. How's that?'

'It sounds fine,' Juliet said shakily.

'Well, it's a start,' Daisy said briskly. 'At least, it will keep Mark from blaming you if James blows this project he's working on.'

'What do you mean?'

'It's drawing to a close, and James has never stuck to anything in his life, so he just might blow it.' Daisy sighed. 'This time, with his university career riding on the outcome, he might get temperamental.'

'What are you trying to say, Daisy? That James would deliberately sabotage his future?'

'It's his usual pattern,' Daisy explained grimly. 'He's trying to sabotage his book, isn't he? I guess you know that Mark is financing this wildcat dolphin thing? Mark—not the Bannerman Corporation!

'James didn't explain anything about it,' Juliet told her.

'That figures. Bannerman's is providing a similar grant for experiment at James's university. James has a place on the faculty if he does his work here under their guidelines. But, in fact, he hasn't bothered to keep in touch with his superiors at the university, and Mark is having a devil of a time to keep him at it.'

'He is?' Juliet asked weakly.

'Indeed he is. Two years ago, when James asked his brother to build this expensive lab and buy the dolphins, he claimed it was all for his doctorate. Mark agreed to finance him and give him time to write his book, but he only asked one thing, that James use it to advance his career. James has done anything but that.

Now that the time is up, Mark thinks he's dragging his heels because he's scared to show what he's done, scared he won't measure up out there in the real world. That's where you come in,' she added crisply. 'You're here to get that book written and, let's hope, get James moving.' She studied the tip of her cigarette thoughtfully. 'Personally, I think his interest in you is a good sign. Unlike Mark, who seemed to think it would be disastrous, I think James needs someone like you to push him into action.'

'Thanks,' Juliet said dryly. 'I'm not sure I like being used as a crutch.'

'No, it wouldn't be wise unless you could continue with it,' Daisy agreed.

'I can't.'

'You're not still nursing any delusions about Mark, are you?' asked Daisy bluntly.

Juliet flushed. 'No, but neither do I like being used. I just want to get through and out of here without complications.'

That was how matters stood until the day Mark returned. Cora brought the news to Belle Vista at an early hour of the morning.

Julliet and Daisy had just finished breakfast and were lounging on the terrace with a second cup of coffee when Cora appeared. She stood for a moment in the doorway, a thin, sour smile on her lips.

'Looks like you two are going to have to get off your backsides and do a little work for a change.' That was a sample of Cora's best attempt at friendly humour. 'Mark just phoned that he's coming home today. He told me to let you know, Daisy, and also to let Mai know he's bringing some additional guests. One of the men is a doctor, the university kind, but he'll be staying with James, occupying the bed Miss Welborn tried so hard to hang on to.' She threw Juliet a savage smile. 'Looks like you're getting the shaft, dearie. This man's taking your place. Mark's making sure his little brother gets that experiment of his approved and is on his way out of here as soon as possible.'

'Go to hell, Cora Bannerman,' Daisy said tranquilly.

'You've delivered your message, now get yourself out of here. I'll see to the rest.'

Cora's mouth literally dropped. It was no secret that she was jealous of Daisy, but she had always been careful how she spoke to her, and until now Daisy had, at least, put up a façade of politeness.

She bit her lips, then whirled and left them, abruptly.

'You've made an enemy,' Juliet said uneasily.

'She was never my friend.' Daisy didn't seem worried. 'I expect she plans to go to Mark with some story. But don't worry—he's my boy. He'll listen to me. He'll be disappointed in Cora, because he wanted to help her out, and he thought she was working out fine. But it won't be the first time he's been disappointed in a woman, and it won't be the last.'

Juliet felt a twinge of sympathy for Mark Bannerman before she realised what was happening and suppressed it ruthlessly. No doubt, if he had been disappointed in anyone in the past, it was his own arrogant fault!

# CHAPTER SEVEN

DAISY did not waste any time in warning James about his visitor. She came away from the telephone looking slightly disturbed.

'Better get over and see the lad right now, Juliet. He was rather agitated when he heard the news.'

James was more than 'rather agitated'. By the time Juliet got there he had worked himself into a state of nerves, mixed with self-pity and resentment. She saw Lallie first and cleared the matter of a visitor with her, and went on into the study, which had been allowed to get back into its former disreputable state since her departure. She found James pacing the floor. Mark, he declared, did not appreciate the pressure he was under, and now he was bringing a stranger into his domain, a man who would criticise and question and perhaps even suggest changes in the way he was training the dolphins. He might even suggest to Mark that the whole project be scrapped because it lacked scientific value.

'That's nonsense!' Juliet said briskly. 'Why should the man do anything of the sort? And anyway, don't you want an honest assessment of your work? If you're wasting your time, don't you want to know why? After all, the object of what you're doing is to get your doctorate, isn't it?'

'You worked for Graham, and my methods are the same as his, aren't they?' James asked sullenly. 'If I'm wrong, then so was he!'

'Da-David Graham had his doctorate. He could afford to experiment,' Juliet said patiently. 'You must work under guidelines.'

'Mark doesn't give a damn about me!' James burst out bitterly. 'He expects me to run to order, like a—a computer! I can't present him with a neat row of figures at the end of the day like a bookkeeper in one of his

123

companies. It's more complex than that. I have to proceed more or less by instinct——'

'Won't the man who's coming here understand that?'

James scowled. 'He can slant the facts any way he likes, particularly if he know what Mark wants to hear——'

'Do you think Mark wants to hear that you've failed?'

He looked at her broodingly. 'I'm not sure. I—he's been rather strange lately, about you. So have you, come to that. You act as though you hardly know him, even dislike him, yet you spent the day with him on the *Sea Witch*. And you jump every time his name is mentioned. I suppose he's been getting at you, trying to get you to leave me, because it's obvious that you can't wait to finish my book.' Apparently her fleeting look of guilt gave him his answer, for he added quickly, 'Juliet, I—I've been trying to tell you for days that I——'

Juliet cut in hastily, trying to prevent him from uttering the proposal that she was sure was trembling on his lips. 'The book has nothing to do with the real issue, which is your doctorate,' she said briskly. 'The book is merely a side issue, something you wanted to write to publicise the plight of the dolphins. Naturally, I want to finish it as soon as possible. I thought those were my instructions.'

'Juliet——'

'Who'll be coming today, James? Do you know his name?'

'I suppose it will be Kennedy or Shopwell.' His voice was sulky.

Both names were familiar to Juliet, although she had never met them. They were part of a team working with Dr Robinson, who was head of James's department. Juliet knew Dr Robinson. He had been a friend of her stepfather's, although they had differed in their interpretation of the dolphin's behaviour. Robinson believed that the dolphin could be taught to communicate in a sign language similar to that which had been taught to the chimpanzee in many universities. James believed the same thing. Yes, either Kennedy or

Shopwell would be the person to meet James, and whatever he might think of it now, he would enjoy the exchange of ideas. He could talk to his visitor on a scientific level, which was something he had not been able to do with Juliet or Mark.

'I think Mark—Mr Bannerman—made a wise choice,' she said encouragingly.

'I thought you were on my side, not his,' he said petulantly. 'I suppose he's gotten to you. I told you before, it won't do you any good.'

'In that case, the sooner I finish the book and leave, the better,' Juliet said expressionlessly.

James looked stunned. He didn't really believe she was in love with Mark, but he had struck out at her through a sense of frustration and jealousy and had expected reassurance from her. Like all people with absolutely no insight into the feelings of others, it hadn't occurred to him that she might be wounded by what he had said.

'*No!* No, Juliet! I—you can't leave!'

'But I can and I will, James. As soon as possible.'

'But I've been planning to ask you to stay! With me—for ever. I want to marry you, darling. I've been trying to say it for days, but you've acted so cool and businesslike, as though the only thing we had in common was that damned book, that I—— That's why I've been taking out my feelings on the thing. You knew, didn't you? The way you know most things about me,' he added ruefully. 'I don't care about the book, my sweet—I only care about you.'

'I'm sorry, James,' she said gently. 'I don't love you and I can't marry you.'

'If you're worried that you'll be marrying a poor struggling university professor, don't be.' His mood had changed and his voice was buoyant, as though he had no doubt of his ultimate success in persuasion. 'I may not be as rich as Mark, but I can give you anything you like. I won't have to *be* a university professor, if you'd rather I wouldn't. In fact, I don't want to any more. We could have our own lab—I could write and work alone, like David Graham——'

'James!' she said desperately. 'I can't marry you!'

'Are you worried that Mark will cut me off without a cent if I marry without his permission? Don't worry, he won't. He might lecture me, but when he learns how much I love you, he'll take it all right.'

'That sounds as though you think I'm only interested in your money, James,' Juliet said wearily. 'Which shows, really, how far apart we are in what we think about one another. You're just lonely, you know, and right now you need someone to talk to, someone on your side, as you put it, because you're angry with your brother. I'm not that person.'

He stared at her blankly. 'I thought you loved me!'

'I do—as a friend. Have I ever given you any reason to think I've felt anything else?'

James conveniently ignored that question. 'You'd marry me in a minute if you weren't afraid of Mark,' he muttered rebelliously.

Juliet thought of a lot of answers she could have made to that, but she merely contented herself with assuring him firmly, 'Mark has nothing whatsoever to do with it.'

She wasn't sure that he believed her, but she wasn't worried too badly about hurting him. He might think of himself as a star-crossed lover, but in reality, he was a spoiled child. Whether his fault or Mark's, he had never been allowed to grow up. Right now, he was searching desperately for a substitute to put in Mark's place, since his brother seemed to be bent on forcing him to become independent. He was more shocked and angry by her cavalier treatment of his proposal than hurt. Until now, the Bannerman money had always got him anything he wanted. In that respect, she thought wryly, the Bannerman brothers were alike.

Of course, she could understand that Mark wanted to see some positive results from James's work. There had never been any doubt that he didn't love his brother and thought him brilliant. He was probably irked to see him plodding along without receiving his rightful recognition. Such a lack of ambition would be utterly foreign to someone as aggressive and self-assured as

Mark Bannerman. He would find it hard to understand James's apathy, and he would certainly never understand James's almost hysterical dependence on her. But he would not like it, and of course, removing James to a university would remove him from her influence.

Juliet had already decided that originally, Mark's primary motive in making love to her was to make her forget James. It would destroy his brother's fantasies about her, and at the same time, provide him with a little playmate who would help him get rid of Serena Cadwell. In the end, of course, his desire for Serena had overcome his duty toward James, although he wasn't reluctant to indulge in a brief fling with her, as evidenced by their last night together.

Well, the book was near completion, enough so that she could finish most of it today. After that, she never wanted to work with dolphins again. So far, they had brought her nothing but unhappiness, and this time it was going to take her a long time to recover. The scars from her encounter with Mark Bannerman would take a long while to heal

She told James she was returning to the house and then walked out firmly, despite his protests. At Bella Vista, she found Daisy bundling up the typescript to clear the desk for Mark.

'I'll take it,' Juliet held out her hand for the stack of pages. 'I intend to get it finished today, no matter what.'

Daisy looked at her shrewdly. 'Something's happened?'

'James proposed,' Juliet said wearily. 'I couldn't stop him.'

'And you said——'

'I said no. I don't think he's heartbroken, although he's certainly frustrated. He persists in blaming Mark. He says I refused him because I'm afraid Mark will disinherit him.' She shrugged. 'It was all very sordid, Daisy. I want to finish this before Mark gets here.'

'Yes. I'm sorry, hon—I'll miss you. But I guess you're right to go. It must be hell to be so beautiful.'

'Yes, hell,' agreed Juliet bitterly. 'I'll go upstairs. I'll be in my room if anyone asks, but I hope they won't ask.'

'Don't worry—I'll keep everyone away.' Daisy smiled a little sadly. She was fond of Juliet and she was going to miss her, just as she had said. But of course, the girl was right. If James was going to be filled with grievances because she wouldn't marry him, Mark wasn't going to want her working around here any longer, even if he had a yen for the girl himself. A man like Mark ruled his desires; he didn't let his desires rule him.

Juliet went straight to her room without seeing anyone but the cook, from whom she got a snack lunch and a thermos of iced tea. She set to work grimly, unmindful of the heat or the drowsiness that overtook her mid-afternoon. She worked without stopping until the late afternoon shadows began to creep into the room, when she sat back with a sigh. She had roughed out the final six chapters of the book, and although they would need more polishing before they were ready for the final typing, her part of it was finished if Daisy could do what remained. She hadn't expected to finish this quickly, but the material was there and it had merely needed some hard work to get it ready. It would not be an extremely lengthy book, but illustrated with plenty of beautiful photographs, it would flesh out into a respectable length. She wondered if James had thought of contacting a photographer.

That wasn't her business, she reminded herself firmly, as she sighed and ran her hands through her hair, then straightened her back cautiously. It ached, along with her head, and she badly needed exercise to rid herself of the kinks and the deep, clogging weariness in her mind.

Hours earlier, she had thought she heard sounds that might indicate that the visitors had arrived. If they had, they were probably around the pool right now, and she had no wish to become involved with whatever guests Mark Bannerman had brought with him.

She stood up and stretched, then made a quick trip to the bathroom, where she splashed cold water on her face and neck. What she needed, she thought, was a brisk walk.

Outside her bedroom, she almost bumped into a couple of strange maidservants, hurrying past with linen and towels. Then she saw Mai standing in the doorway of one of the unoccupied bedrooms, supervising the unpacking of a pair of suitcases.

She was looking a little harassed now, as though she had a problem on her mind, but her face lightened when she saw Juliet.

'Where you been, Julie?' she asked smilingly. 'Mark's been asking for you from the time he walked in the house.'

'I've been in my room working.'

'Your room! I think he looked everywhere but there.'

'I'll go see him, then, if he has some business he wants to discuss.'

'Don't know if it was business, but he's at James's now. He took the man who's come about the fish over there with him. That man will be staying over there, in your old room. One less for me to worry about,' Mai muttered under her breath.

'Is something wrong, Mai?' Juliet asked tentatively, knowing Mai would never admit to a housekeeping problem she couldn't handle.

'Nothing at all, Julie.' Mai was on her dignity. 'Just a little bother that comes up sometimes when we have more guests than we counted on. Until the hotel can take the overflow, I guess we'll have a little squeeze, but Mark put me in charge of deciding what bedrooms to use, and until he tells me different, I'll do my job the way I'm supposed to. If there're some who don't like the way I do it, then they're welcome to leave—or complain—or whatever.'

'Is there some mix-up about the rooms?' Juliet asked sympathetically. 'If it will help, I'll glad to go to the hotel.'

'That you won't, Julie,' Mai said firmly. 'Mark told me to put you in that room, and until he tells me to send you to the hotel, which he won't because he's too courteous for that, then you're staying right where you are! No matter what some people say!' she added ominously. 'Now, where you going, in case Mark comes back and needs to see you about something?'

'I'm going for a walk on the beach. I'm sure he wanted to ask about the book. You may tell him my work on it's finished and I'll be ready to leave tomorrow if he likes.'

'That I'm sorry, to hear Julie. Your pretty face is always sweet and smiling, not like some, I'll hate to see you go.'

'I'll miss Tamassee, too, but my job wasn't ever supposed to last more than a few months. I finished earlier than expected. Please tell Mark—it will save him the trouble of looking for me.' Juliet felt an almost savage pleasure in saying what gave her so much heartache.

The sun was dropping below the horizon and a grey veil was descending, the beginning of the brief, tropical twilight. Juliet walked south, away from James's place, until she was tired; until there was nothing to see but a lonely stretch of beach, the ebbing tide and the wheeling, screeching gulls overhead. Then she dropped exhaustedly to the sand. Over that horizon was Mexico. It wasn't far and she wished she was on a ship steaming towards it right now. She loved Mexico, a land of contrasts, of hot, garish sunlight, stony soil and the lush, tropical playgrounds of the rich along the coast. Some of her happiest memories were of Mexico. There, she thought, she could find forgetfulness and a sort of peace. She dropped her head to her crossed knees with a sigh. Perhaps in Mexico she could forget Mark Bannerman.

# CHAPTER EIGHT

'WHEW! I thought you'd never stop walking, honey!'

Juliet jumped. Jack Tanner stood beside her, barefoot, with his slacks rolled up to his knees. He gave a gusty sigh and dropped down on the sand, his impudent grin reassuringly familiar. Juliet smiled back.

'I followed your footsteps. Didn't you hear me calling?'

'No.'

'I wondered. You certainly never looked around once.' He chuckled. 'I never thought I'd chase a girl this far just to say hello! I'm glad you're not planning to swim—I wouldn't have the energy to join you.'

'Did you have a good trip?' she asked.

'I wouldn't know. You'd have to ask our mutual boss how successful it was. I just pilot the plane and leave the brainwork to others, although from the way he looks, I'd say it was very successful indeed. But Mark never reveals his secrets. Never mind about that,' added Jack, abruptly changing the subject. 'What about you?' He leaned forward and turned her face up gently to the fading light. 'You have circles under your eyes and I think you've lost weight. What's been happening to you anyway?'

'I've been working too hard.' Juliet pinned a bright smile on her face.

'Working, hell! Work doesn't cause this kind of change in a couple of weeks.'

'I didn't sleep too well last night,' she said evasively. 'I guess I got too much sun yesterday.'

'Too much sun, eh? Someone or something's been eating you, and it didn't happen just last night! Not with that weight loss! What's really happened, sugar? Two months ago, when you came to Tamassee, you looked like a little girl who'd just been handed a great big lollipop, but now you have shadows like bruises

131

under your eyes. Who is it?' he added fiercely. 'Has
Mark Bannerman been getting at you? Or is it that sissy
little brother of his? Just let me know who's done this to
you, and millionaire or not, I'll punch him on the nose!'

Juliet tried to laugh and put a hand tentatively on his
face. 'Ah, you're nice, Jack Tanner,' she said warmly.
'No one has done anything to me and I haven't any
complaints to make, and even if I had,' she added
firmly, 'I'd keep them to myself. Do you think I'd allow
you to get fired just because of me?'

'So it *was* Mark Bannerman! What has he said to you?'

'*Nothing!* No one has said anything. It's just that I—I
hate this place! It's too isolated, and that hasn't been
good for me. I—I need city lights instead of a lonely
island where I had too much time to think about myself
and my troubles.'

'So you did have something on your mind when you
came here?' Jack asked tenderly. 'I thought so—it had
knocked you for a loop. But you seemed happy about
coming——'

'I thought it was what I wanted. It wasn't,' she added
firmly. 'As soon as I finish what I'm on now, I'm
leaving.'

'And Mark Bannerman doesn't have a thing to do
with it?' he asked thoughtfully. She could see he was
still unconvinced. 'And his kid brother hasn't begged
you to stay?'

'Well, naturally, James would like me to stay.'

'Aha! I thought so. But you're not going to?'

'No.'

'I can't pretend I'm unhappy about it. I don't like my
girl interested in the Bannerman brothers—Mark
especially. Too many girls fall for his charm,' Jack
added wryly. 'I can't compete.'

Juliet rose and dusted the sand off the seat of her
skirt. 'Come on, let's go back. And you needn't be
jealous of the Bannerman brothers, Jack,' she added
teasingly. 'You have your own brand of charm, and it's
pretty lethal!'

'But it doesn't get me anywhere with you, does it?' he
asked gloomily.

'I'm immune.'

'Precisely. I wonder why?'

'Please don't make a mystery out of this, Jack. I don't need that sort of thing right now.'

'And you're sure it's just loneliness that's inspiring this indecent haste to be off the island?'

'If it isn't, it's my own business,' she said flatly, and Jack recognised that a door had been closed firmly in his face.

So he started talking about the guests who had come and those were were expected. It seemed, he said, that Mark had decided he needed a vacation —and according to Paul, who returned with them, he had been working like a man obsessed lately. He had ordered his yacht south, and the captain to pick up some of his friends in Charleston. Mark planned to spend the next month cruising and there was talk of a trip to the Canaries. But before that, Mark wanted to get in some diving, and they had picked up a scientist and the photographer who was to do some shots for James's book.

The other guests were the three Rackhams. Joe Rackham, a self-made millionaire, was a business associate of Mark's and had been invited to Tamassee for a brief business session. His wife and daughter had shown up, too, at the airfield this morning, and from the wry way Jack looked, it hadn't been a particularly pleasant surprise. Apparently these were the guests Mai was complaining about.

'Mai said Serena left a few days after we did?' he asked casually.

'Yes,' Juliet answered absently. 'But Sam told Lallie she was due back today on the supply boat.'

There was a brief silence.

'That figures.' Jack's voice was dry, and Juliet looked at him curiously, surprised by his hardness. Until now he had treated Serena with a casual mocking amusement. 'She didn't waste any time coming back when she heard that Mark was returning, did she? The girl has a marvellous spy network operating for her, doesn't she?'

Juliet looked at him hesitantly. 'Well, she was still on vacation, and had a right to leave——'

'That never mattered to Serena before. I've known her to take off for weeks at a time just to be with me——' He bit the words off abruptly, looking like a man who had been caught in an indiscretion.

'Jack! Was Serena your girl?'

'Was is the operative word, all right. She was mine until Mark Bannerman took her away from me. Not that it was all that hard.' He laughed harshly.

'What happened?'

'The usual thing,' he said cynically. 'Boy loves girl, girl loves money. Boy loses girl to well-heeled, good-looking bachelor who can offer girl what she loves best. Oh, hell! When I learned they were losing their resident nurse here, I persuaded her to apply through Posenby's for the job. She got it—and I had the quaint idea that I'd get to see more of her if she worked here.' His lips twisted. 'Well, I saw her all right, but so did Mark. He wanted her and she made a big play for him. To give him credit, I don't think he ever knew about us. Serena kept it quiet, naturally, and I had too much pride to let him know how easy it was to lose her. Before long, I was dropping them off for a week at Palm Beach or Las Vegas or wherever her mercenary little heart desired. Just lately, I thought he was getting tired of her. That day at the hospital—remember?—he sounded bored and fed up. She cried later, when she told me about it, and said he was brutal. But she wouldn't give him up and I guess her persistence paid off, because it looked like when we left they were taking up again where they left off.'

He sounded bitter and angry. Juliet could understand the agony of standing by and watching the girl he loved chasing after a man who didn't want her. 'Do you still love her?' she asked.

Jack gave her a shamed, half-defiant look. 'I reckon I do, honey. I tried to fall in love with you, but it just wouldn't work. It's a shame, too, because you're a much nicer person than Serena. I don't even like her, yet I love her.'

'Sometimes it happens that way,' Juliet said sadly.
'We can't love to order. I just hope Serena doesn't find
out too late that it's you she wants, after all.'

'Fat chance! But she may get her eyes opened this
time,' he added sardonically. 'I think Mark is going to
get married.'

Juliet paled. Stopping abruptly, she bent her head
and pretended to dislodge a piece of shell in her sandal.
'What do you mean?' she asked in a muffled voice.

'He said something that made me think he was
considering it. I didn't know what he meant until we
picked up the Rackham kid today. Of course, everyone
knows she's wild about Mark and she has a doting
mother who always sees that she get what she wants,
but Felicia hinted that Mark is expected to propose
soon. Joe Rackham is a good friend of his, which
means if he wants the daughter, he's going to have to
marry her. Joe wouldn't stand for anything else.'

A cold chill settled on Juliet's heart.

'She's just a kid,' Jack went on. 'Mark has always
been sweet to her, but I never thought—— Although
she *is* a man-trap, and Mark didn't even turn a hair
when they showed up unexpectedly at the airport. Poor
old Joe was embarrassed, but if Mark didn't like it, he
didn't show it. Of course, he can put an iron guard on
his emotions when he wants to, then let 'em rip later
over nothing. Like, for instance, when he got back from
James's place a while ago. He was biting everyone's
head off.' He grinned and gave a mock shudder. 'I took
off just to get out of his way!'

By this time they had reached the lights of Bella
Vista, gleaming in the darkness. They approached the
terrace silently, surprising Daisy who was sitting alone
and smoking. She was wearing one of her caftans, a
gold and blue creation this time. Her cigarette flicked as
she tossed it into the shrubbery.

'About time you showed up!' she called. Juliet, who
by this time knew Daisy very well, saw that she was
disturbed about something, although she was making a
determined effort to sound gay. 'Juliet, you'd better get
inside. You had Mark running in circles looking for

you. No one had any idea where you were until Mai said you'd gone walking. But she didn't mention that you two were off together!' she added sharply.

'You're way off base, old girl.' Jack threw his arm around Daisy's shoulder. 'I like to be alone with this girl, but she just won't play.'

'Good thing, too!' Daisy snapped.

Juliet went on upstairs, leaving Jack to make his own explanations. There had been an undertone of disapproval and a hint of—surprise?—in Daisy's voice that made her wonder. Yesterday she would have loved the idea of Juliet and Jack alone together on the beach. She sighed. There was no pleasing some people. As she approached the room, she saw a girl at Mark's door. She was knocking imperiously, and calling.

'Mark—open up! I know you're in there!'

There was no reponse and the girl, with a pettish little sound, turned directly into Juliet's path. 'Oh!' She sounded disconcerted. 'Who are you?'

She was dressed in a negligee. Juliet saw the outline of slim legs through the sheer chiffon and caught a whiff of expensive scent. If she had just got out of the bath, she had delayed long enough to make a liberal use of cosmetics, for her pretty, sulky little face beneath the mop of red curls was carefully made up.

'Juliet Welborn,' Juliet replied politely. 'Are you Miss Rackham?'

The girl flushed awkwardly under Juliet's cool regard and she saw that beneath the red negligee and the careful make-up was a teenager. A teenager with a great deal of brash assurance, however. She said impatiently, 'Felicia Rackham? Yes. I'm trying to get up with Mark. Is he in?'

'I really couldn't say,' Juliet replied blandly. 'If he doesn't answer, I presume he isn't.'

'But the door's locked, so he must be in!' pouted Felicia. 'No one told me about you,' she added. 'Are you one of the guests or one of the hired help?'

'I work for James Bannerman,' Juliet replied, hanging on to her temper with difficulty. She was determined to be pleasant if it killed her.

'Oh—Mark's freakish kid brother!' Felicia looked relieved. 'Then if you just work here, there's no reason for you to keep that room. It's next door to Mark's and *I* want it! Mama told the housekeeper to give it to me, but she said it was taken. She didn't say one of the servants had it, though. You could bunk in with that old woman, Daisy what's-her-name.'

'I really wouldn't know anything about that,' replied Juliet frostily. 'I suggest you take up the matter of your accommodation with Mr Bannerman.'

'I certainly shall! And Mama intends to tell him exactly how that awful housekeeper talked to us, too!'

Juliet wondered at the vagaries of men. How could anyone prefer a spoiled brat like Felicia Rackham to Serena Cadwell's mature beauty? At any rate, she thought dispassionately, the gentleman had certainly proved that he preferred redheads! And if he was going to have to marry someone, she would expect him to pick someone like Felicia Rackham who, besides beauty and that all-important commodity, money, had a certain arrogance that matched his own. He would enjoy the battles they would inevitably have, of course. They would end up in the bedroom—and Juliet could picture that, too. She shivered with a cold feeling of desolation. She supposed it was partly tiredness that was making her feel so depressed.

Excusing herself to Felicia, who seemed prepared to stand and talk indefinitely while wearing next to nothing, Juliet went to her room. She switched on her bedside lamps and stripped quickly out of her wrinkled clothes, then knotted a towel, sarong fashion, between her breasts. Slowly she wandered out on to her balcony, reluctant to face the bath and dressing and going downstairs that would begin the demands of the evening. Standing there, feeling the slight chill of the evening air on her heated skin, she thought that Paradise must have been very similar to the darkened beauty of the garden below. She heard the slight twitter of a bird, then the wind sighed through the palms, conjuring up thoughts of a tropical night—moonlit beaches, waving palm trees and all the magic elements that went to make up a night made for love.

A bleak smile touched her lips and was echoed in the shadowed eyes. A night made for love! she thought cynically. She was getting out just in time, obviously, if she had become reduced to associating Mark Bannerman's garden with maudlin thoughts of love. And with Felicia Rackham headed for the role of Mrs Mark Bannerman, she didn't want to hang around for any more punishment. Perhaps, even now, she could lure him away from Felicia if she gave him what he wanted. Perhaps she could even keep him interested as long as Serena had. What had been the track record there—twelve months? Daisy had talked as if it was something special. Could she make it thirteen—two years, even? Juliet's smile grew bitter. Who was she to complain? Mark's attitude towards love was perfectly straightforward and he did not misrepresent how he felt, for all that she disliked hearing it. A direct exchange of sensual pleasure, then with the coming of satiation, a swift, impersonal goodbye, sweetened on the girl's part by some expensive gifts. And that, she was sure, was done to ease his conscience.

Fool! she categorised herself harshly. You could never do it! Perhaps for a Serena or a Felicia, it might be that simple, but possessions had never meant that much to her, although she loved beautiful things. If she had not loved Mark, if it had been no more than a physical attraction, then she might have been able to receive him as her lover. Which was something of a paradox. As it was, even to ease this gnawing ache that was eating her up inside. she would not appease her physical hunger, for it would make it that much more unbearable later. No, beside that pale imitation of the real thing, her love was too encompassing, too strong and all-devouring to be satisfied with anything less than a total commitment. It did not have to be marriage, since he apparently feared a legal entanglement, but it must be a gladly, even freely given acknowledgment of love.

Wearily, Juliet turned aside to her room. The glare of light was dazzling after the soft darkness outside, and she stumbled and leaned tiredly against the balcony door, her eyes closed.

'Are you pregnant?'

The voice was harsh and shocking in the quietness of a room that Juliet had thought empty of everyone but herself. She started, her frightened eyes opening, and saw Mark standing a few feet away, fully dressed except for his dinner jacket and tie, both of which were slung across his shoulder. He was pale and she knew instantly that he was in a white-hot rage.

'How did you get in here?' She was still trembling.

He ignored the question. 'I wouldn't have thought you'd have time yet unless you're extraordinarily fertile, but if you're not pregnant, then what's wrong with you? You looked as though you were about to faint,' he added tonelessly.

Her eyes darkened. 'Just who do you have selected for the father?'

'James, of course,' he said brutally. 'He told me this afternoon that you and he have been lovers from the beginning.'

'And you believed him?'

'Why not?' he drawled, strolling further into the room. 'It's what I expected. You'll be glad to know that he wants to marry you. He felt he should explain why he was morally obliged to do so.'

The hot colour flooded her cheeks, but she was too winded by his accusation to speak. A wave of hatred swept over her—for James, who had whined his lie into Mark's ear, and for Mark, who had cynically accepted James' version.

'Of course, I knew you were ripe for love after that weekend in Key West, but fool that I was, I failed to take advantage of what I could have had for the taking.' His mockery was savagely directed at himself. 'I'm thankful now that I was too discriminating to accept what was offered. I never did like sharing, especially my women. Sorry, my dear, but I don't go in for kinky sex.'

Juliet flinched. 'Now that you've insulted me in every possible way,' she whispered fiercely, 'I want you to get

out of my room and my life. I hate you both! I never
want to see you and your lying brother again!'

Mark's eyes narrowed. 'Are you trying to tell me
James is lying?' he asked slowly.

'I wouldn't try to tell you the time of day,' she replied
bitterly.

'Did James ask you to marry him?' he asked
insistently.

'Oh, he asked me all right!' The colour flared in her
hot face. 'And like you, Mr Bannerman, your brother
doesn't listen when a woman says no. The only
difference between the two of you is that he made an
honourable offer of marriage, whereas you merely want
a temporary partner in your bed!'

He looked at her oddly. He was impassive, but she
sensed a change in him; an elation simmering beneath
the surface. 'So you decided to run, and that was the
reason for the snooty little message you left with
Mai?' He sounded like a man trying to clear up loose
ends.

'Was it snooty?' she asked wearily. 'I merely left the
message I thought you wanted to hear. I'd finished your
brother's book in spite of every effort he's made to
sabotage it and I want out of this job.' She struck out
then, blindly, her one desire to maim and hurt. 'And I
hope I never have to see you or this island again!'

'Never is a long time.' Mark's eyes glinted at her
beneath his lashes.

'Not to me!' she cried wildly. 'I've been hurt enough
by you to last a lifetime!'

She could have torn her tongue out by the roots
when she saw the triumphant light that leapt into his
eyes as she gave herself away, but he merely said mildly,
'In spite of James's muddled attempt to gain my
consent to your marriage, I haven't changed my mind
about letting you go.' His eyes roved from her pinned-
up curls to her bare feet. 'I shouldn't blame the poor
fool, of course. You're enough to send any man into a
tailspin.'

Juliet swallowed convulsively and tightened her grip
on the towel, a shiver of fear chilling her spine. 'I think

I asked you to get out of my room.'

He grinned. 'I don't like taking orders.'

'I mean it!' she said desperately.

'I'm sure you do. Why are you trembling?'

'Leave me alone,' she whispered.

'No way, lady.' He advanced towards her. 'There's no way—*ever*—that I'm going to leave you alone.'

'I'll scream!' She backed away from him.

'Go ahead, scream. You'll bring them all running, but that's fine with me, too.' He advanced further until he was standing close enough for his breath to warm her cheek. 'This is it, Juliet. You and I. Here and now. I'm not waiting any longer.'

*'No!'* The back of her knees hit the edge of the bed and she fell on to it, the towel flying open to expose a slender length of leg.

Mark grinned. 'Sometimes you can be real accommodating,' he drawled, and fell on top of her, his body covering hers.

She cried out with rage and he kissed her, a swift, hard kiss. She struck at him and he took advantage of her flailing arms to loosen the knotted towel and expose her breasts. She gave an inarticulate cry of shrill fury. 'No! Damn you, Mark Bannerman—stop it!' Her face was scarlet with rage and she struggled wildly as his hand closed over the swelling breast, cupping it tenderly.

He mumbled something harsh and guttural beneath his breath, then lowered his mouth. Juliet's breath broke on a sob and she whimpered as wild tremors racked her body. Her breasts swelled and hardened beneath the moist sweetness of his mouth, and an answering heat spread like fire through the nerve endings of her body. She was dimly aware that he was tearing off his shirt: she heard his shoes hit the floor with a thud, then he gathered her more closely, his hand gently caressing her thigh and belly.

'Darling!' he moaned. 'Darling!' She could feel him trembling and she opened heavy eyelids to stare into the face of a stranger. She did not recognise him in the softened mouth and flushed cheekbones. His eyes met hers. They were filled with a mute appeal and she answered it by whispering, 'Mark—darling——'

'You're not leaving me, are you?' he whispered. 'Tell me! I want to hear you say it!'

Juliet obeyed him, half sobbing the words into his bared chest as she clung to him, her senses afire as he whispered back words of reassurance.

'All right, baby, it's all right! You're staying with me! I'm not letting you go to anyone else! Damn you, you leave me and I'll kill you—do you understand me?'

A whimper dragged Juliet unwillingly out of her erotic haze, in which the only reality was Mark's face and his husky, whispered words of want and need. She opened her eyes reluctantly and focused them on two people standing in the open doorway. Felicia and James. White-faced, they stared at the couple on the bed, their faces, wearing identical expressions of mingled shock and incredulity.

Juliet stiffened and Mark looked around slowly. He was the first one to recover enough to speak.

'Damn!' His voice held mild regret. 'I forgot to lock the door.'

He rose slowly and leisurely pulled the gaping edges of Juliet's towel together, half covering her naked body. He even wore a rueful half-smile on his lips as he turned towards the others.

'What the hell are you two doing, walking in on us like that? Can't a man and his fiancée make love without being interrupted by everyone who cares to wander into her bedroom?'

James made a stifled sound under his breath and whirling on his heel, left. Juliet's wondering eyes took in Mark, his upper torso bared, his hair in wild disorder from her hands. She could imagine, too, how she herself looked, half-naked, flushed, her mouth still swollen from Mark's kisses.

She rose and Mark handed her the robe that was lying across a nearby chair. Defiantly she dropped her towel and pulled it on, tying the sash with a vicious tug. That done, she turned proud eyes on Mark and Felicia.

Felicia was made of sterner stuff than James. She

stood her ground, staring at both of them with a glare
of baffled fury.

'What did you mean about her—her being your
fiancée?' she stammered. 'You c-can't—be *engaged*! No
one told *me* anything about it!' She turned on Juliet.
'You didn't tell me you were engaged to him!'

'Yes, well, that *is* regrettable.' Mark's voice was
smoothly regretful as he shrugged into his shirt and
buttoned his cuffs. 'But it was just decided. I haven't
even had time yet to get the girl a ring.'

'You c-can't marry her, Mark Bannerman!' Felicia's
voice rose shrilly as she faced him, her bosom heaving,
her eyes shining with unshed tears. 'She's—a nothing, a
nobody! Why do you want to marry *her*?'

'Why? For the usual reasons, of course,' he drawled
insolently.

'I hate you! You're a beast!' Tears of outrage slid
down her cheeks. 'You know my Papa expects you to
marry me!'

'Surely you've learned by now, my child, that one
doesn't make something come true merely by saying it
often enough?'

Felicia ripped lose with a string of adolescent gutter
words that had no connection with the present situation
but apparently relieved her feelings a great deal. Then,
turning with a whirl of skirts, she departed, slamming
the door viciously behind her. Mark strolled over and
locked it.

'I wouldn't put it past the little minx to come back,'
he said coolly. 'And we need a few moments of
privacy.'

Juliet stared at him stiffly. She gave the impression of
being frozen with fury. 'How dare you put me in this
position?' she demanded tightly. 'I guess you know that
girl will spread this story to everyone who'll listen!'

'I should think so, yes,' Mark nodded gravely.

'You did this to me!' she gasped. 'You made it sound
as though we—we did this sort of thing all the time!'

His lips moved and parted on a smile. 'Did I? Well, I
didn't notice you trying to contradict me.'

He watched interestedly as a tide of red scorched her

cheeks. As tangible as though it had been spoken was the memory between them of her impassioned response to his kisses. She felt sick.

'James,' she whispered, folding her arms defensively over her breasts, 'he—he must think we——'

'Yes.'

'Oh, God!' She shivered. 'Did you arrange that scene for his benefit?'

'That "scene" was spontaneous—but I confess his appearance was an added bonus. What he saw should get him over his infatuation for you in a hurry,' he said blandly.

'I see.' She laughed harshly. 'Congratulations! You're fortunate indeed, Mr Bannerman! You even manage to turn spontaneity to your advantage!'

He shrugged. 'It was to be expected that Felicia would try your door if she tried mine again and found the room empty. That's the way her mind works.'

'So you deliberately gave her an opportunity to find us in a compromising position? It didn't matter that my reputation is blasted so long as James is cured?'

Mark had seated himself to tie his shoes and now, he looked up quickly. 'Apparently you didn't hear when I told Felicia we were engaged.'

'Oh, I heard you,' she said ironically. 'But I don't intend to allow you to use a bogus engagement as an excuse to make love to me for the day that remains before I leave.'

'I think I told you once that you weren't going anywhere until I said so,' he replied coolly, standing up and sliding his tie under his collar. 'And if I wanted to make love to you, I wouldn't need the excuse of being your fiancé. I think we disposed of that myth a few minutes ago,' he added mockingly.

Juliet flushed, staring dumbly at him. There was nothing she could say to refute his statement. They both knew it was true.

'You need this engagement,' he went on easily. 'You'll find it preferable to be my fiancée than to be known as my latest mistress.'

'Forget it! I'm afraid that story would be too wild

even for your friends to swallow!' she said bitterly. '*Me*—engaged to the elusive Mark Bannerman! They'd soon learn about that witch-hunt you've conducted against me! They'd laugh themselves sick if I tried to pass myself off as your fiancée!'

'They won't if we carry it off together,' he said coolly.

'I'm not stupid,' she said wearily. 'I know you don't give a damn about my reputation. It's James you really want to fool, isn't it? Well, even if I agreed, he would soon know the truth, because he asked me to marry him this morning and I didn't say a word about being engaged to you.'

'Didn't you hear what I said to Felicia? That it had just happened? Anyway, James wouldn't question it; that is, if you did refuse to marry him——'

'It's true!' she countered fiercely. 'It's also true, whether you believe me or not, that I've never been James's lover!'

'O.K., I believe you,' Mark said slowly, almost as though he was surprised at himself. 'Which means he hoped to change your mind by getting my consent. So he'll be looking for a reason, and this is the only one that will make sense to him. James always did credit me with more than my share of success with women,' he added ironically. When Juliet did not reply, he added, menacingly, 'Unless you really do want James after all, and hoped he would get my approval?'

She turned on him with a snarl of fury. 'I've told you the truth! At this moment I don't care whether you believe me or not. I *won't* marry James and I *won't* become your mistress! I just want to turn that damned book over to you and get off this island!'

His face darkened. 'You're staying here and helping me to pick up the pieces you've managed to scatter to hell and back. Whether you like it or not, you have poor old James going in circles, and you owe it to him to stay and apply an astringent dash of cold water.'

'I don't owe him anything!' She glared at him bitterly.

'You do,' he said calmly. 'I told you what was going to happen. Why didn't you do something about it then?'

'Because I——' Juliet stopped, biting her lip. Her hands clenched into fists. 'Oh, very well!' she said scornfully. 'But why this ridiculous pretence? Surely it would be just as effective to pretend we're—we're——' She stopped, swallowing, as she realised what her words were leading to.

Mark's eyebrows rose mockingly. 'Then you're willing to leave the impression that we're lovers?'

She flushed. 'What difference will it make once we leave here? Our paths will never cross again. I'll make sure of *that*!'

His mouth twisted derisively. 'I don't think you fully appreciate the malice of the female Rackhams. You haven't met Vera yet, but she'll be like a balked vixen with one cub. She was depending upon this visit to give Felicia what she wanted, which happened to be me, and she'll be sore and looking for revenge. There's no way she'll let this pass without tearing your reputation to shreds. I'm not talking about this island, or even just Florida. You'll find your name linked to mine in those scandal sheets that are sold on the grocery shelves all over the country. Would you like that?' At her shudder, he added dryly, 'Exactly. There's only one way you can save yourself, and that's for us to announce our engagement. As I did. Joe won't let his womenfolk say a word about you then.'

'Very well, you've told me how this engagement will help me,' Juliet said stonily. 'What are you getting out of it? And don't try to pretend it's because you're trying to protect me, because I wouldn't believe it.' Her lip curled.

Mark moved over to the dressing table and casually used her brush. She saw that he was watching her from the mirror. 'Okay,' he said laconically. 'I need you as much as you need me. This will get rid of Felicia.'

'Felicia?' she queried.

'Yes. This will be an easy way to avoid offending Joe Rackham.'

'I thought so,' she said scornfully. 'I knew you had a reason.'

'You know me so well,' he murmured ruefully.

'Why don't you tell me the rest of it? It will sweep the board for you by ridding you of all your encumbrances at once, won't it? Serena was getting a little too possessive, wasn't she?'

He looked at her sharply. 'Go on. You know everything,' he said sarcastically.

'Otherwise, you would have used Serena as your partner in your little deception. But of course, you needed to disillusion James, too.'

His face darkened. 'Let's leave Serena and James out of this.'

'By all means!' Juliet was hurt and was consumed with a savage desire to hurt in turn. 'Let's leave Jack out of it, too! Poor old Jack! Don't you ever think of how he feels about this?'

'*Jack?*'

'Yes, Jack!' she said recklessly. 'Why don't you open your eyes to how he feels? What do you know about him? Or care? Don't you know Serena was his girl? He found this job for her, and you took her away from him by lavishing expensive presents on her and offering trips to Paris. Something Jack could never do-o-o——' Her voice trailed off as she met his eyes in the mirror. She felt sick at what she saw, but it was too late. His face was gaunt with shock and there was a white line around his mouth.

'I didn't know,' he said bleakly. 'Of course not. Who would tell me?' he added in a stricken voice. 'All the girls love me—didn't you know that? It's because I can buy them pretty things.' His mouth twisted with self-derision.

Juliet's triumph had turned to ashes in her mouth, and she wanted to take that fair head in her arms and comfort it against her breast. But she knew he would reject her sympathy, seeing it as pity.

Making a supreme effort, she replied briskly, 'Well, don't let it go to your head! And don't think you're buying *me* anything, Mark Bannerman! I don't intend to give you an excuse to make love to me!' she added tartly.

He grinned, her acerbity apparently just what he had

needed. 'You're forgetting an engagement ring,' he said
teasingly.

'I'm not forgetting anything! Anyway, you don't have
an engagement ring here on Tamassee, do you?'

'But I do—in the safe. It was my grandmother's. And
what's more, Daisy knows it and wouldn't be satisfied
unless I put it on your finger.'

'That's another thing,' said Juliet. 'I want Daisy told
the truth about this engagement.'

'Why?'

'Because she warned me about you, and I don't want
her to think I'm such a besotted fool I didn't heed her
warning!' she said fiercely.

Mark laughed aloud. 'Ah, Juliet, you're so good for
my ego. Any time it threatens to become swollen,
you're right there to slap it back down to size. Okay,'
he added easily, 'Daisy gets told. Meanwhile, you're
going to have to display a modest show of affection for
the benefit of the others.' His eyes twinkled. 'That is, if
it won't strain your acting talents. Naturally, I don't
expect anything too rigorous—just enough to get our
point across.'

She glared at him crossly. His amusement made her
angry. If he thought she was going to drool over him,
she thought rebelliously, or let him get away with a lot
of pawing in public——!

He was staring right back, and as though he could
read her thoughts, his amusement deepened and he
smiled slowly. 'Yes, I mean what I say. No one will
believe we're in love if we spend the evening ten feet
apart. But it shouldn't be too difficult. Just follow my
lead. In other words, let your natural instincts guide
you, my dear.'

She flushed, all too aware of what he meant.

'Now,' he said briskly, 'if you don't intend to spend
the evening in that towel, you'd better get dressed. I'll
wait for you while you dress in the bathroom. By then
we'll have given them enough time to absorb the news
and get over the first shock.' He glanced at his watch.
'They should be about ready for the first congratulations
by the time we get downstairs. Get a move on.'

Juliet gathered up her clothes and went into the bathroom and locked the door. It didn't take her long to shower and make up her face, using a dash of her most exotic perfume. She swept her hair up and inserted a Spanish comb in it. It had been her mother's—one of the few good things she had—and its fanlike jewelled shape gleamed against her dark tresses. Even at her worst, she was breathtakingly beautiful, and she had never looked better. The touch of haunting shadows around her eyes that Jack had noticed merely made them look larger and more mysterious. Her eyes sparkled; she looked poised on the edge of triumph.

She had chosen to wear the shimmering green dress that had caught her eye in the shop window. As she slipped it over her head and it slid smoothly down her hips, she made up her mind that she was going to surprise everyone tonight by beating Felicia at her own game and not giving an inch. And no one was going to intimidate her tonight, not even Mark Bannerman.

She emerged from the bathroom to find Mark seated at her desk, looking over the manuscript of James's book.

But when he looked up and saw her, his face froze into an inscrutable mask, the cheekbones oddly prominent in the handsome, taut face. His eyes wore an arrested look as he approved of the girl packaged in the shimmering green gown. Then he rose and carefully replaced the pencil he had been using.

'Ready? And wipe that apprehensive look off your face. You're supposed to be happy and madly in love with me. Remember?'

He took her arm and led her down the stairs.

Downstairs, Felicia was sobbing, her head in her mother's lap. She was wearing a tight red dress with a ruffled skirt, and it looked incongruous on her as she cried with all the abandon of a child, knuckling her mascaraed eyes repeatedly. Her father sat beside her, obviously a thoroughly nice man who was out of his depth in the midst of this feminine display of emotion.

Daisy told Juliet later what had happened. Felicia

had stormed into the room where her parents were seated on the sofa talking to Daisy and Serena, and flinging herself at her mother, blurted out the news of the engagement in a loud, hysterical voice. No one, not even Joe Rackham, could prevent her from going into graphic detail of what she had found upstairs, but Joe was able to pull her back from the worst excesses by administering a swift slap before she revealed herself too much. She had responded by collapsing into her mother's arms. During the ensuing commotion, Daisy noticed that Jack Tanner rose and poured a stiff brandy, then presented it to Serena, who had gone as white as a sheet.

By the time the newly engaged couple walked into the room, things had quieted down, although Felicia was still sobbing accusingly, 'But you promised, Mama! You said Papa would see to it! You *promised*!'

There was no sign of James. Felicia hadn't thought to mention that he had been with her, and of course it hadn't occurred to anyone else. Mark had read Felicia's mind correctly. Jealous, spoiled, thwarted for the first time in her life of something she wanted, she had reacted like a woman on the prowl. She was quite certain that Mark was not accepting her very obvious overtures because there was another woman in the picture, so she had gone looking for a rival—and created one. James had merely happened to be on hand when she opened the door.

Daisy was the only person in the room who was enjoying herself. Not even the photographer was wholly satisfied. An embarrassed Paul Bradford, wishing to protect his boss, had edged him into a corner to prevent him from hearing the worst of Felicia's revelations, but the photographer had enough news sense to be curious. He had already learned enough to be able to scoop every newsman in the country with the story of Mark Bannerman's engagement, but he was anxious to hear the further revelations being poured forth amid angry sobs.

'My dears!' Daisy rose and came forward, and to Juliet's horror, there were happy tears glistening in the older woman's eyes. 'I'm so happy about this! I love this girl, Mark! You've made me so pleased.'

'Thank you, Daisy,' he said gravely, sliding an arm around her and Juliet's waists. 'I know you mean those good wishes from the heart.'

Juliet felt wretched. Daisy was nice and uncomplicated, and she was going to be hurt when she learned the truth. It couldn't be helped, of course, but Juliet hated to deceive her even for a few hours. People like Daisy or Jack or even James must be wondering why she had been sending up a smoke-screen of lies and evasions all along. Daisy was going to wonder if there wasn't more to the story than Juliet had told her, and as for Jack Tanner, she felt guilty every time she met his eyes.

Juliet felt no such compunction about Serena. She had been momentarily touched with pity until she met the glittering malice in the angry blue eyes. Serena was very beautiful tonight in a white dress that left one shoulder bare and clung in all the right places. She must have come here determined to stake everything on a final try to win Mark, but now she was looking like a woman who had just seen her last hope falter at the stretch.

It promised to be a thoroughly awkward evening, Juliet thought miserably, as Mark pulled her down beside him and handed her a cocktail. For once, she was grateful for the mantle of his protectiveness, however false it was. Not that he was obvious about it: it was all done with a subtlety and sureness of touch that couldn't be faulted, but somehow he got the picture across that she was the love of his life.

It saved Juliet from an attack by Vera Rackham, who was forced to make a pretence of sincerity when she offered her congratulations. Juliet liked Joe on sight. A big man, with a kindly face and shrewd blue eyes, he wore a faint air of apology whenever he spoke to her. Juliet, taking her cue from Mark, treated the whole episode lightly, and she saw that Joe was grateful. At least his embarrassment with his family wasn't made worse by her taking Felicia's jealousy seriously. Vera was forced to follow her husband's lead, and finally, grudgingly, accepted a few of Juliet's tentative conversational overtures.

It was all a façade, of course, but they kept it up, mostly through Mark's efforts. When they rose to go into the dining room, he pulled Juliet up with him and continued to hold her hand loosely as he led the way into the other room. He placed her at his right side, and after that it merely needed an occasional fleeting touch, an occasional 'darling', to get the point across. She couldn't fault him on his performance.

He and Daisy disappeared briefly after dinner and when she reappeared, her plain face was beaming.

'Mark told me,' she murmured in Juliet's ear as she bent over her. 'And I like it! He wants to see you in the study now.'

*I like it?* Juliet was bewildered. What had Mark told Daisy? Or what did Daisy think he meant? She knew better than anyone the way Juliet felt about Mark. Hadn't she herself warned her it was hopeless? So— what kind of game did she think this was, anyway?

Mark was waiting for her, seated behind the massive desk in his study. An inlaid jewel box was open before him and spread out upon its velvet lining was a dazzling array of jewellery. He was holding a magnificent emerald ring, turning it this way and that in the light.

'The family jewellery,' he said, waving at the display. 'My father's second wife, Lisa, would have given her mercenary little soul to have laid her hands on this collection, but my father had everything locked away for me to give my bride.' He paused, shrugging. 'Well, what does my lady desire?' he added lightly. 'I can offer you an emerald if you like. Thomas Bannerman gave this one to Carlotta on their wedding day. She looked something like you. Or if you prefer the more usual engagement ring, there's this diamond.' He picked up a ring with a single stone in a raised setting. 'Or you might like something like this opal? It belonged to my grandmother. Opals are said to be unlucky, but she never found them so.'

'None of them!' Juliet gasped, putting her hands behind her back.

He frowned slightly. 'Are you superstitious about wearing someone else's jewellery? If so——'

'I—it's n-nothing like th-that!' she stammered. 'I just don't want *any* ring at all! I said I wouldn't accept anything from you.'

Mark's face cleared. 'So you did, but you know, you must have an engagement ring. Think of it merely as a part of your costume while you're acting a part— something I'm lending you to give credence to our story. Stop being a silly girl and put this on your finger.' He rose and came around to where she was standing, then gripped her left hand firmly and slid the emerald on the third finger. 'Personally, I prefer this one.'

Juliet did, too, and in the circumstances, she knew she couldn't refuse to wear it. It was the first ring she had ever owned, and she was fascinated by the way it looked on her finger. Unobtrusively, she tilted it to see the crimson and green flashes in its heart. Looking up, she saw that Mark was watching her, and she reddened.

'Very well,' she said stiffly, 'I'll wear it for now, and give it back to you when this is all over. Is that all?'

'No.' Mark leaned comfortably against the desk and regarded her mockingly. 'I shall have to give the papers some sort of story, or the reporters will be swarming over this island. I'll need some information about you.'

She stared. 'But surely that's not necessary?' she objected. 'How long will this engagement last, anyway? I assumed it would be no longer than a week or two— just until the Rackhams left.'

'I've been thinking about that,' he said smoothly. 'I don't think it's going to work to just be engaged. We're going to have to get married.'

'*Married?*' she gasped, almost doubting her ears. She thought quickly. 'You mean you want us to pretend to be married?'

'Pretend? Of course not, you foolish child! I mean the real thing,' he said calmly. His eyes gleamed with amusement as they met hers and Juliet flushed with anger.

'You're joking, of course!' she said crisply. 'You
don't even like me! Why would you even consider
marrying me?'

'Because I need a wife,' he said casually, 'and you
would suit me better than anyone I've seen, so far.'

'Thanks!' she retorted sarcastically, trying to quell the
trembling that had started deep within her stomach.
Marriage? Did he mean he loved her? She would not
allow herself to believe what she was hearing, yet was it
possible that he—Mark—felt the same way as she did?

He smiled. 'I don't think you need to be told that I
want you. I've already demonstrated that, just as you've
proved you want me.'

He was still leaning against the desk and she sat
down in the leather armchair opposite, because her
shaking legs were theatening to fold up beneath her.
'That still isn't enough to make a marriage,' she pointed
out, trying to sound sane and reasonable.

'Naturally not. I've also taken your other attributes
into consideration.' His voice was light with mockery.
'You're beautiful, of course, and dress with taste and
discrimination, which is important for the wife of a man
in my position. You're tactful—your handling of Vera
and Joe was masterly. You get along well with the
servants, and moreover, you're intelligent—don't try to
tell me you didn't write most of James's book! That, to
me, is the most important factor of all. I couldn't stand
a stupid wife, no matter how beautiful she might be.'

Juliet's face was shadowed by her downbent head,
and with an effort she kept her hands loose and
unclenched in her lap. 'Is that all?' she asked in a
muffled voice.

'I think so,' Mark said pleasantly. 'Except that if you
agree to marry me, you do so knowing what I can give
you: jewels, clothes, the houses, the—oh, security, if
you like. That's the way I like it, with us both getting
something out of it. Oh, I know you're not mercenary,'
he added quickly, as she glanced up in protest. 'I've
already learned that, and I wouldn't want you if you
were. But I want you to know what you'll be getting.
Whatever you want, whether it's a yen to hobnob with

the rich and famous or to make your name as the best party-giver on two continents. It all takes money. Think this over carefully,' he added, as she still did not speak, 'and make your decision on the basis of what we can mutually offer one another.'

Juliet, listening dazedly, was almost persuaded by the reasonableness of his tone, the force of his argument, that she could accept the terms of this marriage. She thought of the luxury, the beautiful things she could put in the home she had always longed for but never had because of her parents' nomadic way of life. It could be hers. She remembered Daisy saying that Mark had only one method of dealing with the women in his life—through bargaining. So far, it had worked for him. Could he be blamed, then, for making a stark business proposition out of his marriage proposal?

'What about children?' she faltered. Her eyes were enormous in her white face.

Mark paused, his thin, ruthless face quite impassive. 'I would want a son, of course,' he said judiciously, 'but if the first child is a boy, I don't think I would need to demand a second sacrifice on your part.'

Juliet's face flamed at his calmly chauvinistic attitude, the sheer coldbloodedness of his marriage proposal. She drew in her breath sharply as she realised at last what he was really saying and what her future would be. A marriage in which one partner loved desperately and the other was motivated only by cold, clinical reasoning. All the joyousness and beauty of lovemaking reduced to the lowest common denominator. She knew then that she couldn't do it. She couldn't bring a child into a cold, loveless union like this one, and she couldn't live like that—holding back, never spontaneously turning to Mark to express her love. He did not want it. It would repulse and embarrass him. He only wanted one thing from her, and if she tried to love him, tried to show him the happiness she longed to give him, he would turn on her and savage her to death. It was like being granted a premature glimpse of hell.

She stood up shakily, her face stark with emotion. 'No, I'm sorry! I—I can't do it. I can't marry you.'

She left the room hurriedly, without waiting to see his reaction, and went straight upstairs to her room, not caring for once if the others found her absence strange. She couldn't help it. She had known heaven for a brief moment, thinking Mark wanted her because he loved her, and the disappointment was too great.

Later, huddled shivering in her bed, Juliet heard vague sounds of movement outside the corridor and knew the dinner party was breaking up. Finally, the house quieted down and grew still, but she still lay awake, her tired brain going over Mark's proposal again and again, looking for a loophole whereby she could accept it. Once, she thought she heard a phone shrilling, but while she was wondering if she had dreamed it, she fell asleep.

She awakened to the sound of a discreet tapping on her door. It was Mai, who had a note from Mark asking her to meet him for breakfast on the terrace outside his study. When she looked up from reading it, Mai smilingly offered her congratulations.

The invitation was more in the nature of a command than a request, so Juliet hurried through her face washing and teeth brushing without bothering with a shower, then dressed in one of her more attractive outfits—a green split skirt with a figure-hugging tee shirt in lime to match. She wore the emerald.

She had expected to be embarrassed at their first encounter this morning, but she felt no embarrassment when she saw Mark's preoccupation. A breakfast table had been laid and Mai was bringing out hot coffee, but Mark was gazing moodily out to sea, his feet propped on the railing. He was dressed in crumpled slacks and a shirt, and was unshaven. Something about the quality of his stillness made Juliet's heart pound uncomfortably. He looked as though he had been up all night, wrestling with a deep problem, and she suspected he was facing the unpleasant task of breaking their false engagement.

'What's wrong?' she asked.

He glanced at her. 'Sit down and pour yourself a cup of coffee. You're going to need it. That will be all, Mai,' he added. 'We'll manage the rest for ourselves.'

Juliet obediently poured herself a cup of coffee and then, at his signal, refilled the cup he had resting on the terrace railing. Her hands were trembling as she lifted silver covers and helped herself to scrambled eggs, grilled sausage and toast. She wasn't hungry, but she took the food more for appearances' sake than anything else. At least, it would give her something to push around on her plate and pretend to eat.

She took a deep breath. 'I guess you've decided to break off the engagement,' she said brittlely. 'I can't say that I'm surprised. Fortunately, it hasn't gone any further than this island, and they're your friends, so whatever you want to say is all right——'

'Shut up!'

'Wha-at?' She stared at him, open-mouthed.

'You talk too much,' he said dispassionately. 'Don't try to anticipate what I'm going to say. If I want out of this engagement, I'll tell you so. You won't have to tell me.'

'Very well,' she murmured, swallowing nervously.

'Last night, or rather about three this morning, Robinson called me. He's the scientist over at James's place, in case you didn't know. He was extremely agitated. James had come back and spent the evening getting drunk. Then he went out and opened the dolphin pens.'

'Opened the dolphin pens? What do you mean?'

'He let the dolphins out.' Then, as she continued to look blank, Mark added impatiently, 'He opened the gates to the sea.'

'Oh.' After a moment, Juliet asked timidly, 'Is that so bad? Letting them free, I mean? I've often thought they should be free. I don't like to see wild things in captivity.'

'I know. But according to Robinson, they may have lost their ability to survive after having lived so long in captivity.'

'Oh, no!'

His voice roughened. 'James was in a state of shock when he sobered up and realised what he'd done.'

'Then you've talked to him about it?'

'Yes,' he said grimly. 'He was suffering from an outsized hangover, but he listened to what I had to say. I told him what I thought of his childish, irresponsible behaviour. This is the end of his project, so far as I'm concerned. He destroyed it himself. Of course, he still has his notes if Robinson will accept his findings without proof. But James is on his own, to make his own plea to Robinson, to make whatever plans for the future he cares to make. And I don't feel a damned bit guilty about it!'

'I do,' Juliet said desolately. 'I did this to him.'

'You did not!' he said flatly. His face was granite-hard. 'If anyone's to blame, I am. James has always been spoiled and I've indulged him because I was too busy making money. It was easier to give him what he wanted. But not any more. He's an adult now, and responsible for his own actions. And the best thing I can do is to leave him alone to show what he's made of. He can make his future a success or a shambles. Robinson says he's intellligent and he still wants him on his team. Now it's up to James.'

'I suppose you intend to endow the university if they take him on?' she asked wistfully.

The grim look lightened a little. 'Not a chance! I made it clear to Robinson that they had their money whether they take James or not, but he still wants him. However, James won't know that unless he does his own talking to Robinson. Makes his peace, as it were.'

Juliet took a tentative bite of sausage and chewed thoughtfully. Mark's chair came down with a bang and he rose and strode over to the side table, where he helped himself liberally. Then he pulled up a chair opposite hers. There was an air of relief about him, as though he had just been over a difficult hurdle. Could he possibly have been dreading her reaction, thought she might blame him? Juliet wondered, astonished. The hard face with the shadowed suggestion of a beard had softened a little. There was even a touch of humour as his eyes met hers.

'Well? What are you thinking?'

'What happens now?' she asked hesitantly.

She meant about the engagement, and the fact that it might not be necessary now, but he deliberately chose to misunderstand her.

'What happens now? Well, James wants to dive—as soon as possible. There's a school of dolphin that's been sighted in these waters and there's a possibility—a bare possibility—that James's four may have joined them. If they have, and James can make contact with them, Robinson said he will accept that, plus his notes.'

'Oh, I hope so!' Juliet cried eagerly. 'Then he's going to dive today?'

'Unfortuately, there's no boat available right now. The only one with diving equipment on board is on other business off the coast of Africa,' Mark explained. 'But there's my yacht. It was in Charleston, picking up some passengers for a cruise, and I've radioed the captain to proceed immediately. He should be here by tomorrow.'

'Then you're expecting more guests?' she asked hesitantly.

'Only a few friends. You'll like Betty and Tom Henley.' The firm lips quirked into a smile. 'Betty's been trying to get me married for years. She'll be very interested in meeting you.'

'Mark, do you think this is wise, to let this thing spread any further? It will be harder to retract later on.'

'Are you suggesting that we become un-engaged?' he asked dryly.

'Well, is it really necesssary any longer—for James's sake?' Juliet pointed out. 'Surely, since his attitude has changed——'

'Nothing has changed!' he said flatly. His face had hardened, become inflexible. 'Including that marriage proposal last night. I hope you've been thinking about it as I told you to.'

'I'm sorry, Mark, I can't——' she began desperately.

'I don't want your answer now,' he interrupted. 'It's too early. Talk it over with Daisy, get some advice before you make up your mind.'

'B-but, Mark, I can't possibly——'

'Will you shut up!' He turned on her with a ferocious glare, and she drew back, startled. 'I don't want to hear another word about it until you've had time to think about it!'

She lowered her eyes and lifted her coffee cup with trembling fingers. She had already learned that Mark was accustomed to being obeyed, but was he really so domineering that he thought he could force her into a loveless marriage?

Apparently mollified by her silence, he went on as though nothing had happened, 'I need today to clear up some business on the island. I have to get someone to take Cora's place.'

Juliet looked up sharply and saw that he was watching her reaction. 'Cora's leaving?'

'She's already left,' he said thinly. His lip curled. 'Jack took her out at seven o'clock this morning. I gave her an hour to pack her things and get off the island, but she got a better deal than she offered you. Why didn't you tell me what had happened, when you arrived?'

'Then Sam did?'

'Yes. Did you think I'd ordered her to do it, Juliet?' he persisted.

'She was following your orders.'

Mark contemplated her thoughtfully. 'She was interpreting them to suit herself, but perhaps it did seem that way to you. Anyway, Cora goes. She's bullied and tyrannised people long enough. On the whole, she's lucky to be escaping with a whole skin.' He clenched his fist. 'It's the last time I disobey my instincts. I never liked, her, but because she claimed some sort of distant kinship, I kept her on against my better judgment.' He hesitated. 'Which reminds me—speaking of misjudging——'

'Juliet Welborn! So it *is* you, my dear, dear child!'

It was Dr Robinson, striding eagerly across the lawn, followed by James. Juliet had already realised, of course that Robinson, rather than one of his assistants, had come to Tamassee, but she hadn't seriously thought about the consequences of meeting him. She stood up uncertainly and glanced at Mark, who was watching Dr Robinson expressionlessly.

The elderly man embraced her, talking all the while. 'My dear child, when Bannerman told me his brother's secretary was Juliet Welborn, I wondered—and then, when he said you'd worked with David Graham, I knew! Why did you slip away so quickly after the funeral, my child? I tried to get in touch with you, as did many others at the university and the institute, but you'd disappeared. I'm just thankful you've surfaced now and are doing this work. You loved it, I know.' He turned to Mark. 'I understand Juliet has consented to become your wife?'

'Yes,' Mark said grimly, his eyes not leaving Juliet's flushed face. 'Yes, we'll be getting married very soon.'

'Ah, an eager bridegroom!' Dr Robinson beamed at both of them. 'I'm happy to know this child has found a safe haven at last. She's been through a great deal. The death of David Graham was a great blow to the scientific world and I personally felt a keen loss from Mary's death. I knew her well, because the Grahams and I had been friends since our student days.'

'Juliet hasn't yet explained to me why there's a disparity in their names,' Mark said gently. Juliet searched his face with convulsive eyes, but she couldn't tell if he was angry and hiding it well or merely not surprised.

'Oh, one forgets about that,' murmured Dr Robinson. 'Juliet hasn't explained? She's his step-daughter, of course, although she was only two when her mother married David, weren't you, Juliet? But I think you always regarded David as your father, didn't you, child?'

'Yes,' she said faintly.

'You'll have to tell me all about it some time, Juliet,' Mark said smoothly.

She glanced at him, half scared. It was stupid to feel guilty. She had been, she admitted, ridiculously secretive, but it had been partly his fault. There had been this instant antagonism that flared between them—and her reluctance—but *must* he look so stern?

'May I speak to you alone, Juliet?' It was James, a

pale, desperate-looking James, wearing an un-accustomed look of humility.

She sighed and rose to follow him, prepared for reproaches. But she had reckoned without James's utter blindness to everything that did not directly affect himself. He was not interested in her relationship to David Graham. Right now, he was wallowing in an orgy of remorse.

'It was all my fault—I had no right to say what I did to Mark about you. And I shouldn't have run down Mark to you. He's always been better to me than I deserve, and I've repaid him by getting drunk and blasting two years of work. I'm sorry, Juliet. You must have wanted to kill me yesterday when he told you what I said about us.' He flushed. 'I hope it didn't make things awkward for you. But I didn't know then that Mark loved you and wanted to marry you, Juliet, I swear I didn't!'

'Well——'

'It was an awful thing to do to a man—tell him you're sleeping with the girl he loves. That's really why I got drunk. I kept seeing Mark's face when I told him. God, he must have wanted to kill me!' James seemed gloomily determined to prove that someone had wanted to murder him yesterday. 'It was so unlike me, too—but then I guess I was jealous. And I've been a little crazy, too, what with the thought of being on my own and you not caring. I came back last night to apologise to you for what I said when——' He stopped, visibly embarrassed, and Juliet saw with relief that the memory was not so much painful as embarrassing.

'I hope you weren't hurt by it,' she said gently, repressing a smile.

'I was at the time. I went haywire, I guess. Then I went home and drank all the liquor in the house.' He looked rather sick at the memory. 'I don't remember letting out the dolphins.'

'I'm sorry that happened. Will they be all right?'

James heaved a deep sigh. 'I probably condemned them to death. Or Tim anyway. He was born in captivity and he doesn't have a chance unless the others

stay with him and teach him what he should know.' He
seemed to be almost enjoying his gloomy prognosis. 'I'll
have to start all over again, and Mark says I'm on my
own this time. He says I'll have to earn my own
living. I won't even have the book royalties to fall back
on, because I've ruined my chance of getting it
published. Without photographs, I haven't a chance.'

'I wouldn't say that——' Juliet began feebly.

'Mark won't want to pay for a photographer after what
I've done to him!' It was obvious that James was not going
to allow anyone to offer him hope. 'I told him this
morning that I'd lied about you, and I thought he'd knock
me down! It would have served me right if he had!'

Juliet changed the subject hastily. 'If the photographer
gets some good pictures of the dive, wouldn't that help?'

'Perhaps,' James said despondently. 'You *are* coming
with me, aren't you?'

'I don't think so, James.'

'For God's sake, don't let me down now! I'm
depending on you!' He sounded panicky. 'Mark hates
me and Robinson thinks I'm a contemptible fool.
You're the only person who doesn't hate me in spite of
what I've done.'

'Now, James . . .' she began.

'You have influence with Mark, Juliet. Please tell him
I'm sorry. I'm the world's worst fool, but I—I love him.
He's my brother!'

'Ah, James, it's just an engagement,' she said
uneasily. 'We're a long way from being married.'

He looked at her as though she was talking in riddles.
'Don't be stupid,' he said bluntly. 'Don't you know he's
crazy about you? Do you know what he said when I
told him I'd lied about you? He said at least I'd shown
good taste in women for a change. I tell you, I was
thankful to get away without getting my teeth punched
down my throat!'

Juliet, who knew that Mark's anger had been
motivated by nothing more than pride, didn't argue
with James's interpretation, because his orgy of
repentance, for whatever reason, was doing him too
much good.

# CHAPTER NINE

BEFORE dawn the following morning, the *Kiwi* steamed majestically into the blue waters adjacent to the little island of Tamassee and anchored just outside the little lagoon. Captain Allen, reacting to his boss's urgent message, had wasted no time in getting here. One hundred feet of trimly proportioned yacht, dazzling white with its brasses gleaming, the *Kiwi* was a sight that brought most of the island out to watch as the *Sea Witch* breezed out to meet it. Soon the *Sea Witch* was back, skimming lightly over the water, bringing the ship's officers and the passengers to the island for a breakfast at Bella Vista.

The Commodore, who had piloted the *Sea Witch*, helped the ladies ashore. There were two of them, a Mrs Henley and the movie actress, Lana Mayberry. In the curious way that news had of spreading on the island, the fact of her presence was already known, particularly by the female contingent from the hotel. To most of them, Lana's face was as well known as their own in the mirror. She had been a star for twenty years. A chill of excitement shook Miss Foster, who had turned out the school for the occasion, along with Mrs Elliott, Mrs Nesbitt and the Monroe sisters. Not even Lana's companion, the equally famous Adam Harkness, created the same stir as he stepped on to the dock. As for bluff, friendly Tom Henley or Captain Allen or the three young officers he brought with him, they were ignored as Lana Mayberry paused theatrically, the famous profile very much in evidence.

Juliet had not expected to like any of them. They were older than Mark, friends of long standing, who might be expected to be critical of his choice of a wife. Instead, she was disarmed by their friendliness. Betty and Tom Henley and Adam Harkness were frankly pleased that he was getting married, and Lana's reaction was a dry comment that she was always glad to see a girl with Juliet's looks spoken for. Especially, she added, when they were going to be thrown together on a cruise.

Before Juliet could correct her assumption that she would be joining the cruise, Lana drawled, 'Adam is altogether *too* susceptible to beautiful women.' This made everyone laugh, for Adam Harkness's devotion to Lana was a long-standing affair. But in the ensuing babble of talk, the spotlight was taken off Juliet, for which she was grateful. She thought ironically that Lana hadn't a thing to worry about, for she was one of the great beauties of all time. And with her clean bone structure and heavy-lidded dark eyes, it was a beauty that would continue to endure when she was an old woman of eighty-odd. She was just thankful that Lana had instinctively sensed that she was not a rival and had made of her a friend instead.

She hated this business of giving everyone a false idea of their relationship, but Mark was adamant. She had not been alone with him at all since the preceding morning when he had learned her true identity. In spite of his subtle hint that he expected an explanation at some future time, he had made no effort to get it, and she supposed he had learned all he needed or wanted to know from Dr Robinson.

He had told her to talk over his proposal with Daisy, but Daisy was proving strangely elusive. And when she was around Juliet, she blandly pretended that they were an ordinary engaged couple, just as Mark did. It would have been funny if it hadn't been so frustrating.

That afternoon Juliet escaped from the guests for a moment's respite in the garden below her window. Their arrival had kept her working at top speed, for Mai had turned naturally to her, rather than Daisy, for assistance with the hundred small details that a good hostess must have at her fingertips. Right now, the guests were resting in the rooms assigned to them, after a day of swimming, sightseeing and lunch. After dinner, they were all, herself included, returning to the *Kiwi* and tomorrow would leave early for the dive.

The garden was at its best in late afternoon when it became almost somnolent with the drowsy murmur of insects and the distant roar of the surf beyond the palms. The stillness seemed to heighten the senses, so that colours and scents became more vivid, distilled in a crystallised moment of time. It was all so beautiful, Juliet thought, struck by the poignancy of the moment. Slanted stripes of light and shadow lying on the vines of the night blooming cereus that climbed the garden wall; the spiky bloom of the bright pink pompom; hibiscus and bougainvillaea blossoms a colourful background for the pale mauve orchids with their speckled, tightly curled leaves. Juliet stopped walking to observe an air plant, one of those rootless, drifting little parasites that literally exist on air, floating weightlessly on the merest hint of an air current.

'Hi, honey—a penny for your thoughts. Or do they come higher these days now that you're going to marry Mark Bannerman?'

Juliet turned, a strained smile on her lips. She valued Jack's good opinion and she had wondered if he thought her a liar—or worse. 'They're still selling for a penny,' she said lightly. 'I was merely thinking how beautiful the garden is.'

He shrugged. 'Good thing you like this place as much as Mark does, because it's his favourite home. I'm leaving, Juliet. I saw you from the window and came out to say goodbye. Mark has told me he's sending me to the West Coast to work for one of the subsidiary firms there. Not exactly a kick upstairs, but I'll be glad to go. The change will be good for me.'

She was surprised. 'You mean he's releasing you? When?'

'Tomorrow morning, the man says. My replacement takes over then. He—he also told me he's buying out the rest of Serena's contract,' Jack added hesitantly.

'What do you mean?'

'He's releasing her. Not that she'd want to stay on, with Mark marrying you, but she's not being allowed a choice in the matter.' He smiled bitterly. 'And the lady has asked her old friend Jack to take her with him!'

'Is that what you want?' Juliet asked uncertainly.

'Yes. I'm still crazy about her—but this time I call the shots. Funny thing,' he added, watching her closely, 'I could swear Mark knew about us—Serena and me. It was the way he looked when he told me about it. Did you tell him, Juliet?'

'I'm sorry,' she said miserably. 'I blurted it out, but——'

'Don't apologise.' He smiled at her distress. 'It doesn't matter. Actually, I never thought I'd feel sorry for Mark Bannerman, but I did, then. Things like that must happen often enough for him to feel he's wanted only for what the dames can get out of him. Serena's a greedy lady, and she made the play for him. I can't blame him for what happened.'

'I hope she's learned her lesson, Jack.'

His mouth twisted cynically. 'I doubt it, but I've learned that happiness isn't that easy to come by, little one. Sometimes you have to settle for less. Just let's say I'm pleased with the way things are now, and leave it at that.'

Juliet did not see him again, and the next morning he and Serena were gone by dawn. Juliet, from her bedroom aboard the *Kiwi*, heard the clatter of the helicopter blades as it rose and hovered over the yacht briefly before starting its journey towards the Keys. She got to her window in time to see it fade in the light of the rising sun.

The night before, after dinner on the island, everyone had returned to the *Kiwi*. They were ferried out to the yacht on the *Sea Witch*, which then returned to its usual spot in the lagoon. Cocktails were served by white-jacketed stewards on the main deck, which was sheltered by a gay awning and furnished with nautical-looking furniture covered by colourful cushions. The deck was lit by a string of twinkling fairy-like lights.

In a few minutes there was a move to the main salon for dancing. Mark seemed content to talk instead, moving around to his guests while he held Juliet firmly and inescapably at his side. His light conversation reflected all that smooth urbanity that made him such a success in the business world. Juliet was silent for the most part, her eyes reflecting her thoughts as she looked around curiously. Except for the portholes and the imperceptible feeling that one was afloat rather than on firm ground, the salon could have been the luxurious drawing room of a penthouse apartment in any big city. Decorated in tones of silver-grey and green with accent colours taken from an antique silk screen mounted on the wall, it cast a mood of restrained elegance. There were a couple of oil paintings, their colours glowing in the subdued light, and Juliet suspected that they were masterpieces, just as she suspected that the antiques in the room were real and not expensive reproductions. When contrasted with the mass-produced modernity of the *Sea Witch*, for instance, the lounge of the *Kiwi* was as different as a castle was from a tenement.

Mark had been watching her face and murmured as they moved away, 'What's the matter?'

'Nothing.'

His mouth tightened. 'Let's dance, shall we?'

His dancing was as smoothly competent as everything else he did. He held her firmly but not so closely that it interfered with their conversation. 'Now, what's the matter?'

A shadow crossed her face. 'All—this. It's all so rich, and I'm not like that. I'm more—a *Sea Witch* sort of girl.'

He didn't pretend to misunderstand what she was trying to say. Shrugging, he dismissed the remark as irrelevant. 'I keep the *Sea Witch* mostly for the benefit of any guests who want to fish. But I live on the *Kiwi*. It's my home. And you fit in as well as anyone else.'

'Did Serena ever stay aboard the *Kiwi*?' she asked.

Mark hesitated, then said bleakly, 'Yes.' There was a long pause, then he said abruptly, 'We have to talk. Let's go out on the deck.'

Outside, he seemed in no hurry to begin but stood with his hands on the rail while he gazed out towards the darkened outline of Tamassee.

Finally, Juliet asked huskily. 'What did you want to talk to me about?'

He looked down at her. 'James wants you to dive with him tomorrow, doesn't he?'

She hesitated. 'Yes, he does. He thinks he won't recognise the dolphins unless I go with him.'

'I was watching your face when James was talking about it. You're afraid, aren't you?'

She flushed. 'Yes.'

'Because of your parents?'

'That—and other reasons. It's foolish, I know. I've dived since I was seven, but lately——' She stopped and her hands fluttered restlessly. 'Lately, I've been afraid. I can't explain it—it's all too stupid. But I have this recurring nightmare of watching helplessly—from somewhere safe—while someone I love doesn't come up from a dive.'

'That settles it,' decided Mark. 'You aren't diving tomorrow.'

'*No!* No, I've got to! I must!'

'Nonsense. You're scared stiff, and that isn't good for the rest of us. I've made the decision—you won't dive. Robinson will back me up on it. James will have enough with the rest of us—besides Robinson and myself, there'll be the photographer. If the dolphins don't see him, too bad.'

'No!' gasped Juliet. 'Don't you understand? I *must* dive!'

'Very well, tell me. Make me understand. I want to.'

She struggled to define her feelings. 'I've got to be there,' she began painfully. 'I know I must. I'm not afraid for myself, but I know if I don't go—I have this sick terror that something terrible will happen if I'm not there to prevent it.'

'To this "someone you love"?' His voice was sardonic.

'Perhaps.'

'Well, that lets me out. In fact, unless you've lied about your feelings for James, that lets out tomorrow's divers.'

'Not necessarily,' she gasped. 'I'm very fond of Dr Robinson, and I shouldn't like anything to happen to you.'

Mark's mouth tightened. 'Oh, spare me the "good friend" routine, if you please,' he drawled with chilling contempt. 'I prefer honest hatred. Anyway, it's all too Freudian for me, but it looks as though you're determined to dive. So—let it be on your head. Come on,' he added abruptly. 'It's getting late. I'll show you to your cabin.'

If Juliet had known anything about yachts, she would have realised that her stateroom was no 'cabin', and too large and luxurious to be anything but part of the master suite. As she stared around the room, dominated by the king-sized bed set between the portholes, her eyes widened with surprise. She had heard that the passengers were having to double up to accommodate everyone, but there was only one set of luggage—hers— on the rack at the foot of the bed.

'I—It's very beautiful,' she stammered.

'Someone will unpack for you if you ring the steward.' Mark showed her a small princess telephone beside her bed, near the buttons that controlled the lights, curtains and television. 'If you need me, I have the room next door.' He motioned towards a door in the wall beside the T.V.

Juliet swallowed nervously. 'Isn't Daisy my room-mate?'

'Daisy is subject to insomnia, so she usually gets a room to herself. And naturally, Lana is sharing Adam's room, so that leaves only one unattached female— Felicia. I thought you'd prefer a room to yourself rather than share one with her,' Mark said dryly. 'If you have a nightmare, just dial "One" and I'll come in and hold your hand,' he added lightly.

Before she could protest, he was gone—through the door into the passageway. Juliet looked around uneasily, her nervousness increasing. This opulent bedroom was, to say the least, suggestive. And that enormous bed! How could one person sleep in it alone? And the connecting door had no key in the keyhole. She walked over and gently eased the knob but it held firm. The door was locked on the other side.

She wandered into the adjoining bathroom. It was

tiled to match the colours of the bedroom and had a
sunken tub with another phone on a convenient shelf at
its head. The bathroom shelves contained everything
any woman could want, from bath powder and a
selection of lotions and perfumes to the more mundane
toothbrush, shower cap and hairbrush, still in their
plastic wraps. And—wonder of wonders!—an electric
hairdryer and hot curlers. She wondered how an all-
male crew would know just what to put into a lady's
bathroom but presumed that, like the ship's owner, they
had had plenty of experience to guide them.

She came back into the bedroom and started
unpacking. She hadn't brought many things—only
what would be necessary for the couple of days they
would be at sea with the dive. When she had finished
hanging her dresses, they looked lost in the huge, cedar-
lined closet, and her lingerie took only a quarter of the
space in one of the built-in drawers that slid noiselessly
out from the wall. As she stooped to put away her shoes
in the closet, she noticed a pair of high-heeled satin
mules in one corner. She stood up abruptly, her face
flaming, and promptly banged her head on the hanging
rod.

She was really angry now. Those mules were jade
green, the sort of thing a redhead might wear.
Obviously they had been left behind by Serena—or had
been put there in expectation of her occupying her old
bedroom. It looked as if Mark Bannerman and his head
steward should get together, she thought viciously.
Another girl was occupying Serena's room now, and if
Mark Bannerman thought he was going to pick up with
her where he had left off, he had another think coming!

She began to fling open drawers and slam them shut,
searching recklessly as her rage intensified with each
passing second. She was looking for evidence of another
woman, and she finally found it, folded neatly in one of
the drawers. It was a matching green nightgown and
robe: not precisely sheer but very, very expensive. It
would fit her, too, but then she and Serena were about
the same size. Swooping it and the mules up, Juliet
stalked over to the telephone and dialled 'One'.

When Mark answered, she said harshly. 'I have some of Serena's things here. Would you like me to give them to Daisy to mail to her, or perhaps you would prefer to hand them over in person the next time you're in California?' It was a nasty insinuation, but she didn't care, as she slammed the phone back into its cradle.

Mark was through the connecting door in ten seconds or less, pulling on a robe as he came. He was partially undressed, but still wearing slacks and his shoes. 'What the hell are you talking about?' he demanded truculently.

Juliet flung the garments at him, but he fielded them neatly, throwing up a hand and allowing them to drop to the floor.

'Damn you, Mark Bannerman, how do you think I felt when I started finding Serena's things in the drawers I was using?' She shivered disconsolately. 'D-do you th-think I like using that bed, kn-knowing that you and she had slept on it?'

He didn't answer but merely stepped over to the telephone and dialled a number. 'Get down here at once, at the double,' he said crisply.

'Who are you calling?' she gasped.

'The head steward.'

Juliet paled. 'You can't! He'll—he'll think I—— Oh, no, it will be too embarrassing!'

'I can explain until I'm blue in the face, but you won't believe any of it until you hear it from him,' he said bitterly.

There was a discreet rap on the door and a thin, elderly man entered. He was hastily buttoning his white jacket and he looked perturbed. His eyes darted from the soft pile of silken lingerie on the floor to Juliet's slim, tense figure, then to Mark's grim, dark face.

'Is something wrong, sir?'

'Ah, yes, Perkins. Miss Welborn was wondering about these things you put in her room. Where did you get them?' Mark asked casually, his toe nudging the pile of clothing.

Perkins picked them up and folded them nervously.

His worried eyes darted back to Juliet's face. 'Are they not satisfactory, miss? Is it the colour? I can exchange them for something else if you prefer it.'

'Where did you get them, Perkins?' Mark repeated patiently.

'Why, from the ship's stores, of course, sir. We keep a supply of night garments on hand in case one of the guests come aboard unprepared to spend the night, miss,' he explained. 'It's because one is so isolated aboard ship that we must be prepared for every contingency,' he added apologetically. 'I—*is* there something wrong, sir?' He broke off to ask again.

'I think—would you happen to have another colour?'

'I might have a blue set, sir,' Perkins replied cautiously.

'A blue set? Would you prefer blue, darling?' Mark's mocking eyes quizzed hers.

A slow tide of red rose to her cheeks. 'No, of course not,' she said awkwardly. She felt like a fool and of course, Mark knew it. Her ignorance of the customs of the super-rich had allowed her to make a stupid blunder.

Mark turned back to the head steward. 'Apparently the green will do. But I think you should explain to Miss Welborn how you happened to guess her size.'

A discreet smile touched Perkins's lips. 'Lingerie isn't like clothing, miss. There are only a few sizes, and I must admit that I've become rather good at guessing the right sizes of Mr Bannerman's guests as soon as they come aboard.'

'I see. Does that explain everything to your satisfaction, darling?' Mark asked solicitously.

She glared at him.

'Then that seems to be all, Perkins.' Mark held open the door. 'And thank you. Satisfied?' he asked Juliet ironically as the door closed behind the steward.

'I don't understand why he put a nightgown in here for me,' she muttered. 'He knows I brought luggage aboard.'

'Perkins is a perfectionist. It's just one of those little

touches he thought of to ensure my guests' comfort,'
Mark said dryly. 'He would be horrified to know the
evil interpretation you put on his innocent little
gesture.'

Juliet said nothing. She was still flushed and
embarrassed.

'Did you really think those things belonged to
Serena?'

'Yes, I did, and I don't want to talk about it any
more!' she snapped.

'She has never used this room nor slept in my bed
next door. Nor in my room at Bella Vista. Nor has any
other woman. This stateroom is reserved for the wife of
the owner of this yacht, and has never been used. So
your suspicions are unfounded. Not that I mind at all,'
Mark added oddly. He leaned over and dropped a swift,
hard kiss on her lips. 'In fact, I find this display of
jealousy enormously reassuring. And just when I'd
decided the best you could summon was a tepid liking.'

'Mark——' she began, but he was gone.

# CHAPTER TEN

THEY made contact with the dolphins about ten o'clock the following morning. The divers had had an early breakfast, and were assembled on deck in their swimsuits while the others sat leisurely drinking coffee, when Juliet appeared.

Dr Robinson, who until then had not known she was diving, protested. 'This girl isn't emotionally ready for something like this! Juliet, what are you trying to prove, child?'

James looked up. 'She has to go!' he cried shrilly. 'She knows Tim as well as I do! And the others—she may see the others—or they see her——!' He stopped, clearly upset. 'You *can't* forbid it!'

Since Dr Robinson was technically in charge of the dive, it was his decision. He was looking troubled. 'I have no wish to *forbid* it,' he said stiffly. 'But this girl is not ready for a dive like this. She may panic and ruin the whole thing. Did you ever think about that?'

Mark's voice broke in, deep, strong, reassuring. 'I think you can depend upon me, Robinson, to keep an eye on her. I promise you, she won't panic.'

Juliet was thankful to see Dr Robinson subside with a relieved, 'Well, if you're sure——' He saw as well as anyone that James was staking everything on his dolphins having joined this school and that some miracle was going to occur, and they would recognise him. Juliet seriously wondered about his mood if he didn't get his miracle.

For James's sake, she had managed so far to control her nervousness, and now she retreated to the end of the deck and took long, deep breaths in an attempt to quell the fluttering in her stomach.

'Are you all right?'

It was Mark. He took her cold little hand between his warm hands, his eyes watching. She sent him a shaky smile.

'I'm fine—no, really I am. I'm nervous—but it's more like the kind of thing one gets—stage fright, butterflies in the stomach. You know?'

He smiled back. 'I know.'

Just then there was a shout from a lookout and he said quickly, 'That must be the dolphins. Remember, I'll be near all the time.'

'Okay.'

Juliet sat down on deck to put on her flippers, then slid into her tanks and picked up her goggles. James and the photographer already wore their gear, and Mark and Dr Robinson were slipping into theirs. The boat, carrying the extra tanks and the photography equipment, was being lowered.

The two sailors who were to row were standing up, and one of them, and Mark, helped her into the boat as she descended the ladder. The dolphins were half a mile away. Although dolphins were gregarious creatures, the sight of a big ship's hull would have an offsetting effect, so the *Kiwi* attempted to get no closer.

As the boat approached, Juliet could see them plainly now, a line of joyously leaping and bounding creatures playing in the waves. It was a sight she had seen many times, but it never failed to bring a lump to her throat. They crowded around the boat like curious children, intent on investigating the strange intrusion into their waters, the bright eyes and smiling mouths reminding one of human children.

'This is it. Now!' At James's command, the five divers slid over the side of the boat, one by one, following his lead. Mark was the last, following Juliet and leaving the boat with the two seamen to wait for them above.

At first, Juliet could see nothing. It was always that way—the dark green water was shadowy and impenetrable. It took a moment, too, for her to acclimatise herself to the shocking change from the warm air above. Then her vision cleared and she gradually made out the others, identified them in her mind. Her eyes darted past James and Dr Robinson in the lead, past the photographer, easily distinguishable because of his camera, and found Mark. He was right beside her, his eyes gleaming behind his mask. He made a thumbs-up sign with a questioning waggle, and she returned it. She saw his teeth flash as he grinned.

After that, it was easy going. She swam with more confidence, knowing that Mark wasn't going to let her out of his sight; knowing, too, that he was safe. As they swam, they were surrounded by gentle, weaving bodies. She had dived into a dolphin school many times before, so the broad grins weren't new to her, but this time there was an extra poignancy. This time they were looking for James's four.

And it would be impossible to recognise them. The dolphins were going to have to find them. Julie swam towards James, confident that Mark would follow her. James had been wandering in what looked like an aimless fashion, but was actually a systematic canvassing of the whole school. He was followed closely by the photographer. He swam with the feeding bucket he had used many times, and hoped the dolphins would identify it. Like Tim's ball, it was bright yellow and had been made with a sounding device that was not heard by human ears. If his four were here, and heard and saw it, they would come.

Suddenly Juliet noticed the odd behaviour of a couple of dolphins. Hadn't that one, that one that looked so much like Jo, butted them repeatedly? Now she was butting the bucket. And another one crowded up eagerly as though she, too, recognised the bucket. Then Juliet saw Tim. Tim was the only one she had any hope of absolutely identifying. He was young, still not fully grown, and he was full of tricks and guile. He butted her now, almost knocking her over, then he swam around her and James delightedly as though he was greeting old friends. James gripped her arm eagerly and pointed. Juliet saw his eyes shining with enthusiasm behind his goggles as he reached into the netted bucket and withdrew a fish and Tim almost snapped it from his hand. Then the dolphin shot straight up to the surface of the water and Juliet knew without seeing him that he was standing on the end of his tail in his 'catch' pose.

The other dolphins were milling around, but as

though they understood the affinity between the land creatures and their four new members of the school, they were leaving all close contact to them. Jo, Heidi, Suzy, and Tim all crowded around, receiving their fish, making their greetings, almost as though they were reassuring the humans of their well-being. And all the time Juliet was vaguely conscious of the photographer beside them, grinding away with his camera.

Then suddenly, as abruptly as though they had heard some sonar warning in the shadowy depths of the ocean, the dolphins disappeared. For a moment longer. James's four lingered, but for a moment only, just long enough for a final gentle push, a final farewell; then they, too, were gone.

Dazedly, Juliet looked around. The photographer was close by, but there was no sign of Mark. James touched her arm and pointed upward and she rose unwillingly, her eyes still searching for Mark.

Her head broke water beside the boat. She clutched its sides and peered inside. Dr Robinson was sitting up, stripping off his helmet, but there was no sign of Mark. Before she could ask about him, she was hauled aboard and deposited in an ungainly heap in the bottom of the boat by one of the seamen while the other reached for James. She finally managed to crawl upright and strip off her goggles. Blinking, she looked around. To her amazement, the hull of the yacht loomed close by, almost on top of them, but there was still no sign of Mark.

By this time, the photographer was following James and Juliet's eyes desperately searched the surface of the water.

'Where's Mark?' she cried.

The seaman were making heavy weather of hauling aboard the photographer plus his bulky equipment, and one of them panted, 'Sharks sighted coming this way. The captain said get you up at once. Did you see how fast those dolphins disappeared?'

'It was a perfect example of their built-in sonar equipment,' Dr Robinson remarked dryly.

James turned to Juliet, his face shining with

eagerness. 'Did you see it, Juliet? They knew me! And
they've been accepted into the school by their peers!
The others are teaching Tim, helping him! He'll be all
right now. I haven't condemned him to death, after all.'

'Where's Mark?' asked Juliet, barely moving her lips.
She could feel the blood leaving her face; the
shuddering start in the bottom of her stomach; the cold,
dark premonition of dread, of fear. She knew in just a
few minutes she was going to want to die. Her eyes
strained, searching the surface of the ocean, but it, the
yacht, the sea and sky were all whirling in a hideously
endless spiral before her very eyes. Suddenly she stood
up, startling everyone in the boat.

'Where's Mark?' she screamed. 'My God, he's still
down there! Mark! Mark!'

She was barely conscious of the hands that held her
back as she fought like a maniac to leap back into that
cold, dark sea. She did not see the ominous fins cutting
the water, but the others did, and frantically pulled her
backwards into the boat. She screamed Mark's name
over and over until someone slapped her face with a
resounding crack, and someone else shook her.

Her eyes focused unwillingly on James's grim,
desperate face. 'He's safe, Juliet! He's on the yacht!'

She turned her head unbelievingly towards the yacht.
Standing on the dock at the foot of the ladder was
Mark, an air rifle in his hands, watching her anxiously.

'He waited until he was sure you were safe, then he
swam to the yacht for a rifle to shoot the sharks.'

She barely heard James's explanation. Her whole
being was concentrated on Mark as though she had only
to take her eyes off him for him to disappear. As soon as
the boat scraped the side of the yacht, she hurled herself
into his arms. By this time tears were streaming down her
cheeks, but she touched his face and damp shoulders
repeatedly, fumbling with cold, wet hands, reassuring
herself by touch that he really was there.

'I thought you were dead!' she sobbed. 'You damn
fool, why didn't you stay with me? You said you were
going to! I thought you were *dead*!'

'I couldn't stay with you, darling,' he said gently.

'That young male dolphin pushed me out of the way. I made sure you were safe before I swam towards the yacht. Didn't you see me? I didn't take my eyes off you the whole time.'

'You're crazy!' she scolded shakily. 'Don't you know better than to swim when sharks have been sighted? Why didn't you stay with the boat?'

'Because I'm a fool—and crazy—just as you are.' There was a thread of amusement in his voice as he pulled her closer into his arms. 'No, don't try to get away. I've never had anybody weep over me before, much less try to jump into shark-infested waters in an attempt to save my life! It feels good.' He tilted her head back and gazed into her eyes. He was wearing a very smug look. 'Now that I know you're willing to die for me, I don't intend to let you get away.'

He kissed her then, very thoroughly and taking his time about it as he disregarded her panic-stricken efforts to pull away. All Juliet could think was that she *had* given herself away—very devastatingly—and she hadn't a prayer of disguising the way she felt after this.

'We'll defer the rest of the conversation until we have more privacy,' Mark added, his eyes filled with a strange warm light.

Juliet gave a guilty start, appalled to see that the boat's crew and the diving party were watching them with interest. At Mark's signal, James jumped on to the dock beside them.

'Congratulations, brother!' he grinned.

There was a gentle cheer from above. Juliet looked up and saw everyone hanging over the side of the yacht, peering down at them. She buried her flushed face into Mark's chest and felt it move as he laughed.

After that, it was just a few minutes before she was on deck, being stripped of her diving gear and thrust into a robe by Daisy, whose eyes were frankly sparkling with delight.

'I knew if I kept out of the way and let you two work it out, you'd get together,' she said smugly. 'Fake engagement, indeed!' she added in a lower tone.

Mark wouldn't allow her to be questioned. 'The rest

of you can do what you like,' he said impatiently. 'But Juliet needs a hot bath and a rest.'

'Well, I can tell you already what *I* saw,' piped up Adam Harkness. 'It was a dolphin standing on his tail. He nosed a yellow bucket to the surface and tossed it our way as though he was trying to net a basketball score. I got a perfect picture of it, too,' he added, patting the camera hanging at his side.

Downstairs, in the luxurious stateroom, a cup of hot coffee beside her, Juliet faced Mark with outward composure. They had both showered and she had put on her robe and wrapped her hair in a towel turban. She wished she had taken time to dress—clothes were an armour for the interview that was undoubtedly facing her. Mark had apparently dressed in a hurry, for the loose-fitting shirt that had been tucked impatiently in his jeans was half open, exposed a broad expanse of masculine chest. He looked calm, but he was pale. As for Juliet, her heart was pounding so hard she was sure he could see it knocking against her rib cage.

'Were you really going to jump overboard to save my life?' he grinned. 'No, don't answer that—I know you were. It's just that it gives me so damned much satisfaction to say it that I have to keep reassuring myself I didn't dream it.'

He came across and took her hand, pulling her towards the bed. She followed him reluctantly; he was looking so boyishly complacent, it was hard to deny him anything. He sat down and pulled her into his lap. She held herself stiffly, her face wearing a hunted look as she desperately tried to regroup her shattered defences.

'Well, now that you know how I feel, you can just forget it!' she snapped. 'I still have no intention of marrying you!'

Mark threw back his head and laughed joyously. It was the first free, untrammelled laughter she had ever heard from him, and she was stunned at the difference it made in his face. 'That's right—slap me down! Prove to me all over again that you're one tough, cussed little dame who doesn't intend to give an inch. But don't expect me to stay slapped down, love, because I feel as though someone has just handed me a slice of the moon!' He gave her a hard, exultant kiss. 'It's too late to pretend you don't love me. You've given yourself away.'

Juliet stared at him mutely, then burst into tears. 'I don't care!' she sobbed. 'I won't marry a man who doesn't love me!'

'Is that why——?' He stopped, bit off an oath and pulled her closer. 'Darling, don't you know, even now, that I love you? Surely it's obvious? Why do you think I asked you to marry me, and jumped at the chance to announce our engagement? I could have even kissed Felicia for her timing, bless her bitchy little heart! I even told Daisy how I felt,' he added ruefully, 'because I wanted her to talk to you. I hoped she would persuade you to marry me. I thought if I could make my offer sound attractive without scaring you off until I'd had time to change your opinion of me, I—— *One child!* My God!' He broke off, his voice shaken. 'I tried to put it coolly, but I was in one hell of a turmoil inside. The last thing I wanted to do was frighten you with protestations of love that you didn't want to hear. Instead, I succeeded in giving you the impression I didn't give a damn, didn't I?'

Juliet, who has been listening to this rather incoherent explanation in bewildered silence, began to appreciate for the first time *his* apprehensions, *his* uncertainties, *his* love. It had been there all along, only she had been too fearful of being hurt to meet him halfway. She had been a coward, too blind to see his needs because she was too wrapped up in her own.

She reached out a tentative hand and touched his lips. He drew a sharp breath, then turning her palm inward, kissed it softly before removing it gently.

'Later,' he promised, giving her a look that sent the hot blood coursing through her cheeks. 'Explanations, now, or we'll never get them made.'

'Mark, you didn't even hint that you loved me.'

'I don't think I knew it,' he said slowly. 'At first, I put the unaccountable feelings I was having to an extremely strong sexual urge. I told myself I was concerned for Paul, for James, but inside, I knew I was seething with jealousy. And when you turned me down, I was determined to humiliate you. That's why I behaved as I did in Key West, but it boomeranged on me. By the time we left there I knew I wanted more than just a weekend. I wanted to get you into my bed so I could entice you into a permanent commitment.'

Juliet stared at him reproachfully. 'You wanted a mistress!'

A shadow of shame crossed his face. 'That's what I told myself. Quid pro quo. Something for something. That was the way I had operated with women in the past, and it had always worked very well—until you came along. It had never mattered before if I didn't score, but I was getting desperate. When I saw that you were jealous of Serena, I pushed my cold affair with her for all it was worth, hoping to get a reaction from you. But you only turned that cool little face towards me and ignored whatever I did. I was so damned frustrated I thought I'd go crazy!'

'It probably did you a lot of good,' she said primly.

He laughed reluctantly. 'Uh-huh. I wondered if you realise how you left me the night I found you crying? I wanted you so badly I would have given you the moon to get you into my bed. But I wanted you to know what you were doing, not be just carried away by the emotions of the moment. When you turned me down, I nearly went out of my skull! I made up my mind then that if it was marriage you wanted, I'd marry you. The idea even appealed to me: I saw it as one way of making sure of you. When I had to leave you the next morning, I was scared to death you'd take the chance to clear out while I was gone.'

'I almost did,' Juliet admitted. 'Daisy talked me out of it.'

'I didn't dare ask Daisy to help me. I knew she'd take me apart if she had any idea what was in my mind.' A fleeting grin crossed his face. 'But I left orders with Cora that if she let you leave the island, I'd break her. I knew it was a bad time for me to leave, although it accomplished one thing.' He paused, then added slowly,

'I was able to send someone down to the Graham Laboratories with instructions to find out whatever he could about you. What he uncovered made me feel like dirt.' His voice thickened with self-contempt.

'You didn't trust me,' she said sadly.

'We didn't trust one another,' Mark reminded her gently. 'Why didn't you tell me the truth about yourself, Juliet? Instinct told me that you were keeping something back and I made my own guess about what it was. Being a cynic, I guessed wrong. When my man came back and told me how you'd walked off after the funeral in a kind of daze, I knew what real fear was for the first time in my life. I'd insulted you, accused you—and it would serve me right if you never forgave me. That ring,' he nodded towards the table, where Juliet had left the emerald that morning before the dive. 'It wasn't my grandmother's. I bought it—and a wedding ring—as a sort of hostage against the future, intending to come back and try to persuade you to marry me.'

'And when you got back, instead you were met by James's lies. No wonder you behaved so badly!' she sympathised.

He grinned. 'It didn't seem to make any difference. You were mine and I didn't care how many men there'd been before me. The last one was going to be me. My old rule of no entanglements no longer applied. I wanted you secured with every legal bond the law provided. But enough of talking about that,' he whispered huskily. 'You know what I want. When will you marry me? When, my heart's treasure, will you come sail with me?'

Recognising it as a paraphrase of an old quotation, she gave him an answering smile. 'Tomorrow?' she suggested provocatively.

'Tomorrow it is.'

She sat up straight. 'Mark! Is it possible? What about the cruise?'

'Anything is possible—and to hell with the cruise. My guests can go to the Canaries or wherever they like on the *Kiwi*. Me, I prefer something smaller, something we can handle ourselves. How about taking the *Sea Witch* and going cruising among the islands? I know of one nearby, much smaller than Tamassee, where there's plenty of fresh water and a long sandy beach. And plenty of privacy. We can anchor a hundred yards offshore and swim and snorkel as much as we like. At night, we can sleep on board the boat.' His voice dropped to a sensuous murmur.

'Mark.' Juliet half hid her head on his shoulder. 'Do we have to wait until tomorrow?'

She almost cried aloud as his hands tightened spasmodically about her waist. Then he levered her gently to the bed and stretched out beside her. 'Do you really mean that?'

She met his eyes steadily. 'With all my heart.'

Gone was the old Mark, the hard mask of cynicism he wore to fool others. His eyes shone with a light that took her breath away, making a mockery of her fears. She had always dreaded this moment, this final, unreserved giving of herself into another's hands, because she had had nothing with which to compare it. Her long, lonely childhood had been a barren wasteland. The love which she had poured upon her parents had not reached them in that ivory tower in which they dwelled. They had wanted nothing but each other—and their work. They had had no room for her.

She had not thought their preoccupation with themselves had damaged her, but it had. She had learned a lesson in childhood that had stayed with her: to love was to be rejected, and rejection meant pain. She had grown up seeing love as a danger to be avoided at all costs. To love was to be vulnerable.

She had seen her love for Mark as a dark, empty pit, this gateway that she was now prepared to enter as the gateway to pain and humiliation. She had not trusted him, and so she had created her own unhappiness. Now there was no holding back, no more shadows on their love. She could receive him now with open arms, on equal terms, knowing that only by being together they could experience the completion that was due every human being; that is, if each was willing to forgo a little something of that former self that had once dwelled alone.

# Coming Next Month in Harlequin Romances!

**2689  DARK NIGHT DAWNING  Stacy Absalom**
An injured concert pianist hides her suspicions about the hit-and-run nightmare that destroyed her career and crippled her faith in her ex-fiancé...until he starts pursuing her again!

**2690  STAG AT BAY  Victoria Gordon**
Following a disastrous marriage, a young widow retreats to her father's Queensland deer farm and tries to turn her back on men, especially her father's partner and his improbable dreams.

**2691  A TIME TO GROW  Claudia Jameson**
A Yorkshire woman is no longer the difficult teenager her grandfather's protégé once rescued from one humiliating scrape after another. She's grown up and determined to be acknowledged as a woman.

**2692  YEAR'S HAPPY ENDING  Betty Neels**
Is it a young nanny's destiny to settle into a permanent post caring for other people's children, or will an infuriatingly cynical widower be proven wrong?

**2693  MAN AND WIFE  Valerie Parv**
Running her father's Australian property-development empire would be simpler if her home wasn't in such a mess. What she needs is a wife. What she gets is a man and a world of complications.

**2694  BRIDE BY CONTRACT  Margaret Rome**
For a price—the ancestral home for her grandmother and employment for her disentitled brother—an English aristocrat agrees to marry a shrewd Canadian millionaire with an eye for bargains.

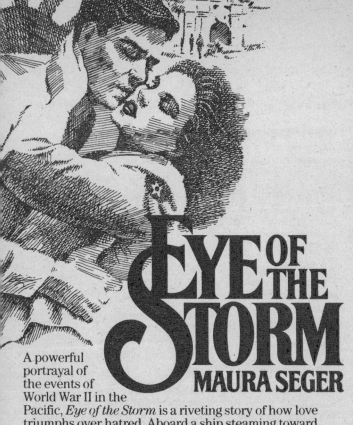

# Eye of the Storm

## MAURA SEGER

A powerful
portrayal of
the events of
World War II in the
Pacific, *Eye of the Storm* is a riveting story of how love
triumphs over hatred. Aboard a ship steaming toward
Corregidor, Army Lt. Maggie Lawrence meets Marine Sgt.
Anthony Gargano. Despite military regulations against frater-
nization, they resolve to face together whatever lies ahead....
A searing novel by the author named by *Romantic Times* as
1984's Most Versatile Romance Author.

At your favorite bookstore in March or send your name, address and zip or
postal code, along with a check or money order for $4.25 (includes 75¢ for
postage and handling) payable to Harlequin Reader Service to:

In the U.S.
Box 52040
Phoenix, AZ 85072-2040

In Canada
5170 Yonge Street
P.O. Box 2800
Postal Station A
Willowdale, ONT   M2N 6J3

EYE-A-1

*Harlequin American Romance*
*Premier Editions*

# BANISH MISFORTUNE

## ANNE STUART

Jessica Hansen was tired of living on the razor's edge. After years of corporate climbing she yearned for a change. Someone who would make her feel alive again....

Available in April at your favorite retail store or send your name, address and zip or postal code, along with a check or money order for $3.70 (includes 75¢ for postage and handling) payable to Harlequin Reader Service to:

**Harlequin Reader Service**
**In the U.S.**
Box 52040
Phoenix, AZ 85072-2040

**In Canada**
5170 Yonge Street
P.O. Box 2800,
Postal Station A
Willowdale, Ont.
M2N 6J3

APE5-A-1

# 4 FREE

## *Harlequin Romances*

# TAKE THESE 4 Harlequin Romances FREE

Delight in **Mary Wibberley**'s warm romance, MAN OF POWER, the story of a girl whose life changes from drudgery to glamour overnight....Let THE WINDS OF WINTER by **Sandra Field** take you on a journey of love to Canada's beautiful Maritimes....Thrill to a cruise in the tropics—and a devastating love affair in the aftermath of a shipwreck—in **Rebecca Stratton**'s THE LEO MAN.... Travel to the wilds of Kenya in a quest for love with the determined heroine in **Karen van der Zee**'s LOVE BEYOND REASON.

Harlequin Romances . . . 6 exciting novels published each month! Each month you will get to know interesting, appealing, true-to-life people . . . . You'll be swept to distant lands you've dreamed of visiting . . . . Intrigue, adventure, romance, and the destiny of many lives will thrill you through each Harlequin Romance novel.

### *Get all the latest books before they're sold out!*

As a Harlequin subscriber you actually receive your personal copies of the latest Romances immediately after they come off the press, so you're sure of getting all 6 each month.

### *Cancel your subscription whenever you wish!*

You don't have to buy any minimum number of books. Whenever you decide to stop your subscription just let us know and we'll cancel all further shipments.

Your FREE gift includes

- MAN OF POWER by **Mary Wibberley**
- THE WINDS OF WINTER by **Sandra Field**
- THE LEO MAN by **Rebecca Stratton**
- LOVE BEYOND REASON by **Karen van der Zee**

# FREE *GIFT CERTIFICATE*

## *and Subscription Reservation*

## Mail this coupon today!

## Harlequin Reader Service

In the U.S.A.
2504 West Southern Ave.
Tempe, AZ 85282

In Canada
P.O. Box 2800, Postal Station A
5170 Yonge Street,
Willowdale, Ont. M2N 6J3

Please send me my 4 Harlequin Romance novels FREE.
Also, reserve a subscription to the 6 NEW Harlequin
Romance novels published each month. Each month I will
receive 6 NEW Romance novels at the low price of $1.50
each (*Total–$9.00 a month*). There are no shipping and
handling or any other hidden charges. I may cancel this
arrangement at any time, but even if I do, these first 4 books
are still mine to keep. **116 BPR EAVE**

_____

NAME                    (PLEASE PRINT)

_____

ADDRESS                      APT NO.

_____

CITY

_____

STATE/PROV              ZIP/POSTAL CODE

This offer is limited to one order per household and not valid to
current *Harlequin Romance* subscribers. We reserve the right
to exercise discretion in granting membership.

® ™ Trademarks of Harlequin Enterprises Ltd.      R-SUB-3US

If price changes are necessary you will be notified